THE CALADRIUS

THE CALADRIUS

EDWARD ANDREWS

ARCHWAY
PUBLISHING

Archway Publishing books may be ordered through booksellers or by contacting:

Archway Publishing
1663 Liberty Drive
Bloomington, IN 47403
www.archwaypublishing.com
844-669-3957

ISBN: 978-1-6657-6654-8 (sc)
ISBN: 978-1-6657-6656-2 (hc)
ISBN: 978-1-6657-6655-5 (e)

Library of Congress Control Number: 2024920774

Print information available on the last page.

Archway Publishing rev. date: 12/12/2024

CONTENTS

DEDICATION

The book was written because of the love and belief of my wife. We were sitting around one day and I told her about this dream I had and how it continued for several days. I felt that it was some kind of a sign but I didn't know what. She told me that since I had written several other books that I was in the process of updating and changing because they were out of date from when they were originally written that I needed to write these thoughts down. I thought about it and she was right. I started to write down the dream and in less than a month I had everything on paper. She read it and after making minor changes she thought it was a great read. I had to think about some of the things I wrote to bring some characters more to life and then the research started into this unknown entity, to most of us, called space. So for the love of my life I wrote this dream and decided to make it my first entry into the world of being an author. Hopefully my other books already completed will follow.

CHAPTER 1

THE TRAINING SESSION WAS GOING AS PLANNED. THERE WERE A few issues that we still needed ironed out but we had weeks of training left to make sure we got it right. The water tank was the hardest part of the training as far as I was concerned. It was the best at simulating weightlessness but the process to get in there took hours. But we were floating around doing our maneuver training to simulate a space walk. We had been in the tank for three hours now and I didn't know how the others were doing but I was in misery. Mexican food last night was now doing its dance on me. The container bags inside the suit to handle such a mess in my mind were too small to handle my problem today. I was hoping that the exercise would be concluded soon. We went over the antennae array issue one more time and then they called it a wrap. It took a good hour to be lifted out of the tank and moved to the training room where we could finally start the process to remove the suit. We each had two permanent assistants that were with us all the time to help with anything we needed. The main items were getting in and out of the suits. The main guy I had was a fellow who was a practical joker which kept the air light most of the time. He removed my helmet when we were standing on the platform next to the tank. As he was putting it on the rack he turned and grimaced. "What the hell is that smell?"

"Jim, that is the wonderful aroma of Mexican food making a statement on day two."

I started to laugh as the smell came flowing out of my suit.

"Let me turn off that pack. God, that's terrible."

"Hell no, I need it to force the air out of the suit. I don't need to keep all that inside for just me. Everyone needs to enjoy my dinner."

He walked behind me and I slowly felt the air system cycle down.

"I am going to get very hot inside here now and with what is in here that created that great aroma, you're gonna regret turning the air off."

He looked at me and disappeared behind me again. Soon I felt the air system come back on.

"Smart move there kimosabee."

He started moving me to the suit room so I could get out of this thing. The removal of the suit didn't take half as long as getting in it. So in about forty five minutes I was standing there in the under garment. I looked down at the bag and saw in was totally full. I told Jim I needed to go and empty that thing right now. After about twenty minutes I returned to the suit room and they were all standing there in a group. When they saw me they started to clap. I smiled and walked up to them. As I got closer I could smell a strong odor of air freshener.

"What is that smell, fruity flowers?"

"We emptied two cans of room deodorizer trying to get rid of your stink."

They were all laughing hysterically. I took a bow and we joked about never eating Mexican food before a dive suit day again. After a while we headed into the debrief room to listen to the boss tell us we sucked again. He wandered in and everyone took a seat. One of the aides started throwing water bottles to each of us. They were nice and cold and felt great going down. Soon the boss walked up to the front and started to write on the white board. He listed the exercise as bullet points and then listed plus items and minus items under each bullet. After a while he started to discuss each item and then sorted out the issues by person and what he expected next time in the tank.

"Phil, when is the next tank session?"

"It should be scheduled on Wednesday."

"Well, that gives you two days to drain the water and scrub it down with bleach. None of us will get in that water after what Vince did in there today."

Everyone broke out laughing at what Tom said. It took a long time to get control again. Then Jim spoke up.

"I am not going to be the one that cleans his suit either."

Again the laughter took over the room.

"OK! OK! Let's get to some serious stuff here. I was not pleased with the time that it took today. You took forty minutes longer to do the same thing you have done seven times now. It is supposed to be taking less time each exercise, not more."

"Sorry boss, but I had trouble staying grounded out there. I guess I just had too much gas in my suit today."

That started everyone again. Phil just shook his head and walked out of the room. Sarah stood up and said the meeting must be over since the boss left. We all got up and left heading back to the dressing area to finish getting out of the suits. About an hour later I came out and saw most of the crew standing at the mission board. I walked over to them.

"Look at this. This is not good. They are adding even more to our plate than before. As it is we have five EVAs to do. This is pushing us too far."

Carl was not a happy person concerning something that was on the board. I walked up to the board and looked at the schedule. Whenever there was something changed they put it in green so we could see it. Our mission was going to take us on a ten month trip and there were hundreds of experiments and five EVAs from setting up the antenna arrays to checking the skin of the ship for damage. Now they are adding another EVA but it doesn't specify what for. It just lists a four hour EVA about three fourths down the list. That would mean it would be somewhere after we arrived at Mars or on the way home. Then on the training board they added six new tank excursions. So we were going to be going in the water at least fifteen more times. We were scheduled to finish training in five weeks but there was no way we could add more tank time and still end training on time. I turned towards the guys and looked at each of them.

"This means they have added something to the mission. So, we need to find out was it pre-scheduled and just not listed until now or was it a last minute deal. Either way we need to know what it is. I guess I will be back in a few."

As the captain of the mission it was my job to be sure everything is acceptable before we go on the mission. I was not going to accept this mission without knowing everything about it. There was not going to be any secret parts to this. I headed for the office. I was still in my skins but I didn't care. The skins were not to be worn outside the training area. I left the training building and headed across the lot to the administration building. I entered the back door and was met by a guard.

"Sir, you're not allowed in here dressed like that."

"Get out of my way."

I pushed him aside as I started down the hall. The guard and I knew each other quite well anyway.

"Sir, don't make me lock the place down. I need to see your pass."

I just ignored him and entered Philip Nelson's outer office.

"Leanne, buzz me in, now!"

I still was walking as I reached for the boss's door. I turned the knob just as I heard the alarm going off indicating a breech in security. I entered seeing Jim sitting at his desk as he looked up.

"What the hell are you doing here dressed like that?"

"You will explain right now what the added EVA and mission is that showed up on the board today."

"What are you talking about? Nothing should have been added to the mission."

"Don't fuck with me Phil, as captain of this mission I don't like surprises."

Phil stood up and started to walk around the desk when several guards came through the door with guns drawn.

"It's OK! I have this under control. I will deal with this. Please!"

He motioned for them to leave with a hand wave towards the door. After they left he put his arm around my shoulder and started to speak very softly.

"Vince, if there is something new on the mission chart then I will have to look at it and see what it is and find out why it was added. I am not aware of any changes that were planned for today. So, let's go back and take a look at that board. OK!"

"Don't patronize me Phil, I know when I've been had. Something new is part of this mission and it was deliberately kept secret until now. You didn't want this schedule to be public and you knew that after last weekend the press received no more updates on training. So what is it and why were we not told in private about it earlier?"

He started to walk towards the door pulling me by the arm as he went. "Let's go look at it."

He just kept nodding his head and smiling.

"You could get bumped from this mission for being in here dressed like that. I will catch hell explaining this to the council later. What am I going to do with you? This is the third time in four months that I have had to explain your actions to the council. You're lucky I want you as my mission lead or else I would have to give it to Anthony. Hell, they may demand that anyway."

He was still talking very low as we headed out the door over to the training building. When we entered the building we started towards the office area. As we rounded the corner we saw the entire crew and support staff standing in front of the message center. Phil walked straight up to the message board and stood in front of the schedule. He looked at it for a long time. There was too long of a hesitation to have just read it once. I figured he was trying to formulate a response. He then turned around and looked straight at me. All the others had formed a semi-circle behind me as he was reading it.

"There is some kind of mistake here. I know nothing of these additions and I promise you I will get you an answer before you leave here today."

He reached into his pocket and pulled out some keys. He fumbled around for a moment and then opened the case and pulled out the schedule. He locked the case back up and started to walk away. "That was a pretty lame statement coming from the Director of Operations. Especially one who should have known everything we did in advance."

Hank spoke up rather loudly and throwing the words like they were meant to stick in his back like a knife. Jim slowed and started to turn but after a short hesitation he kept walking and went out of sight. We all stood there in a circle now and pondered what he was keeping from us. It appeared that he knew about this change but we definitely got the impression we were not supposed to know just yet. Slowly we went back into the suit room and we each went to our changing rooms. After getting into our uniforms we met back outside in front of the message center.

"I will head back to his office and get his official answer and give each of you a call at home later. I really don't think we are going to get an answer tonight. For some reason I feel a stall move coming." Everyone seemed to be in agreement over that. They walked out of the building and headed for their cars. I made my way back to Phil's office and entered the outer room. His secretary was gone but I saw his door open so I went up to it and entered. Phil was not in his office. I looked around and called his name but received no response. I sat down in the chair across from his desk and waited. It was quite a while later when I could hear conversation coming from the hallway. I just sat there knowing he would soon walk in. After a few more minutes I turned and watched Phil and a P R man named Scott Douglas come into the office. Phil stopped dead as soon as he saw me sitting there. "Vince, what are you doing here?"

"You told me you would have an answer for us before we left. I am here waiting for that answer." "Well, as I expected there was a huge mistake. Scott here had given his secretary some information on scheduling, and she put in on the wrong schedule. It was not meant for the TALON PROJECT training mission."

He stood there looking at me. I just sat there looking at the two of them back and forth.

"Well, that's it. There is nothing more to it than an error, right Scott?"

"Sure thing Mr. Nelson, just a mistake."

Phil moved around to his chair and stood behind it. Scott was standing off to one side of the room. I looked at both of them and then stood up.

"Do you really thing I will buy this crap without something to support your words?"

"You will have to take my word for this. That's all there is going to be. It was a mistake and there will be consequences if this is pushed any further, understand?"

"Oh, I understand but I still think you are lying to us."

Phil just stood there and then pointed to the door. I looked at him and turned and left the office. I headed out the door and made my way to my car. Later that evening I called each of the crew members and filled them in on the story I was fed. We agreed to not push it any further but planned to meet somewhere over the weekend to discuss what had happened in private. Things were not being placed on the table here and I wanted to find out why. We were going on a mission that had the potential of being very hazardous and I was not going to accept a hidden agenda.

CHAPTER 2

THE NEXT MORNING CAME EARLY AS I HEADED OUT THE DOOR. I looked up and saw that the sun still had not made an entrance over the horizon. I drove the thirty minutes to the Lincoln Center and parked in my usual spot. I noticed that there were several cars already in the lot including Phil's. Now why would he be there before 7 A.M. I was there early to meet with my co-pilot for the mission, Anthony Politta. We talked for quite a while last night but kept it very general. We had a code between us and set up the meeting this morning just in case our phones were being monitored. We really didn't trust too many individual around here. Everything was a secret and we knew they planned to try and keep it that way. Past history told us they were monitoring everything we did including our phone calls. As I was walking to the mission building I saw Anthony pull up and park. I waited by the entrance door for him to catch up to me. He also glanced over and looked at the boss's car sitting there as he walked past it. I opened the door with my pass key and we entered. Just inside the door were 2 guards who immediately questioned our presence. We flashed the ID's and they continued on with their routine. We headed for the crews office and entered making sure there were no followers. Once inside we entered the lounge area. I immediately started a pot of coffee and then we sat down.

"Tony, what happened yesterday was a mistake on their part. I firmly believe that training was meant for us but it was not supposed to be posted. I think they were going to add it secretly as we trained. I don't know what it means just yet but we need to watch and listen for anything that is out of the ordinary."

"I agree! That posting got by them but had to be in the schedule for the secretary to have printed it out. They just didn't read it before it hit the board."

We looked over our previously listed schedule we had in our logs and compared it to the now newest one posted in the lounge. There still were a few minor changes mainly on time lines. It left holes in certain places that were not there before. Enough of a hole that things could be added without any problem at a moments notice. We checked it out thoroughly and saw five holes that were not there before. Each hole covered a time line from 3 to 7 hours. Most of the holes seemed to be at the end of tank sessions. That would allow them to add extra time onto the existing session. We determined we needed to watch these holes in the schedule very closely. We made a copy of the schedule and decided we would copy it every day to watch it. Just as we were done putting the schedule back on the board we heard the door open. In walked Phil and two senior engineers on the mission.

"Vince! Anthony! What are you doing here so early? You're not supposed to be here for another 40 minutes."

He was looking at his watch as he spoke.

"Since when have we become clock watchers for our arrival time in the morning? I have spent the night here before and you never questioned me on that. Why now?"

Tony was quick to throw a comeback at him. He just smiled and said he just was startled to see us, that's all. He walked up to the day board and pulled down the schedule and folded it and placed it in his pocket.

"The guys here seem to think we might now be doing the right training in the right sequence. They are going to revamp the schedule and see if we can get everything accomplished in a more timely manner so we can guarantee to be ready a week before fly out."

It was my turn to pipe up.

"Really! For an organization that prides itself on precision and exact science of detail you are admitting your system of training is flawed?"

He looked at me and then they all walked out with out saying anything. I looked at Tony and said, "This is their way of putting in the training modules they now need to cover the new mission that was added. We will see what that is by tomorrow."

He agreed and as we were talking more and more of the crew started to come in the door. We gathered all of them together and filled them in on what had occurred this morning including how we surprised them by being very early. We sat around for over two hours waiting for someone to give us a training syllabus for today but no one ever came in the lounge. Finally at just after eleven one of the training specialists walked into the lounge and informed everyone that all training was cancelled until Thursday. He put it very clearly that we were to go home and not to return tomorrow at all. He said consider it a free vacation day. Before he left the room I made it very clear that losing two days of training was going to make it even harder to catch up when they add the extra training into the system. He did not acknowledge me or my comment as he exited. We stood around for a while longer discussing and speculating when he walked in again.

"Ladies and Gentlemen, this is not a request. I will be locking up in five minutes and you all are to be out of here, now."

We all agreed to meet at the diner in town at noon to continue our conversation. The man who gave us the word was one of the system engineers and heard us make our plans to meet. I made sure of that, to see who else would show up at the diner. We all drove out of the lot and one by one cleared the check point leaving the compound. There still was another check point about three miles down the road. It was a large complex and access was very limited having only four roads that went around the complex and two that made it out to the main highways. We all lived in a community just outside the property limits that was still considered part of the complex. It consisted of approximately 400 houses and six apartment complexes for the single folks. All the houses were standard government built prefab homes that consisted of three or four bedrooms and the rest of the house's layout was identical to each other. It didn't matter if you owned a regular house in or outside of town you were required to live here when you became part of a mission. So most just lived in the community all of the time to keep from constantly moving. We cleared the main check point and drove past the housing community heading for town. It was a nine mile trip to town. The population of the area was less than thirty thousand and most of the people were support contractors and their families for the Space Complex. Without the Space Center Complex the town probably wouldn't exist. One by one we drove into the diner and parked. When we entered I went over to the owner, Carlos Martinez and asked him if we could use the side room that he had built onto the diner as a banquet room. He said no problem and we went around the corner into the room. We all sat down around one of the three larger tables in there. Soon the waitress came in and asked if we were planning on eating. I told her no but we could use some iced tea and a couple of plates of Danish. She turned and left leaving the door open. We started our conversation letting everyone chime in on their concern and theories of what was going on. After about ten minutes two waitresses came in carrying everything. I told her I was paying for everything and she nodded and left. We were in serious conversation when I noticed someone standing in the doorway. I motioned everyone to shut up and leaned back in the chair. "You can hear a lot better if you came in the room."

Just as I finished speaking Phil and two others walked into the room. With Phil were the two big bosses of the Space Complex. Leonard Pyler was the overall Director of the complex and his assistant, Jerome Sturgis walked in.

"Vincent, how are you today? Didn't realize you were having a private meeting here. Sure hope it is not concerning mission sensitive material against agency policy?"

"Why do I feel that this is not a chance meeting? You obviously knew we were here, so what can we do for you?"

He looked around to each of the crew.

"I would like to speak to you in private."

"We are part of a crew here. If it has something to do with our job then everyone hears it. Of course, no mission conversations permitted, so don't see the need for a private meeting. We all came here to plan an outing for our families before we left town. You seem a little nervous Phil, like you really just got the shaft or something."

He stood there just looking at me for about twenty seconds before he spoke again.

"Outside! - Now!"

He turned and walked out the door. I just sat there pondering whether to go or not.

"Vince, go ahead and go. You're committing suicide if you don't. They will drop you like a hot potato."

Tony whispered in my ear as he leaned over towards me. I slowly got up and made my way outside. Out in the parking lot was the Director smoking a cigarette. I went out the front door and stood there on the small porch. He just stood there about thirty feet away not moving or doing anything. I moved off the porch as others were entering the diner. I very slowly made my way over to him. "There is always someone who has to be a show boater. Usually it's one of the mission specialists who are a dime a dozen to me. This time it's you, the commander of the mission. Well, this will put the mission back about three weeks but you are no longer part of this mission. You can collect your stuff in the morning."

He threw his cigarette on the ground and walked back towards the diner.

"Well, when you get in there you will find out that you will need a completely new crew. But we figured that's what you wanted anyway."

I stood there watching as he stopped walking but he did not turn around. After a moment he walked up the steps and into the diner. I walked over to my car and stood next to the door waiting to see what happened. I knew the crew and I felt confident of their reaction. It took about five minutes then I saw three of them come out the front door. It was Carl Petterson, Sarah Meyer, and Tom Parker. They walked over to where I was.

"So did he tell you I have been fired from the mission and I guess the program?"

Sarah spoke up first.

"He said that starting on Thursday Anthony would be the new commander and one of the others from another program would be brought in to be the co-pilot. So training will have to be re-scheduled because of this unfortunate incident."

Then it was Tom's turn.

"I guess I started the flood gates to swing open when I told him he needed a new Navigator and stood up and walked out. Sarah and Carl followed me out the door. He was yelling quite a bit when we left."

Just then we saw the rest of the crew coming out the front door. Every one was now outside except Anthony. Michele looked at me as she came out smiling and gave me a thumps up. When they came over to the car she told us they all said they were done and left but they grabbed Anthony and was arguing with him so he is still in there.

"Thank guys but this is what you have been waiting for your whole life, you should not have thrown it away just to support me."

"Support you!"

Sarah blurted it out.

"We would not be here if it wasn't for you. I heard the story. You hand picked each of us personally."

I looked at her for a moment before I answered.

"Yes I did, but that was not common knowledge. How did you know that?"

She just smiled and shook her head back and forth indicating she was not going to tell me.

"OK! Well, it is done now anyway so let's get out of here and how about if we all meet tomorrow at; say one, in the lodge at the State Park."

"You mean Hidden Branch State Park out on 40?"

"Yes! I will tell Anthony later."

Everyone nodded and we all headed for our cars. I waited for a while as everyone drove off. I wanted to see Anthony come out first. I was there about ten minutes and still none of them came out. I decided to leave knowing he would call. I pulled out of the lot and headed home. It took me a while to finally get home since I drove around thinking about what just happened. I worked hard for almost fifteen years to get where I was at and it was over in less than a few minutes. I pulled up to the house and when I entered the driveway I saw Susan standing in the doorway looking at me. I got out of the car and started up the porch to where she was standing holding the screen door open.

"So, it's over!"

"Where did you hear that?"

"Anthony just called looking for you. He told me what happened. He is on him way over here now." I walked past her and straight to the kitchen. I grabbed a beer and went in and sat in the living room. "I have told you before I would always be behind your decisions and have never complained but I just need to know what happened and why."

"It was stupid but we as a crew wanted answers to something and they refused. We or I guess I, took a stand and I have been released from the mission and I have a feeling from the program."

"Anthony told me everyone is united and he was coming to tell you the new terms. That's all I know."

She walked back towards the kitchen. Just before she entered she turned and looked at me.

"This life is not what I call enjoyable. I can't stand this boredom and all I see is it getting worse."

She continued into the kitchen as I stared at her. I sat there with my mind going a hundred miles a minute but I could not get an answer to any of the questions I was asking myself. I was all alone inside my own head. Anthony was going to have to explain why in the hell he was telling Susan anything concerning our mission. I was going to have to deal with her later about this boredom issue. She knew my job and what it was going to entail when she decided to marry me. It was alright them but for some reason it was not alright now. I was getting this from both ends now and I was not happy about it.

CHAPTER 3

I WAS SITTING IN THE KITCHEN HAVING A LARGE GLASS OF RUM AND occasionally taking a sip of a soda. I then heard some talking going on outside the kitchen. I did not hear anyone at the door so I figured Susan was on the phone. We have been married for six years and she talked daily to her mother and sisters. I was sure glad I didn't have to pay by the minute for phone calls. The talking got louder and I saw Susan, Tony, Sarah, and Tom come into the kitchen. They stopped and looked at me as I was taking a good sip.

"You might want to put that down. You don't want a hangover when we go to the office at eight tonight."

"Why would we be going there at eight?"

"Because Phil finally was shown the light of what Pyler did and how he was going to be on the hook to explain to the press and Washington why the mission was scrapped for six months while he tried to find qualified people again to be trained. I explained how this was a very stupid move based on very stupid reasons to take such drastic measures."

Tony finished and then Sarah started.

"And when he found out we all would walk away from the mission he started to squirm. He is having a change of heart now."

"How would you know that? I watched you leave the diner and drive away."

"I remembered you didn't pay the bill so I went back to take care of it and I stayed and backed up number two here."

She patted Tony on the arm a few times.

"He really kept his cool and took them down a notch."

"OK! So now we have another meeting to try and iron this out?"

"Phil was going to meet with Pyler and Sturgis and then call me to confirm things are settled. He said if that happens he wanted us in there at eight to go over the ground rules."

"So nothing is settled, only the hope of a settlement."

Tom started to put his two cents into the conversation.

"You are our leader and we want to move forward and be the team that goes around Mars. So for us to do that you have to take charge and be our leader here."

He walked up to me and took the glass out of my hand.

"So, get your head back in the game and get us back on the mission."

I looked up at him and then stood up.

"So what are our chances to have them back off everything and tell us what is really going on?" "That's why we are here. To go over everything we know and you then will be the crowbar to make it all happen tonight."

We spent the next hour writing down everything we knew and formulating a plan to put their backs to the wall so they had no choice but to tell us the facts. It was soon four in the afternoon so we all decided to retreat to our respective homes and wait for Tony's call that the meeting was either on or off. Susan decided that we would eat out tonight since she really didn't have time to prepare a meal now. She really seems to be upset over this matter. So we went and had fast food. That was not supposed to be part of my diet but I decided I wanted it anyway. It was well after eight when the phone rang. I sat there staring at it for a moment. Susan mumbled something about being lazy and she went over and answered it.

"Hello!.....Hi Anthony, Vince is here, just a minute."

She held out the phone for me to come get it. I got up and walked over to her. I took the phone from her and reached around her and held her up against me tight.

"Tony!"

"Vince!"

There was a pause for a moment.

"OK! What do we have?"

"We have a meeting first thing in the morning in Pyler's office. That's what we have."

"That's it, no other information as to the outcome?"

"He just said be prepared to get back to training as soon as the meeting was over. Cha-ching!" "Good! But we still need a full disclosure and I don't see that being given up very easily." "Tomorrow will tell, have to make more calls, later."

With that he hung up and I turned Susan around and told her that I guess we won't be moving after all. She hugged me and told me to make sure I took a chill pill in the morning then laughed. Morning came very early for me. It was just after four and I was up and drinking my second cup of coffee. I wasn't able to sleep trying to formulate a plan to get everyone back on the playing field without any sanctions. Every angle I came up with I eventually rejected for one reason or another. I finally made up my mind that I was just going to be humble and sit there and ask questions and not get off the subject until we got some answers. Calm was the word for today, to be very calm. I went in and dressed and gave Susan a kiss on the cheek since she was still sleeping and headed out the door. I went into town to the diner since it was open 24 hrs. I sat down and ordered breakfast and coffee. Soon I was eating and I felt someone sit down next to me at the counter. There were only three people in there so there were plenty of seats all around but they decided to sit right next to me. I turned and looked at Phil as he stated it was a good morning. I just nodded and went back to eating my breakfast.

"I guess I wasn't the only one who couldn't sleep last night."

I didn't answer him. I asked for more coffee and then Phil ordered something but I was heavy in thought and barely heard the words coming from his mouth.

"They are going to offer you your job back without any strings if you will agree to keep your nose out of issues that are supposed to be secret."

"I am not interested in secrets. I am only interested in knowing exactly what our mission is and why we are going to be training on items not part of our listed mission."

He looked around to see who might be listening.

"No more now. Let's keep this for the meeting."

"You're the one talking, not me."

He received his food and we ate without any more words for over ten minutes. I finished and just sat there drinking my third cup of coffee while he finished. I looked at my watch and saw it was 6:10 A.M. People were now starting to file into the diner on a regular basis. The town was waking up. I saw a few that I knew who worked at the Center and then in walked Jerome Sturgis. He walked up and stood behind Phil.

"Are we having a nice conversation this morning?"

Phil turned and looked at him. I think he was startled and at the same time lost for words. So I spoke up for Phil.

"Since this is an eating establishment I think what we are doing here is eating. So if you are looking for conversation then I think you need to look somewhere else."

I turned back around and picked up my check and paid it. I looked at Phil and stated that I was sorry we were rudely interrupted but I would see him at the meeting and left. Sturgis was still just standing there as I walked out the door. I got in the car and saw Pyler pull up and park. I figured that Pyler and Sturgis planned to meet there this morning and prepare themselves for the meeting. I didn't think that Phil was aware of their plans by the way he was acting. I could see through the window that Sturgis was now sitting next to him talking up a storm. I knew that the meeting was going to be a real shootout just by the attitude of that jerk Sturgis. I started the car and after watching Pyler enter and go to a booth and then Sturgis went and joined him leaving Phil at the counter, I drove off. I went to the Center and drove in and parked in my normal place. There were three others already there. They were just sitting in their cars. We all got out and walked into the main office complex building together. There was a large sitting area just inside the main entrance so we made our way to the front of the building to relax there. We knew we would be waiting at least another hour before they would get to their offices and then I was sure they would not start the meeting until after eight. They had to have their secret meeting to discuss again what they planned on doing and with the developments of this morning I was hoping nothing major changed from our leaked information. We made a lot of small talk about the town and some about the mission training we had completed. Everyone was trying to keep their stress under control. Soon we saw the secretary for Pyler open up the office and then the main receptionist came to the front desk area. She was startled for a moment when she saw all of us sitting there. Then after she figured out who we were she went about her business of getting ready for the day. It was now the bewitching hour and still we did not see Phil or the henchmen. Soon Pyler's secretary came out of her office and walked towards the main lobby.

"Mr. Mariani! Your crew and you are expected in conference room C."

She turned and walked back to her office. I looked at my watch and saw it was 8:21 when we started to get up and make our way to the conference room. As we entered we saw the three amigos sitting at one end of the oval table. There were about 20 chairs around the table but my crew all sat at the other end from them leaving a gap of empty chairs between us. After we all got comfortable in our seats Pyler started talking.

"The last two days have been filled with very unfortunate incidents. First there was a mistake concerning printed information that was inadvertently put on your schedules. Then there were unfortunate words beings said to higher authorities that only could be construed as insubordination. From there it seemed to get even worse. Classified information being discussed in open public areas, more insubordination remarks in public, and then clear violations of policy taking place not once but numerous times around here."

He stood up and picked up a pile of papers that was stacked in front of him. He started to walk around the table placing a set of papers in front of each of us.

"So, I am dealt with all this and trying to decide just what needs to be done to resolve these incidents. Some are easy fixes and others have grave consequences."

He finished with the papers and went back to his seat.

"Before we get into the papers in front of you I am going to make a few remarks. I have been a part of the space program for twenty-eight years now and I have never had to deal with such flagrant violations of the program like this before today. I have one thing that is a positive note here today and that is there was no leak to the press or to Washington concerning this matter. So that means that my hands aren't tied behind my back. If any of these incidents make their way to either the press or to Washington then my decisions will have to be changed drastically and this mission will be forever marred."

He paused for a while and then picked up some papers he had in front of him.

"As you see in front of you there are papers and each of you should have a cover page with your name on it. So that means that the papers inside are not all alike and therefore are personal and private to each individual. We will call this round one in this matter and I hope to god for each of you that we don't have to go to round two. Round two will be dealt with individually and decisively." He turned a page over and then looked up staring directly at me.

"So turn to page one. Read the page as it applies to you individually. It will list the violations that you have committed and the penalties that will apply to each violation. When you are finished please indicate so."

He leaned back in his chair. Phil was sitting there with his head down. I knew that he didn't have much input into this at all. I read my page and saw seven items listed. They were from insubordination to clothing violations. The penalties were from a fine to several of them indicating termination. I read them again and then looked up noticing that I was the last one to look up. I also glanced over to Sarah's papers and saw she had one line on hers. Pyler started talking again.

"So, now you have read the serious matter that each of you is going to have to deal with. The next three pages for each of you are the same. They spell out the policies of the agency and the discretion on how to enforce each of them individually. So after you read that we will continue."

I laid down my papers and looked down the table.

"We all are aware of the structure for our job. You have indicated what you feel are violations you believe each of us have committed. I think we can proceed to where you list the supporting witnesses and or accusers to each of these charges. I know for a fact that two of the charges listed on my sheet are false. So I definitely want to see the proof behind these charges."

He stood up and I could see his face muscles tighten. But he did not say anything. He just stood there gleaming at me.

"If everyone is in agreement then we will proceed to the next page."

He blurted it our loudly and sat back down. When he looked up he saw everyone turning pages.

"OK! Then let's look at page five. Here you will see an overview of your assignment on the current mission you are training for. On the right side you will see a name. That name is your counterpart that had been training for the same mission out in California. We decided many months ago that we needed to ensure there were two fully qualified crews just in case we had to replace someone for any reason."

He sat there for a moment smiling as he looked at the paper. I looked at mine and saw a name I knew very well. We had been on a shuttle flight together and we both were classmates at MIT. I sat there trying not to show that my body just sank to my feet.

"They are all training as we speak, and in fact, they are actually a good four days ahead of you in that training. So, as you see, we are very prepared to conclude this incident today, here and now."

When I looked up at him he was smirking back my way.

"Now there are only two more pages and they are again personal and private to each individual. So you may look at them now."

I turned the page and saw a statement that started out with the phrase,

'I agree that the following statement is true and by signing this statement agree to any and all stipulations held within'.

I knew that we were about to sign confessions of guilt. I started to read the statement. It went on to paraphrase things of wrong doing but never stating what they were. It made references to violations and again not listing what they were. Then the bombshell stared at me in the face. There was a statement,

'That if any of the current or future policies or procedures whether pre-established or added were ever violated or questioned that termination would be the result of that action'.

I couldn't believe what I saw. They were going to hang everything over our heads individually but do nothing to us at the moment. I knew one of two things just occurred here. Either they did not have a second crew and made that up or they wanted to keep everything hush and not lose the program. Because if any of us were removed from the program the press would pick up on the change of crew and question it. That was the gleaming sign that flashed in front of my eyes. Having to explain a change might mar the mission enough to delay or even cancel it and there was way too much money at stake here. Not to mention their careers and reputation if the fired party started to talk. I decided to make a few comments before he continued.

"I have come to the conclusion here that two things are happening here. First, you have decided that you don't want to waste the training and effort already put into this mission fearing a major delay or bad publicity. Second, that you feel by making us sign such a statement that we will be under your thumb, so to say. I for one have no problem signing a statement if it contains facts and actual issues at hand. I will not sign a statement that is ambiguous and at best a general blanket coverage statement to cover any issue. Especially issues that never happened or are false accusations against us."

Just then Tom Parker stood up.

"I agree totally. I feel we did nothing to warrant this. We asked questions that dealt with our job and the safety of our mission and we still have the right no know the truth. I also will not sign a general statement."

He sat back down and moved the papers towards the center of the table. I pushed my stack forward also. In unison each of the others moved their papers forward. Pyler stood up and slammed the papers he had down on the table.

"You are all making a huge mistake here."

He looked at Sturgis and Nelson and pointed and yelled.

"Outside!"

They got up and left the conference room. I stood up and took a deep breath.

"I took a chance there and called them on this. They don't want this to be public at all and by not listing any violations they thought they could cover it up. I don't know what they will do now but I feel strong that they will not fire any of us because of the public and government negative involvement afterwards."

I looked at them and they slowly started to see what I was getting at. I went over to the phone on the credenza and called Susan. When she answered I asked her to get me the number to Steven Fralinger out in Nine Palms, California out of my phone book in the desk. After a few minutes she read me the number and I hung up. I dialed the number and soon I heard his voice.

"Hello!"

It was a groggy Steve being woke up.

"Steve, Vince here, at Lincoln."

"Vince, what's up? Is there something wrong, why so early a call?"

"Steve, I am sorry for that but answer me one question and that's all. I will call you back later and explain everything. But answer me this one question. Are you currently training for a special mission that has to do with the name of a bird? A cousin to the Hawk."

"I know of that mission. If my memory serves me right you are on that mission. The answer is no. In fact I am in no training at all right now and have never trained for that mission."

"Thanks, I will call you later."

I hung up the phone. I went back to my seat and sat down.

"Well, what did he say?"

Tom was anxious in his voice.

"No!"

They all started to talk low to each other.

"They are out there trying to regroup with their next volley to get us to sign. They don't know we now know they were lying about a second crew. Stay strong people."

About two minutes later Phil returned to the conference room. He stood at the end of the table for a good minute before he spoke.

"You are all to go home and wait for a call giving you each our next decision."

"No Phil, we will remain here. You don't want this public and you certainly don't want such a stupid incident to get blown so far out of proportion that it causes you and the agency national disgrace. We will resume work and there will be no further discussion of this incident. All we want is an honest answer concerning the training issue and why there is a secret mission modification."

I stood up while I was speaking.

"Let's go crew, we have some training to catch up on."

I headed for the door and my crew followed as Phil stood there motionless. We walked out of the conference room and I purposely walked past Pyler's office on our way to the training building. We entered the building and we were met by all of our assistants at the door.

"Vince we were just called by Phil and told to get you into the tank as soon as possible. So you all better get suited up fast."

He smiled at me and everyone went to their dressing areas and started the long process. While we were getting ready I wandered over to the bulletin board to look at the mission schedule. I wasn't very surprised to see that the schedule was not posted. There was nothing at all concerning our mission on the board. Everything had been removed. I went back to the dressing area and let the crew know that there was no schedule so our training today was going to be just a general in tank session going over what we have already done for weeks. When everyone was dressed we strolled out to the tank and saw the crew waiting and I asked the head trainer what the plan was for today. He smiled at me and told me we were going to get very wet. I asked what was the training mission for the day and all I received in return was a comment about more of the same as usual. I told them that we needed to work on satellite assembly issues and they said that they were not going to cross that bridge until told to do so. So we all got ready and made our way into the tank for the session. Everyone was training in the tank but we were just going over maneuvers since no one actually knew what we were supposed to train on. But we were training and I was happy about that.

CHAPTER 4

I T WAS MID AFTERNOON AND WE WERE HEAVILY INTO THE TANK
training when I heard over my earpiece that I was to be extracted from
the tank. Everyone else was to continue on with their training. I knew
then that Pyler was coming to read me the riot act but in essence he was
caving in. I knew he had no choice in the matter but he needed to try and
save face, at least he thought so. I soon was lifted from the tank and brought
over to the side. I had my helmet removed and then I saw Jerome Sturgis
standing on the side far enough as to not get his expensive suit wet. I flung
my arm knowing I had a lot of water lying in the creases. I saw him jump
but I knew I got him. As I was unhooked from the system I was told he was
standing there waiting to talk to me. I turned towards him. I could see the
major wet spots on his light gray suit.

"Sturgis, you need to talk to me, here during training?"

He moved a little closer but was still five feet away.

"We have decided to hold off on enforcing punishment for you and your
crew for the time being. But just so you know that any further disruptions
will not go un-noticed."

He started to walk away.

"That's it! No apology for being wrongly accused. What a guy."

I turned slightly towards my assistant but I could see him stop and turn.
I guess he thought about coming back but thought better of it. I was hooked
back up and then after being pressurized again, lifted and put back in the

tank. Once I was down there and resumed command I made the general announcement so all in the tank and support personnel could hear.

"The boss had a change of heart. He gave me a kiss and said all was forgiven."

I could not see anyone visually but I knew they were smiling or maybe even laughing at that moment. I also knew the command crew topside who monitored everything heard it as well. Training went very well this day and for the next week we put a lot into catching up for lost time. Nothing was said about the schedule issue and none of us pushed for any answers either. We were in a briefing meeting with the training managers when they put up on the screen the time frame for us to conclude our training. We knew we had only a few weeks left before we went through our final stages before departure for the cape. We all looked at the training that was left knowing that our tank time was only supposed to be for one more day. There in black and white was a whole week of tank training with nothing listed as to what type of training. All I could think was here we go again. As it was crossing my mind and the rest of the crew started to mumble and look at each other, Phil came in the door.

"So, now let's get this out in the open finally."

He blurted it out as he walked in front of the slide. He looked around the room and told a few people to leave. When he was satisfied he had only who he wanted in there he started again.

"On the screen you will see another week of tank training that was not scheduled before. It is for you all to train in deploying a satellite. You have all trained for this before but we want to refresh your brain. We have no set mission here but we are aware of a satellite that might need to be grabbed and fixed and then deployed again. So, we want you to be up to speed on the procedure. This is the error you saw weeks ago that should not have been included in training at that time. It is just refresher training. Any questions Vince?"

"This satellite; is it already in orbit?"

"Don't have that information."

"But you just stated it needed to be grabbed, fixed and then deployed again."

"I don't have that information."

"OK, then is it military or civilian?"

"Again, don't have that information."

"What information do you have concerning the satellite that we are taking up with us?"

"I know of nothing that you seem to have a lot of questions for. What I do know is that you are to train in the art of deployment if needed to do so, as a precautionary measure if needed."

"OK, but the biggest question is when would we be passing by a satellite on our way to or from Mars? I have never heard of a satellite out there in deep space."

He stood there staring at me before he spoke.

"So we will have five days of refresher training and then we will resume the final part of the training as scheduled previously noted. Thank You."

He walked out of the room. For the next half hour we all pondered the idea of pausing to fix a satellite during our mission. It all seemed so out of place. There was a launch next week from the cape. Why wasn't it added to their mission instead of ours? But at least now we had a little insight into what the training was going to be for, even if it was a very little insight. We also reviewed the fact that with the new regime in power we were scheduled to be the one and only last exploratory mission to be funded. And then there were only two more regular space station missions left in the budget as well. But those missions were strictly to bring back our people and equipment when they power down the station or leave it for someone else. We as a power in space were about to take a back seat. No one in the space industry was very happy about this. We all wondered why the new administration was determined to destroy our presence as a leader in exploration. Something most of us in the industry felt was necessary for our future survival. But that was something none of us had any power to change so we just needed to do the best on this mission as we could do. We all hoped that a new and more dedicated individual to the space industry became the next President and overturned these decisions. So the rest of the day was spent reviewing the training schedule and setting up the equipment needed for the week. We finished before four and everyone called it a day. Since it was Friday and the training was not scheduled until Monday morning we had a good weekend coming up. I decided that I was taking Susan to New Orleans to relax. I went in and told Phil of my plans and he approved the days off. So I left for home and to break the news. Soon I entered the house to see Susan in the kitchen baking. There was a cake and two pies on the counter and she was making something else as well.

"What is going on here? Are we going into the baking business? You never bake pies or a cake for that matter."

"No, this is for the party tomorrow silly."

I stood there for a moment with a blank brain. I did not recall having a discussion concerning a party coming up.

"What party?"

She turned towards me and gave me a very scornful look.

"You don't know what day it is tomorrow, do you?"

I stood there again trying to get my brain to cycle through all the numbers locked up in there.

"OK, I can't remember."

"It is the 10th. So what is special about the 10th?"

I walked over to the calendar on the side of the refrigerator and stared at it. There in front of me was the 10th and a star in it with the words Deborah and Bryan written on it.

"Oh shit! I forgot all about it. Damn it!"

It was my brother's and her sister's birthdays. And the party was going to be at Deborah's house. My brother lived in Florida and was flying in tonight. I just remembered that I was picking him up at the airport at seven. Deborah and her husband lived here in Lincoln. Her husband was also employed at the Space Center as a Meteorologist. He was always very busy working so we didn't see them together as a couple very often.

"Well, that just let all the air out of my sails."

She looked at me as if I was crazy.

"I can't believe I forgot about this. I just made plans for us to get away for the weekend. I will have to call and cancel everything. I just plain forgot. Work has not been kind to my brain lately."

I turned and went in the living room and sat down. I had not made any reservations but I said it anyway. I just sat there and thought about the whole weekend that I had prepared in my head. I had myself geared up for fun and now I was going to be playing host and trying to make conversation about something other than work. I went back into the kitchen and asked if there was something I could assist with. She looked at me and told me to go have a drink since I looked like I really needed one right now. I chose to get changed and watch the television for a while. At about six I got up and went back into the kitchen.

"I guess there is no dinner right now and soon I have to get to the airport to pick up Bryan."

"No I figured dinner would be for when you two got back from the airport. If you're hungry take a few cookies."

I went to the fridge and took a beer and then grabbed a piece of cold pizza that had been in the fridge for two days. I headed out the door not saying anything else since I caught the tone of her voice. I knew I would just get into trouble. I headed for the airport and after the thirty minute ride I pulled into the short term parking and entered the terminal. I wandered around and after hitting a fast food place I grabbed a drink and drifted over to his arrival gate exit point. Soon I saw him on the edge of a herd of people coming out of the concourse. I motioned to him and he returned the gesture. He was still single but I knew he was dating so I expected him to not be arriving alone. But to my surprise he was all alone.

"I didn't expect you to be alone today."

"Just here for the weekend and I figured it was easier this way."

We embraced and headed for the luggage bin to retrieve his baggage. After a few minutes the ramp started to move and out came the luggage. After he retrieved his bag we headed to the car and headed out onto the highway.

"Hope you are hungry, Susan is making dinner for when we arrive home. I had to wait so I am ready to eat."

"I'm good but there is still room for more."

We talked about life in Florida and how things were going for him. We enjoyed the conversation for the short time we had as we drove into the driveway. We entered the house and threw his stuff in the spare bedroom.

As we entered the kitchen we saw everything was on the dining room table already but Susan was still in the kitchen, still baking for tomorrow.

"Hi Bryan, how are you?"

"Just fine, I think someone here has over done the occasion."

He looked around at everything on the counters.

"I am just making some desserts for tomorrow."

We joked about it for a few minutes then we went in and sat down to eat. After dinner we went into town and to the local sports bar and had a few drinks before heading back to the house. Everyone was tired so we called it a night before it was even eleven. In the morning I made breakfast for everyone as they started to rouse around eight. I put out the normal spread when I get into the cooking breakfast thing. I had a plate of hash browns, bacon, home fries and I was getting ready to cook eggs to order as they arrived in the kitchen. We ate until we were over filled and then relaxed in the living room for the morning talking about old times and current events both in Florida and here. We briefly discussed my future away from Earth that was fast approaching. He was fascinated with the thought that I was actually going 'out there'. He gave me a little medal that he was given many years ago when he was in Italy visiting the Vatican. He told me the story about a Cardinal he had met and befriended. I had heard it before but this time I was holding the medal that he gave to Bryan. Bryan wanted me to carry it, on loan, during my mission. I agreed and put it on the table to be gathered later. Soon we found it to be almost noon and we need to start gathering everything to make the trip across town. The party was a great success. Everyone was having a wonderful time. They were both celebrating their 30th birthdays so it was a big deal to the families. It was close to eight when we gathered everything up and we headed back to the house. We pulled into the driveway and I could see a note attached to the front door. We walked into the house and I retrieved the note and once inside I opened it. It was from Carl Petterson, the Science Officer on the mission. He wanted me to call him this evening indicating it was important. After we put everything away I grabbed a beer and headed out onto the porch and sat there for a while. Susan and Bryan joined me and we talked about life in general and Bryan mentioned he was going to visit our parents after he left for a few days before he headed back home. They still live in the Carolinas and were getting close to retirement. They had owned their own business for over thirty years and really didn't want to quit any time soon. I had once told them that after I could no longer be part of the space program that I would consider coming back and settling down there and taking the business over so they could just relax. They liked that plan and kept reminding me of it. I soon got up and went into the house and over to the phone and dialed up Carl. He answered the phone and I sat down in my chair to carry on the conversation. After the normal greetings he got serious.

"Vince, I am going out on a limb here with some information I received this afternoon."

"If this has anything to do with out mission it might be best not to discuss this on the phone." "You're right how about if I come over there."

I agreed and after about ten minutes he came walking up to the porch. As soon as he did Susan and Bryan excused themselves and went inside. Carl sat down and looked around the street before he looked back at me.

"I received a phone call from someone at the center who said they were involved with the satellite deployment system operation. He said that our upcoming mission had a satellite twist to it. When I asked about the satellite we were going to capture and fix he was speechless for a while. I had to ask him if he was still on the phone before he spoke again. But what he said floored me Vince. He told me that he didn't know what they told me but we would be taking a satellite with us when we launched to be deployed when we arrived at Mars. It was designed to orbit Mars for a while and then return back to Earth and go into Earth orbit for the rest of its mission. That is all he would tell me saying that was more than he planned to say but we needed to know. He then hung up on me. I didn't recognize the voice but he knew us."

"Well, I think we should keep this to ourselves. I don't want the rest of the crew to know anything you told me here. I am not sure I will even tell Tony until after the launch. This is obviously meant to be a secret deployment and they don't want the press or any foreign government knowing about it. I wonder if I can get in to take a sneak peek at this satellite?"

We talked a little more and then he left. The rest of the weekend went by very fast and I took Bryan to the airport at five on Sunday. He was flying into Charlotte and renting a car from there. Monday started our last ten days of intense training. I snooped around and asked some general questions to try and find out where this satellite was being kept but I didn't get any solid answers. So by Wednesday I decided I was just going to have to wander around through the dozen or so buildings myself. I started after we finished the daily exercises. I managed to check all the spaces in our main building but there was nothing out of the ordinary going on in there. The next day Carl and I both together went through the next building adjacent to us. We managed to go through more than half without any interference but when we came to a section of rooms on one end we found there were some security guards monitoring the area. So we tried our best to get into one of the spaces but we were rejected by the guard for not having the correct access badge. I made like I didn't know and got a good look at the badge he was wearing to try and find a duplicate to it. Over the next two days we roamed other building and came across many spaces we were refused entrance to. Everyone one of them had difference access badges. We knew that this was going to be a feudal attempt so we decided to quit while no one suspected us from our leadership team. So the last six days of tank training went as planned and the team was pleased with the results so we were finally finished with the underwater training. Now we had a couple of weeks of book training and a few days to go over again the space capsule orientation. Then our final physicals and we would be ready for the mission to begin. We were into the middle of the next week when everyone was told to take the afternoon off. This wasn't planned so we knew something was up. Most of the crew went home but a few stayed to do some back log work. Carl and I went out to the open lot where we could see the area pretty clearly. We were not there very long when a security car came up to us and told us we had to leave the area. As we were discussing our options as to where we could go we saw a large flatbed semi-truck go past us over to the rear of the building adjacent to our training building. The security ushered us out of the area quickly after that. We were completely on the other side of the buildings and could clearly see security cars everywhere making sure no one could get to the other side of any of the buildings. While we were there waiting to get over to where our cars were Phil came walking out of the building towards us. When he approached be had a very serious look on his face.

"Vince! Carl! What are you two doing here? You were told to leave hours ago. Sturgis called me and told me you were still here and that over the last few weeks you have been identified on surveillance tapes and being in areas you didn't belong in. Don't open this can up again Vince. This time it will not go well."

"What are you talking about? We stayed to go over some of the mission aspects and when we tried to leave we were ushered over here and told we can't leave. You tell us why."

"I am not going through this again. When it is cleared you will leave immediately."

He turned and went over to a security guard and after a conversation with him he re-entered the building. It was about twenty minutes later the guard came up to us and told us he was going to escort us to our cars. He did just that and we drove off the center grounds. Nothing more was seen so we never had any conversations about it that night. We just went home and spent the evening trying to relax.

CHAPTER 5

I AWOKE TO THE SOUND OF BIRDS CHIRPING AND THE SUN SHINING through the drapes. It felt good to sleep in on a Monday morning. The last few weeks were all simulator days going over for what felt like the ten hundredth time all the pages of the flight plan. I knew we would do this three or four more time this week. But it was nice to not have to be there at the crack of dawn. I leisurely got up and showered and then dressed for work. It was almost nine when I left the house heading for the center. I was met in the lot by Sarah Meyer, the Bio Chemist who had a lot of experiments to do on this mission. Her payload was full of experiments and tests that would keep her very busy. She was also the doctor on board so I was glad to have her around. I remembered my last shuttle flight when one of the astronauts got sick and we were guessing and making suggestions from a medical book. It was going to be nice to have a full fledged doctor and Internal Medicine surgeon on this flight. When I was told there would be a doctor on the mission I was given a dozen names and their qualifications. Her resume' stood out like a beacon and there was no question she was going to be a crew member. I knew she was married but I never saw him at any functions we had so I didn't know any of her history. I just knew she had great qualification and she was a looker to boot. She was also the smallest crew member size wise being 5 foot 3. The other two women were both 5 foot 7 and didn't have that small petite frame Sarah carried.

"Captain, I think you need to see this."

She handed me a piece of paper. On it was hand printed in what appeared to be crayon.

'Your mission is a secret mission to destroy the world. Why else would you be putting a satellite in orbit with twenty nuclear missiles on it. You are the bearer of D O O M!'

I looked at her and asked where she got this. She told me it was on the windshield of her car when she came out of her house this morning. We headed over to Phil's office and after we entered I gave it to Phil and told him he had someone who knew the project that appeared to be a little unstable and he needed to deal with it. Phil read the paper and told us not to worry since there wasn't anything there to concern ourselves with. We left his office and saw him immediately pick up the phone as we went out into the hall heading towards the training building. We knew that he was going to try and hunt down where it came from. His quick action also told me that the note hit a nerve and really raised some questions in the back of my mind as to what this satellite really was for. But I dismissed it all figuring it was a ridiculous thought. It was just a crazy dude trying to create a problem. We entered the conference room and sat down with the rest of the crew and after telling them about the note we all got down to going over procedures again. Later in the afternoon Public Relations man, Scott Douglas came into the room. He broke in on our studying letting us know that there was a planned meeting with the press next Tuesday at ten in the morning. Everyone needed to be in their blue traveling flight suits and that the questions were basically a briefing as to who we were and our backgrounds. We would also be giving our official duties as part of the answers. He passed out papers listing everything we would say in response to the questions that were pre-set for the press. Then there was going to be an answer period that I was going to be the only one giving answers to. There was a couple of paragraphs outlining my responses to certain types of questions and what to say on questions they didn't want us to give answers to. So we looked it over and he left stating he would be with us at the press event and not to worry about it. After a few minutes we went back to going over the mission logs. The next two days were spent in the simulator going over launch sequences and orbit and de-orbit procedures. We would be docking with the space station and transferring to the space craft which was already up there being prepared for the mission. It would take two days for us to transfer and check our list to ensure we had everything we needed for the mission. Everything was being duplicated to insure there was not going to be any problems if we met with time delays during the mission. If all went as planned we would take about five months to get there and then spend three weeks in orbit around Mars and then heads home again. So when you add the week on each end stopping at the space station we were going to be gone almost a year. We didn't want to talk about that part of the mission but we knew that the press would be asking that question as well. Our final weeks on the schedule had four hours of visits with a psychiatrist listed. I guess that was our mental training part of the mission. The simulators were my favorite since you could really get your head into thinking you were actually out there. We went over all sorts of problems and situations that required one to know every part of the system to be able to fix or bypass situations. After a week of this we moved to the capsule simulator that we will only be in for two days getting us up to the space station. This was a unique mission in that the space craft we will be taking to Mars had been brought up to the space station three months ago and has been fitted with the fuel tanks and supplies since then. Every three weeks or so a mission went up to support our space craft which was at the space station waiting for us to get up there. Soon we will go up and take control of it. Someone else will bring back the shuttle craft. The last mission to the space station will bring back those two crafts and everyone that is still up there on the station. We were very aware that we would be the last craft left in space soon. Everything was going great in these last few weeks. The press conference was scheduled for today and we were ready for it. Soon the time came and we headed outside to the area set up for the press. We all walked out in order file and stood side by side in front of the large press corps and several hundred others. The families of the crew and all the workers were invited. Soon Leonard Pyler came walking out and up to the podium.

"Good afternoon! Welcome to the Space Center Training facility. We are happy to introduce the eight astronauts that will be taking our exploration of space to the next level. This mission has now, finally, been officially named. It will be called 'TALON'. There has been speculation of several names including this one over the past months but we officially named it yesterday. The mission these great individuals will be embarking upon will be to take a space craft from the Earth to Mars. They will orbit Mars for several weeks taking samples of the atmosphere and sending down a rover and then retrieving the data and samples that the rover has gathered on the ground surface. Then they will return home after what we expect to be a highly successful research mission. As you know this is the only planned mission that has been funded by Congress and we hope that we can show them and the world that other missions need to follow. I would like to introduce to you and the world today our crew that will be taking this historic and record breaking mission."

He turned slightly and looked over towards me pointing.

"First of all we have Captain Vincent Mariani. Vincent has been in the space program twenty-one years now and has flown on several space missions, most recently as co-pilot on a shuttle flight last year. He came to us from the U.S. Air Force and at age 45 is our most senior astronaut and well deserving to command this, our most adventurous mission. He is married to his wife Susan for 6 years now. He is a graduate of the Air Force Academy and hold two masters from MIT. He holds Engineering degrees in Aeronautical Engineering and Mathematics. Next, we have Commander Anthony Politta. Anthony has been in the space program for sixteen years and he also has flown a space mission in the program. He came to us from the U. S. Air Force and at age 41 is the co-pilot of this mission. He has been married to Gabriella for 16 years and they have three children. He is a graduate of the Air Force Academy and he also holds a Masters in Aeronautical Engineering from MIT. When we made our choice for pilot and co-pilot we wanted to make sure we had two of the best the system had to offer. These two gentlemen then were given the task to select their own crew. From their initial selections we approved every one they hand picked. We also approved the five backups that are not out here today that they selected. So you will know that this team is very compatible in that they all were hand selected and work together extremely well. Third, we have Carl Petterson. Carl has military background as a pilot in the U. S. Coast Guard.

He later went back to college and received his Masters degree in Space Science. He also holds a degree in Astronomy. He became an astronaut 12 years ago. Carl at age 39 is married to Helen for 16 years now and has three children. Our fourth member, and our first of three women aboard this mission, is Sarah Meyer. Sarah has been in the space program for 13 years and was our first choice when it came to her field of expertise. She is a Medical Doctor holding a Masters in Medicine from Duke University. She is also a board certified Internal Medicine Surgeon. She also holds a Masters in Biology and a degree in Bio-chemical Engineering. Sarah is 40 and has a husband named Robert. Our next member is Lt Commander Thomas Parker. Tom comes to us from the U. S. Navy and is a graduate of the Naval Academy. He also has a Masters degree in Science from Cal Poly. Tom will be the Science Officer on board for this mission. He has been an astronaut for 17 years and is 41 years old and married to Barbara. They have one son. Next we have Henry Lempster who also came to us from the U. S. Navy. Hank has a Masters degree in Construction Engineering and is one of our Mission Specialists. Hank will be one of the team that will be conducting the space walks during the mission. Hank is 34 and he is single. He has been an astronaut for 9 years. That leaves us with two more. They are not the least important. They have the distinction of being the two with the more critical tasks and having to do the most during this mission. For that we chose two that had great energy and determination. First we have Lt Karen Collins. She comes from a family of pilots and herself a graduate of the U. S. Air Force Academy. Karen has a degree in Space Science and has been an astronaut for 7 years now. She is a Mission Specialist for this trip and will also be doing all the space walks. She is 31 and she is also a single lady. Next we have Michelle Powers. Michelle came from the civilian community. She has a degree in Nursing and will also be a Mission Specialist with space walk duties as well. Michelle has three duties on the mission. First, she is the nurse taking care of any minor health issues that arise. Next as I mentioned, she will be doing EVA's. And last she is the one person on board that knows where everything is located. Her packing skills are crucial to the rest of them. Michelle is 37 and has been an astronaut for 7 years now. She is married to a gentleman named Stephen and they have one daughter. This is the first space mission for both Karen and Michelle. So, I think I have spoken long enough and you now know the crew. I will turn this meeting over to our Captain Vincent Mariani to take any questions you might have. Thank You for coming out today."

With that he turned and walked over to his seat. He was supposed to take questions before I got up there to weed out the heavy mission questions that only he could answer but he bailed out. I could see the look on Sturgis's and Nelson's face when he sat down. I stood up and walked over to the mike. There were several press people standing already.

"OK, let's do this. I know there will be a lot of questions so I will try and get to everyone. Please be patient and I will call on those with a hand up."

I pointed to the first one.

"Have you seen the space vehicle you will be taking to Mars? And if not, how can you feel comfortable piloting something you have never been in before."

"Well, that's heavy right off the bat. The answer is yes, I have seen it, but you are correct in that we have never had the opportunity to fly it since it is its first adventure also, we are both rookies on this mission. But saying that, I assure you that every pilot who goes up in a plane for the first time feels very confident because of all the training in a simulator that is exactly like the real thing."

I pointed to another.

"When was the space craft taken up to the space station? The press was never informed of this launch."

"I really am not sure, but I believe it was launched from California three months ago. Next question."

"We have heard rumors that this mission is two fold. Can you tell us the two objectives you have to perform?"

"I'm not sure what you mean by two fold. We have a mission to take a space craft to the planet Mars, do exploratory research and then return. If you are referring to piloting a new era space craft, well, yes we are excited about that as well."

"No, I was referring to the secret military part of your mission."

"OK! Well as you said you heard rumors. Let me tell you they are just that, rumors. We have one mission and that is to get to Mars and return. That is more than enough to keep us busy. If there is another part of this mission we as the crew have never been told about it. Only the agency could answer that one."

Selecting another reporter was done quickly.

"Your families will be left here on Earth for a year wondering how things are going. What are your feelings about the length of the mission and the loneliness it will bring?"

"We are going on a mission for the betterment of Earth so there is no feeling of leaving loved ones behind. We will feel times of missing our families but believe me we will be so busy doing our job it will be no more different than a sailor going to sea for 120 days. And we still will be able to communicate with them."

"We were at the cape this weekend and could see a third section on the rocket. So I will ask as my fellow reporter did. This extra section we have been informed is most likely containing a satellite. No where is a satellite listed in the mission briefing. So what is the secrecy of this mission and what is in this section of the space vehicle?"

I looked at Pyler and then back to the audience.

"I have not seen the rocket or what is on top. It should be the space capsule we will be flying to the space station in. We are carrying the Mars rover and because of the mission, one hell of a lot of fuel. There is nothing more to this mission to my knowledge. Mr. Pyler needs to answer that one."

I saw Phil walking up to the podium. I stepped aside and he took over.

"That section just below the capsule is the rover lander that will be attached to the space craft once they reach the space station. We were not able to include it inside the shuttle since we have a lot of cargo still to get up there for this mission."

He walked away from the podium. The rest of the hour we were mainly answering questions concerning the rest of the crew. Some still tried to hit on a secret mission but we remained firm on our answers. I felt that if the press was picking up on an extra area of the space craft then I sure was wondering what it was myself. I had surmised that it had to be the satellite though. I wanted to see pictures or see it in person soon. Finally after almost two hours they ended the press event and we went inside. They called a meeting to go over the event. During the meeting several people other than my crew questioned the added section and what was really in there. All the questions were indirectly not answered. We knew that the rumors of a satellite being on this mission were starting to look pretty good.

CHAPTER 6

THE LAST WEEK OF PREPARATION IN THE SIMULATORS WAS MORE stressful than it should have been. The atmosphere around the center was very tense. The rumors of the reports about the satellite were rampant and everyone was asking questions and getting no answers. They had a real problem on their hands. Tempers were on short fuses and no one would make any decisions when it came to a problem that needed resolved. I gathered the crew together and sat them down for a talk. I told them they needed to get through this week and just button it up so there was nothing anyone could blame us for their attitude. So for the next four days everyone was tight as a group and we didn't do anything alone. There were always at least two of us together to protect each other. It was the worst week of my life. I wanted out of there so bad. Finally Friday came and I told the training crew that we were done at noon today. We as a group had a scheduled meeting in town with the mayor and his staff so there would not be any afternoon training. There was nothing said but I knew that Phil or his cronies would be calling soon. Noon came and no one questioned my orders. I gathered the crew and told them we were done with all training and next week was our physicals and psychological reviews for the last time. So everyone needed to get a good rest this weekend and I would see them at 0900 Monday morning right here in the conference room. They all left and I sat there all alone for about an hour. Then I got up and went into town and bought a few things for the weekend. I planned on relaxing and doing a cookout with real food everyday. I was going to eat all my favorite things because I knew it would be a long time before I ate real food again. I gathered up the bags and headed home. I called all the crew members and told them what I was doing and said that if they wanted they were all invited on Saturday for a cookout. I told them there was no need to explain if they chose not to come. We all had our fifteen minute meeting and ceremony with the mayor at three in the afternoon and then we were done. We were leaving for the cape the following Thursday since the scheduled lift off was for eight days from now. So the rest of Friday was spent sitting on my porch and drinking beer. I went to bed real early mainly because I was exhausted. Saturday came to an early start when the phone was ringing. I leaned over to see that it still wasn't seven so I was trying to wake up and getting pissed at the same time. I picked up the phone and yelled,

'Hello!'

"Vincent this is Phil. I need you and the crew in my office by eight."

"Bull shit! This is our last weekend Phil. Can't you just leave us alone for once in your life?"

"Vince, have you seen the paper this morning?"

"You just woke me up so how in the hell would I see the paper."

I was really getting heated.

"Go look at the front cover of the paper and then call everyone and get in here."

He hung up. I laid there for a little while and then rolled out of bed. Susan never budged. I knew she was awake since I was yelling. I put on my pants and went outside to retrieve the paper. My neighbor across the street was standing there holding his paper then looking at me.

"Wait until you see this one Vince. This is not going to be good."

He looked back at the paper. I leaned down and picked up the paper and unrolled it. There on the front page were three pictures and the headlines read,

'Nuclear satellite part of mission.'

The pictures were of the rocket on the launch pad with a circle around the area just below the space module we were going to be in. The second picture was a picture of the supposed satellite showing missiles on its sides. And of course the third picture was of the crew. I stood there and started to

read the article. It stated that a source who worked on the project provided
the information and the pictures for the article. It said we all knew about the
mission and we were going to deploy the satellite aimed at our adversaries.
All I could think of was,

'Oh Shit!'

I went in the house and started to make the calls. Some were already
up reading the article. So soon we all showed up in Phil's office. Phil was in
a meeting with Pyler and Sturgis. We discussed the situation and all agreed
that this was their issue to deal with and we needed to hide from the press.
Finally Phil and Sturgis came in the office. "Ladies and gentlemen, we have
a serious situation here that needs to be taken care of."

I broke in on his talking.

"I am sorry to interrupt you but we do not have a serious situation, you
have a serious situation. As far as we are concerned it is not our problem
and you need to make sure the press leaves us alone. We have asked for full
disclosure on this mission and you have repeatedly lied to us so as far as we
are concerned it is only your problem. We expect to be protected from the
media effective now."

He stood there looking at me. Sturgis walked up to Phil and whispered
into his ear then he and Pyler left the room. Phil stood there until after he
left before he spoke.

"You are right! It is our problem and you need to all go home and we
will get word to you as to what we decide."

We got up and we all left. We stood out in the parking lot and talked
for a while. We all decided that any calls to each other would be made
only on the hour. We made up a call format and agreed that we would
only try between the hour and 5 after so we would not be answering the
phone otherwise. If that didn't work then we just had to meet at each
others houses. Everyone left and went home. Saturday's plans were all
ruined but I still planned on cooking out. It was hard listening to the
phone ring all day long and not answering it. Susan was livid and could
not be talked to at all. Cars were driving past the house constantly and the
press had two cars sitting just outside my driveway. The neighbors were
all good about the situation especially when I told them we knew nothing

about any satellite on our mission. I told them that this had to be a hoax for publicity by someone who was trying to stop our mission for some reason. I was preparing the cookout in the back yard when a helicopter flew overhead and hovered. I looked up to see a news helicopter so I waved and continued on with my preparations. It was almost noon and everything was set up so I gathered up the cooler and put in a bag of ice and a case of beer. I set two bottles of wine in there for Susan as well. I reclined in the lounger and watched as the helicopter occasionally flew by overhead. It was around two when I heard talking coming from inside the house. I decided to check it out just in case there were reporters at the door. When I entered I saw Tony and his family and Sarah but no husband. I could see walking up the front steps a few more of the crew and their families. I had a small swimming pool set up in the back yard so the kids could enjoy themselves. I had wondered if I had wasted my time and money when I bought it but now I was glad I did. We were having a good time just relaxing and talking about everything under the sun. And occasionally we were drowned out by the helicopter overhead but we just ignored it. I cooked up the food and we went inside to eat to get away from the press who occasionally snuck into a neighbor's back yard to take pictures before they were chased away. Eventually the sun started to set and everyone started to head home. Susan and Sarah were still sitting there yapping. I finally caught some of their conversation. She was trying to set her sister and my son up for a future date. I shook my head thinking that was never going to happen. Bryan loved his freedom and took off on trips on the spur of the moment. Not the settling down type just yet. At about nine Sarah started to say her goodbyes and she headed out the door planting a kiss on my cheek and thanking us for a wonderful relaxing day. I agreed it was well needed with all the stress going on around us. My neighbor came over just as Sarah drove off. William worked at the center just as everyone living in this complex did. He walked up on the porch and we shook hands.

"What a mess some asshole has made of all this. Why can't people just mind their own business?" "Yes it is a mess. I can't figure out why someone would send such a far fetched story to the press just before we leave."

"So you really don't know anything about all this?"

"Not at all. I know nothing about a military satellite with missiles. That's wild. We would have definitely been training for a satellite deployment if that was true."

"Your right, nothing gets done without training to the excess around here."

"The press is a real pain in the ass too."

"Yes, but that will all go away in a few days when they find out their story is a fraud."

We talked a little while longer and then he left. I walked back into the house and Susan asked what that was all about.

"It was William prying into the press thing. I told him it was a fraud and all of it was not true. So he will spread the word around quickly. He still is the worst gossip in the neighborhood. He puts you women to shame."

We laughed and retired for the evening planning on doing most of the cleanup tomorrow. Sunday came and went without any major confrontation with the press. It seemed they finally settled down. The morning paper still had an article concerning the mission and added more things in there about the satellite. But their tone had changed indicating they were still looking into the source to verify its accuracy. So they were gracefully trying to back out of the hard line they ran with on Saturday. I had heard from Phil and he told me they were hitting the press hard and that Washington was having real issues with all of it. One would just have to wait and see what was happening at the center when we went back to work on Monday. The one thing I really noticed from the pictures in the paper was that the compartment below the capsule we would be riding in was very large. It appeared to me to be too big for just a rover. I was starting to rethink the story of there not being a satellite in there as well. In fact I was starting to believe everything the press was reporting and that the agency was feeding us a real big line of bullshit. But we were in the final week and I was determined to get to the cape and be on that space craft. I was not going to tell the rest of my crew my feelings but I was very nervous about the whole situation. I knew that once we were in space that the media would quiet down and we in space would not hear about this anymore. But the problem was that if it was true about the satellite them we would be sitting on a time bomb and then we really had to deal with it all alone out there in space. And I was the one who had the responsibility to get it done and I was very worried about that.

CHAPTER 7

I PULLED INTO THE PARKING LOT AND SAW EVERYONE WAS ALREADY there. I looked at my watch to make sure I wasn't late. It still wasn't nine so I guess everyone was just anxious to get this last week over with. I entered the training building and went to the conference room. When I entered there were a lot of people in there. It was really packed full. I thought I had made a mistake and was in the wrong place. Then I saw Tony and when he spotted me he gave a whistle and everyone got quiet.

"Here he is. The man who is going to take us on a mission that will create new and bigger missions for the future."

Everyone started to clap. I looked around and saw a large cake on the table and bottles of water everywhere.

"To our boss! May his guidance be strong and true. May no issue be greater than a hang nail. May his leadership pave the way for the center to be here twenty years from now. May there be no Mexican food in the food machine."

The group cheered and then Tony came up to me and shook my hand.

"This is for you boss. For being the one who was the strength in our training and all the issues that we had to deal with, actually, what we had to not deal with. So thank you from everyone here at the center."

Again everyone was cheering and clapping. It took a few minutes before there was enough of a calming effect that I could speak.

"Well, this was a surprise. I really don't deserve this but I will accept it for my crew. We have only everyone here, that was a part of getting us to today, to thank. Without your help and persistence we would not be here today. So, thank you."

Sarah made her way to the front and went over and started to cut the cake. While everyone was enjoying themselves, in walked the three stooges. Pyler, Sturgis and Nelson came in the room.

"We know this is from the training staff for the crew but we wanted to stop by and also thank Vince and his crew for a job well done and we look forward to next week and the start of our future in long space exploration. Thank you!"

One could tell from Pyler's face that he spoke the words but there was no meaning or feeling behind it. They mingled for a few moments and then left. After they left the group noise level went back up 40db. For the next hour everyone was enjoying themselves and then the P.R. man, Scott, came in and told us the doctors were ready for us. So we went around the room thanking everyone and headed out the door over to the clinic. The whole day was spent going through physicals and tests to make sure we all were still in top notch shape. When we were finished each of us went home individually. The physicals were more exhausting than the training. One was actually weak from all the blood samples taken and then the stress tests. I plopped down on the lounger in the living room and stayed there for the evening. The next day we started the two day event with the group of Psychiatrists to see if we were sane enough to go into space and isolation for a year. We wondered if some of these individuals were on the verge of being loony themselves. But it was a more relaxing day since there were three hour sessions for each of us with three different shrinks. Nothing else was scheduled so our down time was relaxation in the crew lounge in between sessions. I played a lot of pool today. Thursday when we arrived there were press people everywhere. Apparently they were there to make one last attempt to get to the truth of the satellite issue. The center slammed them because they printed their story and never confirmed the source. Since no one came forward as to ownership of it they were back tracking trying to create their own version of it to try and save some face with the public. That would be hard since the whole community was basically employed with the space complex in one way or another. They wanted another interview session with us but the center denied any requests for any one on one interviews. They gave them their generic statement and had them escorted off the grounds. Everyone had their evaluations presented to them on their physicals and their mental state of health. As expected everyone passed but some of us were yelled at for having a few higher than normal levels for eating a lot of meats and other things that were supposed to be on our do not eat list, and we were now ready for our mission. We had the required final meetings with each department head and went over the mission critical issues one last time before we called it a day. It was early evening with the sun starting to set when we each made our way home for the last time. The evening was a subdued time at my house. The night was spent with very little sleep. It was a sad time in some senses of it all. You wanted to leave on the mission but you didn't want to leave your loved ones at home. So for the most part the last ten hours of your family life seemed like twenty hours but the clock was spinning very fast every time you glanced at it. I did manage to get a few hours of rest before that alarm clock went off. Susan on the other hand was not even in bed. She had been awake all night. One could see it in her face, the look that said she wanted to say – don't go. But she knew I waited my whole life for a chance at a mission like this. She also knew I wanted to leave and soon this morning. I packed a light bag just for the few days I would be at the cape before we launched. Most of everything was provided for you when we got there. You didn't want for anything once you were on site. Susan was not coming to the center this morning. She didn't want to have to go through saying goodbye twice. We said our goodbyes and held each other for a long time and then I walked to where a car was waiting to pick me up. It was a policy that if you needed a ride to the center a car would be sent to give you a ride there. I approached the car and saw Phil sitting in the back seat so I got in the back with him. We started to make our way to the center when he handed me a piece of paper. I looked at him and then opened it and started to read.

'I could not let you leave today without telling you a few facts. The stories that were leaked are not all wrong about having a military satellite on your mission. The fact is that there is a satellite and it does have top secret implications. You will be informed once in space. I just wanted you and me to be the friends we are supposed to be. Please keep this to yourself. I have added a folder to your cargo pack to be opened once you're on your mission to explain some things. Take care my FRIEND.'

I looked up at him and he reached over and took back the paper. He folded it and put it in his pocket. We said nothing on the drive to the center. Once we arrived we embraced each other to say goodbye and he went to his office and I headed for the lounge. Some of the crew were already there, all the single ones anyway. I walked in and grabbed a water bottle. One by one they entered and some had their families with them. I called out to the flight operations building to ensure the four planes we would be flying out of here today were being prepped. The morning had a somber attitude and except for the kids running around everyone was quiet. Sarah told me there was another note on her car but she threw it away without reading it. Nothing was going to upset the thoughts of the day for her. Hours were dragging by this morning. People were coming in and out wishing us all well. I reached into my pocket several times an hour just to make sure I had the three medals I wanted with me on this flight. Bryan's was the most important at the moment. Everyone had at least one personal camera that was packed for the mission. I took two and a video camera. One of the experiments Sarah had on her agenda was cell phone related so we were all interested in that experiment. The though of calling from space on a cell phone was intriguing. Sarah walked up to me and grabbed my hand.

"Just wanted to see if you're as nervous as I am?"

She held my hand and I could feel her hand shaking.

"No Susan?"

"No! She doesn't like saying goodbye twice."

She nodded and let go of my hand and placed it on my back and rubbed it up and down in a gesture telling me that she understood. They brought in snack food and light drinks for everyone but I did not feel like eating. I wanted a stiff drink but that was out of the question since I was piloting a plane in a few hours. Phil came back in and walked up to Tony. The two of them were having a serious conversation about something. I could tell from Tony's face he was not in agreement with whatever was being said. Finally the time came when everyone was given their final periods of saying goodbye. Each went into side offices and did what they had to do to get through the moment. Wives and kids left the room with most having teary eyes. After about ten minutes the only ones left in the room were the crew and a few support personnel. Phil asked them to leave and when it was just us he gathered us all in one area.

"Well, it has been a while in coming but we have made it. We are now in the final days of watching you make history. The whole aspect of our life as a space oriented agency lies in the success of you all. I wish I had a glass of the bubbly in my hand so I could raise it to your good fortune on this mission. I will add one thing before I finish. This mission will have its moments and you all are the ones I know that will be up to the task to deal with them. Remember one thing, I am always behind you. I would never allow you to go on a mission I did not feel was 100 % safe. Well, as safe as we can make it anyway. Vince here will brief you all on parts of this mission that none of us, in this room anyway, knew about weeks ago but are now built into the system. I can not say anything more than that."

They all were looking at me.

"Don't judge him yet. He does not know what I am talking about. He has his instructions waiting for him sealed in the space capsule at the cape. I just wanted to let you all know I just became aware of them recently myself and I am sorry you were not told."

He paused for a while.

"So, to all of you, go and venture into the unknown and come back heroes."

He reached out and shook every ones hand and walked out the door. Sarah and Tom both in unison asked what that was all about. I told them I was in the dark as much as they were at the moment. I didn't want to let on about the conversation Phil and I had in the car earlier. Each of us went and gathered up the few belongings we had that we were taking with us and started to head for the flight operations building. I grabbed a piece of sandwich and another water bottle as I headed out the door. We all walked slowly, meeting all the support people that were lined up on our path wishing us god's speed and farewell. It was a nice gesture on their part but it made me feel like I wasn't coming back. Not a feeling I wanted right now. Finally we made our way to the flight operations office and we went over the flight plan to the cape and after signing the appropriate papers and getting our needed flight gear we walked out to the planes that were sitting out there on the tarmac. There were four of us that were still current pilots so we would fly the planes with the other four as passengers in the two seater jets. We had to leave at 1 to be at the cape for the customary arrival ceremony that was scheduled for 4:30. So we had fifteen minutes to prep the plane and head for the runway. It was not prearranged as to who was flying with whom. As we walked to the planes everyone seemed to start pairing up without saying a word. I looked next to me and I saw that Sarah was moving up to my side. I nodded to her and then looked at each of the others who now had a side kick. We climbed in the planes and got settled in. I went over the instructions for her and told her to enjoy the ride from the back seat. We fired up the engines and soon were taxing out to the runway. We got the go ahead and one by one started moving down the runway. Each plane slid upwards into the sky and when we made our turn around heading east, we passed directly over the center waving our wings to say goodbye. We could see a group in the parking lot waving as we went over. After the low pass by we climbed to the altitude we needed and made a direct line for the cape. There wasn't much talking during the flight and most of it was over water so there wasn't much to see. So it was a relaxing smooth flight that went rather quickly.

CHAPTER 8

W E WERE ON FINAL APPROACH TO THE CAPE CROSSING THE
Walt Disney World resort when Carl came over the radio
mumbling very low,
'When I get home I am going to Disney World'.

I could hear some laughing from the others as we looped south to align
ourselves with the runway at the cape. About eight minutes later we were
putting down the landing gear on final approach. After we all touched down
and taxied to the designated area where there was a large crowd and what
appeared to be a hundred press set ups. All I could think about was the press
we received this last week before we left and found myself saying out loud,
'here we go again'.

I didn't realize I had said it out loud until I heard Sarah say,
'Amen'.

We maneuvered the planes into the proper positions and shut them
down. One by one we popped the canopies open and climbed out of the
planes. The crowd was cheering and clapping as we walked up to the stage
where the press had been set up. The director of the space agency at the
cape was at the podium already talking to the crowd announcing our arrival
and giving a short brief history of the mission and our training leading up
to today. We stood there listening to him go on and on about how great we
were. Then to our surprise he started to introduce someone else. We then,
at that moment, realized the presence of someone sitting off to the side. We
didn't see them at first since there were a lot of people standing around that

area. Up walked the President of the United States as he was introduced. We glanced at each other since we did not know of his presence in advance. He rambled on about the importance of this day and then he went on to state how important of a mission it was and that the Americans in this country needed to be grateful for the knowledge and ability to conduct and carry out such a mission. All along I knew that at least I was saying to myself how his words were meaningless since he was the one who was axing any further projects for the future. I came back to the present as the director returned to the podium and started to introduce each of us. Upon completion of the introductions he introduced me and I stepped up to the podium. I gave a very brief acceptance of their gratitude speeches and told them how we planned on creating history so future missions could and needed to be conducted. I was sure they all were cringing about that one. When I was finished the director ended the ceremonies. We were then shuffled off into several cars and headed for the administration building. After all the obligatory welcomes we went into the lounge and took a seat to relax for a moment. The director and the President entered the room. He made his way around talking and shaking hands with each of us showing that smirkish smile he was famous for. He wished us all well in his political way and he left the room. The director talked to us for a while letting us know what was planned for the next two days. After he was done several others gave us the real version of what we would be doing leading up to launch day, five days from now. We were shown our quarters and then taken to the main facilities where we would finish our training on some of the specialized equipment on the space craft we still didn't know very much about. Other than the training on the simulators concerning the cockpit there were no training simulators for the rest of the space craft. We asked to see the rocket and after they received approval we were taken out to the launch pad and we walked around there for a while. We took some pictures with one of the cameras one of the crew had with them. I saw a man coming down from the gantry and I walked over to him.

"Henry!"

He turned and looked at me for a moment before he recognized me.

"Vince, damn good to see you! I see you got the big ride this time."

"Nice huh! What can you tell me about what's up there that is going to be under my ass."

He looked up at the rocket.

"If you mean that extra space, well, I'm not at liberty to talk about that."

He paused reached out and touched my arm and we drifted off to the side away from the others. "That is one hell of a satellite. Never before have I seen a satellite that had its own full propulsion system. It can go on its own mission and no one would know about it."

"So where is the rover located in all that?"

"The rover went up to the station three weeks ago. You mean you didn't know that?"

I looked at him and nodded saying thanks. I walked back to the others and we finished up and left going back to the main assembly building. It was now getting quite dark as the sun had already set. We were taken in and shown a mock up of our space craft in full scale. I was told that it is exactly like ours and it has full power, in fact it could be used on a mission. So it essentially was a back up craft. I guess they needed a back up.

"From what I hear they are going to use it for any problems you encounter so they can simulate everything you do."

That made me feel a lot better. At least I knew they had something to reproduce situations. I asked if we could get a walk through to see what it looked like inside since none of us had any clue to what it looked like inside. We were told that would have to be arranged at a later time. We eventually made our way back to our quarters and were told to be in the crews lounge at the end of the building by seven in the morning. We all just looked at each other and we each went into our quarters to check them out. I walked down to the lounge to get an eyeball on it. It had not changed from the last time I was here. As I was walking back Tom met me and told me that dinner was being served in ten minutes in the cafeteria just for us since it was so late in the evening. I said alright and we headed for the rest to let them know just in case they haven't received the word. After dinner Tony and I showed everyone around the complex. That took a while since we had a few who had never been at the cape before. Soon it had reached almost nine and I told everyone that I planned on retiring early so I bade them good night and left. I went back to my room and opened by bag that was already in there. I saw my carry bag on the chair so I opened it also. I noticed an envelope just inside it that I knew I had not put there. There wasn't anything on the outside of the envelope. I then remembered Phil telling me he placed an envelope in my baggage. I broke the seal and took out a single sheet of paper.

'I know you will be in Florida when you read this. I just want you to know I can not handle this. I will be leaving as soon as you are gone. I am going to stay with my mother and then my sister for a while. I just can't be in Lincoln while you're gone.'

It was not signed but I knew it was from Susan. There was no real ending nor was there any I love you. Wow, she was taking this harder than I expected. It was like she didn't expect me to return and she was preparing herself for it. This is just what I didn't need before my mission. Things were piling up and I was not happy about it. I sat there and brewed for a while but I chose not to call and not to let it get to me again. I had to forget it and try hard not to bring it back up even though I knew that wouldn't happen. I threw the paper in the trash can. I went in and showered and went to bed. I was woken by a knock on the door. I opened my eyes but could not see anything. It was dark and since there were no windows I could not tell if it was still night time. I heard the knock again so I got out of bed and went to the door. I opened the door and saw Carl standing there.

"Sorry to wake you Vince but I need to talk to you about Susan."

I told him to come in and I closed the door.

"Susan is having a rough time Carl and I know she left for her mother's place today. If you were going to tell me she wasn't home, I knew."

"Well, then I guess it is alright. Talked to the wife and she said she called Susan and she told her she could not take any more and she was leaving. What bothered me was the statement she made to the wife about not knowing if she will ever return."

I sat on the bed and looked at Carl. I went over to the trash can and pulled out the crumpled paper and gave it to Carl. He read it and said that it was just between us and nothing more would be said about it. He apologized for waking me again and left. I looked at my watch to see it was only eleven so I went back to bed. This time it took me a while to finally fall asleep again. The alarm went off and it felt like I had just fallen asleep. I laid there for a few minutes but knew I had to get up or I wasn't going to get up at all. I sat up and looked at my watch to see it was six. I slowly got up and after a while got dressed and ready for the day. I wandered out into the hall and then went back inside but left the door open. A few minutes later Karen, Sarah, and Michelle wandered by and stepped into the room.

"Hello!"

I answered and they came in. They said they were heading to the cafeteria and wanted to know if I was going. I told them yes and I put on my shoes and we all left my room to go eat breakfast. We soon met everyone and after a small breakfast we headed for the crews lounge. We weren't in there very long when they came to get us. We were escorted to the training facility where we immediately got down to work. We were training on modifications that were made to the rover that we would send down to Mars. That took about five hours before we broke for lunch. After lunch we went back to a simulator. There Tony, Tom and I were given changes to the thruster controls for the capsule. These changes were made to accommodate the satellite unit attached. We then found out that we had to do an EVA to move the satellite module from the capsule to the new space craft. It was going to be a very long EVA. The rest of the crew was taken to a different area where they were actually walking through the EVA of that move. I questioned why we were not trained to do this in the tank in Lincoln. We were told that this was rather a sensitive issue and there were unfortunate incidents happening in Lincoln that would not permit that to happen. We were also told that the satellite was supposed to be already up at the space station but it was too big for the shuttle bay. So we have to suffer by doing several walk troughs instead of real training. I was real upset with this. This is why there was the change in the scheduling that we did not know about but then was never really added. We went to where the crew was training.

"Vince, this is pure bullshit. They want us to do an EVA with no training on it at all."

Karen was livid as she kept on about the EVA. I finally calmed her down and we all went to a room and sat around a table.

"OK, here is the situation. Back in Lincoln, remember the added water training that we complained about but they wouldn't tell us what it was for so they removed it. Well, here it is. This is the EVA that was added. So let's look at it from a difficulty level first then safety."

We went over what they wanted done and determined after some discussion that it was not very difficult. Undoing 48 bolts on each end and then hooking it back up to the new space craft. Karen told me that the new space craft only had 24 bolt connections. So that meant less work as far as I was concerned. They finally calmed down totally and we agreed that it was not difficult and since there would be three out there it was rather a safe EVA also. We all went back to the training room and everyone walked through the EVA many times. When the day was ended we decided that a few more times in the morning and we all would be ready. We left and all went back to our quarters. I was sitting at the desk in my room with the door open waiting for the others to go to dinner when Karen came in the room. She apologized for the way she acted but was very nervous and upset because of having no training on the EVA. I told her to relax and breathe in for a moment and listen. I told her that this was actually perfect training. That when we are out there and if we need to do an EVA on something we hadn't planned on fixing you would not have any training for that. You have to do what you have to do to stay alive. She sat there and finally shook her head and understood what I was saying. Again she apologized and started to cry. I stopped her cold. There will be no crying here. If someone sees you crying you will not go on this mission. She stopped immediately.

"I am just stressed right now and I don't know why."

"I know why. This is your first time for everything. You, Michelle, and Hank have never been into space before. So you are having trouble right now because you finally realize it is for real and in three days. You will be fine. Take long slow breaths and keep quiet about being nervous."

She was getting ready to say something when a few more of the crew walked into the room. After a minute they all were here and we went to dinner. Later that evening I was sitting there with the door open. That was the policy here. If the door was closed you didn't want to be bothered. If open, anyone was welcomed in. I was reading a manual on the satellite system that was left in my room while we were at dinner when in came Karen and Sarah. Karen walked up to me and gave me a hug and thanking me for earlier. I just stood there looking at Sarah. Karen told me that she told Sarah what happened and it was alright now. I put my finger to my mouth indicating to keep it hush and they both agreed. We talked about fear and how to make sure it didn't take control. We talked for some time before they left and I closed the door and retired for the night. Morning came early again but this time I finally received some good sleep. Today everyone went through their EVA practice several times again and then after lunch we trained on paper the transferred of all the equipment, food, and water we would be doing during the other two days we stayed attached to the space station. I talked to the boss and arranged for the crew to get out for a while this afternoon. We were told that the walk through of the backup craft was not going to be possible since they were still working on it. So around four they took everyone over to the main entrance building where visitors had access to. We went up on a stage and addressed the visitors at the complex for about thirty minutes. That was a real good nerve breaker. We went back to the secure complex and after dinner I went over the final days plans. I saw that it was going to be a half day of training and then the famous words showed up at 6PM on the schedule.

'Confined to quarters'.

I knew what that meant but the new ones didn't. They didn't know they were in for ten hours of forced sleep. I was going over all of this when I realized someone was standing in my doorway. I looked up to see Sarah standing there.

"What's up!"

"Nothing, just going for a stroll and saw you sitting there deep in thought and thought I would see if you were alright."

"Sure, everything in fine. Has Karen settled down yet?"

"She is fine. Nerves got to her that's all."

"Looks like you have something on your mind."

"No, just thought about how you handled Karen and now I know why you are the man you are and why they chose you to head this mission. So, I will continue with my meandering. Bye!"

She walked away from the door. I sat there for a minute and then went back to reviewing the satellite manual. That took me hours and eventually I got too tired of reading and went to bed. The next morning was the same as the others, breakfast and then training. Most of the morning was for any questions to be answered so there were no concerns. When the trainers and mission chief were satisfied we were comfortable it was over. I told everyone we had an appointment with the doctor at four before dinner. So everyone went back to their rooms and if they were like me, packed everything to be stored until our return. At almost four I gathered everyone and headed for the clinic. We had a group talk with the doctor and then a nurse gave everyone a zip lock bag. Inside were four small pouches each being labeled with numbers. I smiled at some of them and they looked at the pouches with surprise. I finished the meeting with a thank you and addressed the crew with words concerning the pouches. I let them know that I would explain them at dinner and we headed that way. We went to the cafeteria but went to a side room and told them to sit down. In a few minutes in came eight covered trays. Everyone was given a tray and the veterans all had smiles on their faces while the rookies didn't know what to think. The lids were removed and they saw a small serving of cut fruit, soup, and two vegetables. They sat there and stared at the plates.

"Welcome to the program's version of the last supper. The food in front of you contains everything you need to feel full tonight. It is bland and there are no condiments available. With this you will take the pills in bag nr 1 in your pouches. It is recommended to take them with the soup to mask the taste. When dinner is completed we will talk about the rest of the night."

Everyone started to eat. Some just picked through what was on the plate. So I spoke up again.

"I am not your mother but I would say that whether you like it of not it would be advisable to eat everything in front of you. You will be very thankful later if you do. If you decide you don't want to eat everything, then, remember later when you are having issues that I warned you."

I went back to eating. When I was finished I looked around to see everyone except Hank had finished everything.

"Hank, are you sure you are finished. That soup has a special purpose later."

He looked at me and then started to eat it. He ate most of it but then quit.

"I have had enough. That's it for me."

"Ok, then here is the plan for tonight. Everyone has taken package number one. When you get back to the room you will be busy packing up everything you have. You will have those items taken in the morning for when we return from the mission. No perfume! No snacking! At seven you will take package number two with some water. At that point you will need to be close to the restroom for a while. After that episode is over it would be in your best interest to take a shower and go straight to bed. You will be sleeping very soon afterwards. I will be coming by around nine tomorrow morning to make sure you are awake. I will tell everyone again in the morning but package number three is taken at nine and then number four gets taken before we enter the van out to the launch pad."

I started to laugh before I continued.

"So, basically you have taken pills to clean you out. Next pills to put you to sleep, then in the morning pills to not make you feel very bad later and then pills to make sure you keep your pants empty during the flight into orbit."

Carl and Tony were having trouble holding back their laughter.

"Those of us that have been through this will tell you that the next few hours are uncomfortable but you will feel great tomorrow."

Then Tom stood up and held up a water glass.

"To US! To the crew that will rebuild the space nation."

Everyone stood up and took a sip of water and then we left for our rooms. The evening went as scheduled. I checked in on each of them to make sure they were following the instructions on the last packages they took. I had conversations with each of the new crew members to reassure them that all was good. After I made the rounds I headed back to my quarters and prepared myself for the reactions of the package and then got ready for bed because soon I knew like me, everyone would be sound asleep.

CHAPTER 9

I FELT THE LIGHT TOUCH ON MY SHOULDER AND A GENTLE SHAKE AS I opened my eyes to see someone standing over me.

"Sir, it's 8:30 A.M., time to get up."

I sat up in bed and took a deep breath.

"Thank you! Any changes to the schedule I need to know about?"

"No sir, everything is still a go and on time. They will be expecting you in the crews lounge at 9:30 sharp."

"We will be there with bells on."

He smiled and walked out the door. I put on a shirt and pants and headed out the door to awaken the crew. I went into Tony's room and rousted him. I told him everything was on schedule and he stated it was going to be a beautiful day. I then went down the hall to each one's door and did the same. So now everyone was up. I checked in with each one again and reminded them to be in the crews lounge at 9:30 sharp. I went back to my room and took a hot shower. I stood under it for quite a while knowing there would be no more long or hot showers. I dressed and put all my papers in a pile on the desk. I wrote a short note to Phil Nelson and placed it on top of the pile. It was 9:20 so I headed out the door and down the hall. The two televisions were on, one on their channel showing a slide variation of different views of the launch pad and area. The other was on a weather channel strictly for the local area. It was showing great weather for today. The launch was set for 3:48 P.M. The bottom part of the screen listed the status and time for the launch with a count down clock. I sat down and waited for everyone to arrive. The mission control people came in first and then the Director of Operations and then my crew. Right on time they started the briefing. It lasted about thirty minutes and then a very light breakfast was brought in. About ten minutes later their prep crew came back in and said it was time. We were all escorted out of the building into a van and taken over to the mission prep building. We went in and entered a large room divided into sections but open in the middle. Everyone went and used the facilities for the last time. We were then told to take package number three. So we all put the three pills in our mouths and swallowed. Each one was taken to their area and the dressing in the suits began. It was almost noon when we finally finished getting into the massive space suits. We were now connected to the mobile air units and I was very comfortable considering the weight involved. I was assisted into the middle area and joined two others already there.

"The only things missing are the helmets and they are already up on the entry gantry."

Tony was telling everyone since I guess someone asked about their helmet. The flight Operations man came by and gave us a little pep talk and said that the van would be outside to take us to the launch pad at 1300. I saw by the clock on the wall it was 12:39 P.M.

"Ok crew of TALON! Time to take your last pill. I would like to say at this time I am extremely proud to be part of this mission. I know it will be a success and the future of the space program will benefit greatly by your efforts. As they used to say, happy hunting."

He saluted us and went out the main doors. One of the others came in the doors as he left. He told us there was a huge crowd of press out there waiting for final pictures for when we left. When all my crew was ready I saw we still had five minutes to go. I decided now was the time for my speech. "Crew! Three years ago I was asked to be the leader of a special mission. I accepted it without hesitation. I also had Tony here as my side kick so I knew whatever the mission was it could not fail. Tony and I over the next year hand picked each of you. There was no selection board and certainly no competition. You were all picked for your special fields and your dedication to your profession. I am proud to walk out those doors today in your company. So now let's go and kick some cosmic ass."

They all smiled and I turned and headed for the door. Each of us had two helpers as we exited. They opened the double doors and we walked out in single file. The crowd outside gave out a roar for a reception and then the clapping overtook the air. We all waved to the press corps as we walked past them on our way to the RV. One at a time we climbed into the RV taking a seat. As I sat there I watched the faces of each crew member as they entered the RV. When Karen entered I looked at her and smiled. She put a huge smile on her face in return. Everyone was now on board and we started to move.

"This is the last chance you have to back out. Any takers?"

Everyone chuckled and the RV made its way down the road to the launch facility. After about 10 minutes we were climbing out of the RV and entering the launch facility. When we arrived at the elevator three of us got in and made the trip up. When we reached the top and got out the elevator went back down for another group. After about fifteen minutes we were all up on top of the launch facility. The view was wonderful.

"Look at that view."

Karen was reaping the effects of the last pill. She was happy. I answered her very softly.

"Wait until you get up there and see the view you get."

I pointed straight up. She slowly tilted her head and looked up to the sky. One by one we entered the outer chamber and our helmets were put on and locked in place. When we were all ready they started putting each of us in our seats inside the space capsule. That process took about ten minutes for each of us. Soon I was the last one going in and I was ready. When we were all strapped in the gantry boss man came to the door and bid us farewell and as the customary salutation, god's speed. He then closed the hatch and sealed it. Tony reached over and threw a few switches.

"CAPCON THIS IS TALON."

"LOUD AND CLEAR TALON."

"ROGER."

I set up and secured the flight book in its place and so did Tony. I saw Tom arranging his book and equipment as well. The rest of the crew was watching us as we went through our routine. It was going to be new to them since they were not involved in flying this big bird at all. It wasn't long until mission control started going through the check list. That took almost an hour just by itself. Then they checked all the other systems dealing with the launch pad and soon we were at the stage when we heard mission control give the words I was waiting for.

"TALON – MISSION CONTROL."

"GO AHEAD."

"ALL SYSTEM ARE GO. WE ARE IN A HOLD. THE COUNTDOWN WILL RESUME SHORTLY. WE ARE AT 20 MINUTES AND HOLDING."

"ROGER MISSION CONTROL."

I looked over to Tony and made eye contact with him. He put out his arm over towards me. I returned the arm swing and we bumped closed fists. I then gave the crew behind us a thumbs up. In the small mirror I saw them nodding their heads and looking at each other as best they could. "TALON MISSION CONTROL – THE COUNTDOWN CONTINUES AT THIS TIME."

"ROGER."

Soon we heard mission control calling each sector and getting a go or no – go from them. Everyone was a green light. I looked at the screen in front of me and watched the clock count down. I knew there would be a short delay at the two minute mark. Soon there it was and moments later they started the clock again. Now the check list verification process started again. We were quite busy from here on down to lift off. We were going through everything one right after another then all of a sudden it hit me. I was hearing single digit numbers. The checks stopped and we braced as the capsule started to vibrate as we heard nice and loud,

"3 – 2 – 1 AND IGNITION."

Everything around us was shaking. We were shaking in our restraints as if we were at sea in heavy waves but more quick violence. Then we felt the pressure starting to build against our body. We were rising off the pad and starting to rise up into space. Mission Control was still talking and asking questions or making statements and I was responding in kind still trying to keep focused. The pressure kept getting heavier. The feeling went from someone pressing on my chest, to now having bags of cement across my body. That was the feeling of the G forces as we hurled up through the atmosphere. Soon it peaked and then there was a jolt when the booster rockets were separated. All along I was keeping communications going with Mission Control. There was a good reason why most of this part of the flight path was on auto control. A human could not manage all the switch control functions that were being done as I watched the panels in front of me with their dancing lights. After about ten minutes everything started easing off. The pressure went away gradually and the shaking was bearable again to function. We were getting more involved in making adjustments and confirming readings back to control. It wasn't long until we were in orbit around the Earth. The engines have now shut down and we were floating in space. We were busy for a while confirming and setting the computers for our rendezvous with the space station about 20 hours from now. We checked out the internal communication system that seemed to have an intermittent problem during our ascent. But it seemed to be working just fine now. I asked the ladies if everything was alright since I seem to have heard an awful lot of,

'Oh Shits' earlier. They laughed and reassured me everything was great. We spent the next few hours going over check lists again and making more adjustments to line up better with the space station. Before we knew it we had orbited the Earth a half dozen times already. Everyone was in good spirits and yet mission control was keeping us busy with little tasks that needed done. It was not yet registering that this was day one of three hundred and thirty-eight. Since Tony, Tom and I were piloting this ship we didn't have the luxury of taking the wonderful happy pill the rest of them were still enjoying. But it would soon wear off and everyone would be grounded so to say, once again. I finished doing the last of the ground checks and was able to sit back and relax and take in the view for a few minutes. I checked to see that the capsule was indeed pressurized and all seems normal so I motioned to Tony and we removed the helmets from our heads. The rest of the crew seeing that went to work getting theirs off as well. There wasn't much room with eight of us in there to take off the suits so we were in them until we arrived at the space station. The holding bags would be well used after the other pills we took started to wear off. The next ten hours was spent checking and rechecking our position as we slowly crept up on the space station. It was a familiar sight for me but the new ones were excited to see the changing from sun light to darkness over and over again. After a while Lincoln told us that we were making another adjustment to line up with the space station. At the twenty-one hour mark we saw it on the radar screen and out one of the windows when they turned on a spot light. So now came the task of lining up the capsule for a docking maneuver. That was Tom's job and one that he has done live before. We all watch as the hour came around and soon we were directly behind the station and the sights and sounds of the system telling Tom where he was in reference to being perfect. I fired the thrusters a few times to make sure we were turned around and sliding at the right speed and he was using mini thrusters to get it right on the bulls eye. Then there is was a soft thud and a very small jolt. Tom gave a big smile and said,

"Welcome to the space station. Do you think anyone is home?"

We pressurized the connection and Tom got out of his seat and locked us in place so we became one unit for the time being. It took us a while to go through the shutdown log and then complete the files to end this flight. After making communications with them in the space station we both opened the hatches and made the link to our new friends. Life was indeed very nice right now.

CHAPTER 10

A FTER A FEW MINUTES OF REARRANGING THINGS ONE BY ONE WE entered the space station and one by one we removed the heavy suits that got us there. After about three hours of getting organized we finally started to enjoy each others company. Soon after that we went on a live broadcast back to Earth and to the world via television. The day was working on being a good one. There was no stress and everyone was jovial and the world out the window was an amazing sight especially for the first timers. I caught the ladies staring out through the window several times as we were trying to sort out the lists we needed to start the loading process into the space craft. I was not able to see TALON from inside the space station except for the tail section. I wanted to see the workhorse we were going to be riding to Mars. Since we came up in a space capsule there weren't any opportunities to see out the forward windows because there weren't any. The shuttle would be coming up in a few weeks with a crew to return the capsule we brought up back to Earth. So I drifted back to the storage module and with my clipboard in hand I started to look for the numbers on the storage packs that matched the list. Nothing seemed to be matching at all. I drifted to the space station commander and questioned where all our storage packs were at so we could get organized for tomorrow. He indicated they had already loaded some into the craft because they had a lot of free time lately waiting for us. The rest are all around, is all I got out of him. This was an all European crew at the moment on the space station and it seemed there was no pressing time frame for anything. They were acting very care free and loose. I felt they were all drifting in space for too long because nothing at all seemed to have any importance at all to them. I went over to Hank and told him things were a mess and we needed to know where the packs were for the transfer. He agreed to start looking and took my list and the other two lists we had and with a station's crew members assistance he and Michelle went to our new home and started to see what had been already taken there. After about an hour Hank came back into the main bay of the station where I was and told me he saw everything they took over already and he checked it all off and also marked where they were located. He also told me it was all wrong and needed to be fixed. I went back to the capsule and contacted Mission Control and asked what instructions had been give for the transfer of some of the packs. They took a while but then came back with sending us a copy of the correspondence emailed to them. I opened the computer file and printed it. It showed they were supposed to transfer approximately 50% of the packs and it specified exactly where to store them. I sent back an email stating that they transferred about 10% of the packs and they were everywhere and more important not secured, some were found drifting about. I also noted we were not having any luck locating our packs in the space station either. So I left and went back to the station and gathered my crew. When I finally managed to get them together I told them the situation.

"I know we need to crash for the night and get this rolling in the morning but nothing was properly completed that should have been already finished. So we need to form two teams and we will work in four hour shift to get all our equipment and packs transferred and stored where they belong. I will head one team and Tony will head team 2. So Michelle and Hank your team 2, Carl and Sarah team 1. Tom you will go into our new home and take Karen with you. You will take a list or where everything is to be stored and then reorganize what is thrown in there to its proper place. Buy then we will or should be ready to start bringing the rest of our stuff over. Team two how about some sleep."

"Well I understand your goal but I think we are all wired right now. How about we all work for two hours and then we nap."

I looked at Tony and said that was agreeable. So Tony and I separated the three large lists and we each took half the pages and we started. Tom took the storage file and they headed for TALON. It took us over an hour to locate the first set of packs we were looking for. We started to move them to TALON. Others on the station offered to assist but I told them we had to do inventory so we had it under control. Six hours later we had rearranged and moved a total of sixty-three packs. The three lists had a total of 312 packs on them. I told team 2 to go get some sleep and they left for the capsule and some needed sleep. The remaining three of us kept moving packs over. Tom said that he finally had things in their proper places but noted that a lot of the hard packs for the mission had been tampered with and opened. He gave me the numbers of the packs and I went back and sent another message to Earth about it. While I was waiting I received a secure call so I set up to take it.

'TALON – MISSION CONTROL LINCOLN'.

"TALON HERE'.

'ARE YOU SECURE?'

'ROGER.'

'OK, THEN THE NUMBERS OF THE BROKEN SEALS NEEDS TO BE CONFIRMED. SEVEN OF THOSE CONTAIN MEDICAL SUPPLIES AND THE OTHER SIXTEEN ARE FOOD PACKS.'

'ROGER, WILL CONFIRM AND GET BACK TO YOU. DO YOU WISH WE OPEN THEM TO SEE IF THE CONTENTS WERE DISTURBED?'

'ROGER, YES.'

'ROGER OUT.'

I went back to TALON and told Tom we need to check the broken seal packs. We stopped the pack moving and started to open each one that had a broken seal. After two hours of this we finally finished the medical packs and had a large list of missing items, mostly drugs and some of them very controlled drugs. I told Tom he needed to stand guard while I went and reported the results. I told Sarah and Hank to go get some sleep. They were dragging so there was no argument. I went and set up the secure link.

'LINCOLN – TALON.'

'LINCOLN'

'I HAVE INITIAL REPORT OF FIRST ELEVEN BROKEN SEAL PACKS.'

'ROGER SEND.'

'EVERY PACK IS MISSING ITEMS. SOME VERY SUSTANCIAL LOSES. MANY CONTROLLED ITEMS MISSING. OVER.'

There was a very long pause.

'TALON – LINCOLN.'

'TALON.'

'SEND HARD COPY ON LIST AND SECOND LIST SHOWING MISSING ITEMS.'

'ROGER – OUT.'

I sent them the two lists they wanted and then went back to TALON. Tom was sitting there trying to rest. We talked for a while and then I sent Tom off to bed. It was almost an hour later when the commander of the space station came into TALON. He asked me to come with him back to the space station and I decline to do that. He started to insist and I advised him that he needed to not start an international incident out in space. I told him that we had a serious problem here and I had every intention to get it resolved. I went on about the space craft being up here for about three months now and they had only transferred a very small part of what they were supposed to do. I was furious with him about not being organized and then chastised him again for being such a poor commander. He stood there looking at me for a while and I could see he wanted to say something but did not. After a long period of silence he then told me his government had contacted him and told him that we had reported that controlled drugs had been stolen from the American supplies. He assured me he would find out who and what but wanted me to be there when he confronted the station crew. I declined again stating that was his concern and unless he wanted an international uproar over this he best find out who and what and have everything returned immediately. I informed him our mission could not start until everything was in place so if it was delayed because of him there would be hell to pay when he was returned to Earth on the next craft. He told me that he and his crew were going to be up here for another four months so it was not proper to threaten him. I informed him that when I finished my report since there were some serious medications missing that he or who ever was involved would be leaving very soon. Once again he stood there for a long time before he finally just turned and left. I was not feeling comfortable being there all alone and in such a tired state. Another hour passed and then I saw the hatch opening again. I felt anxious immediately. Then I saw my team 2 come in the craft. I smiled and let out a big sigh of relief. They waved as they entered and came over to where I was sitting. I filled in Tony as to what was going on and he started to curse. I told him that there had to be one in here all the time as they went and brought packs back. I insisted that only our crew handled the packs and I wanted Tony to verify every seal and the missing contents. We knew it was going to be a very long day doing this and everything else was going to be put on hold for the time being. I felt we were not going to be leaving the space station anytime soon as long as we had this problem. We talked about the time table and expected the mission would be delayed at least three weeks. I was sure that Lincoln would come up with some reasoning for the world was surely going to hear about the delay. They also needed to add a few packs on the next flight up to replace the missing things we found so far. Who knows what else had been stolen. While we were talking the station commander came back in the craft. He made his way over to us and asked to speak to just me. I said no and Tony and I stood there. He just stood there looking at Tony.

"Captain, my crew says they have taken nothing. There must be a mistake."

I took him over to a pack and opened and showed him the empty spaces when things were supposed to be. I told him there are forty-one broken seals in here. That eleven were medical supplies and some controlled drugs were missing from all of them. I made it very clear that there was a thief on his crew and most likely one or more that were turning into a drug addict. I let him know that Earth has been notified and given a list of all the missing things to far. I also told him we were bringing in packs and checking every one. We would not be going anywhere until our checking the packs was completed. So, if he did not have the items returned, then someone or most likely everyone assigned to the space station would be in serious trouble very soon. I also reminded him that since he was the commander of the crew he would be held responsible for the actions of everyone assigned to the space station. I also warned him that if there were any more problem he would be relieved of his duties immediately by me. He started to speak and mumble in his native language as he turned and left. Michelle and Carl were making round trips bringing in packs. Every pack was checked to see if the seals were broken. So far we were good with these. I told Tony that I thought they might have only broken into the ones they brought over thinking they were safe since they were in our craft now. I went over a few things about the commander and then I went and found a place to get some sleep back in the corner. I was out very quickly knowing I had been up for over a day now. I stirred and opened my eye to see Sarah standing in front of me.

"Sorry to startle you Sir, Tony wants to see you."

"I hope this is good, I really was sound asleep."

I got up and we both ventured over to where they were sorting through the packs.

"Vince, we found three more with broken seals and I have made the two lists required. But we have more to the story now. There seems to have been a total effort of their crew to go through the packs. It seems one or two of them did it and then they all got involved at one point or another. One of the crew members has come forward and started talking to Hank who speaks some of that man's language. We contacted Lincoln and advised them of the information he gave us. Lincoln has issued a global condemnation of the station crew and has demanded total change out immediately. They also have made it public world wide with pictures and names of all the crew members. We have been asked to relieve them of their duties and send them back immediately in our capsule. Lincoln is sending another shuttle up in four days to bring us everything we need and a new temporary crew for the station."

"So are we to arrest them or just let them roam freely?"

"They are currently confined to one section of the space station until we put them in the capsule for its return. They have been informed by us and their government that they no longer have any assignments to perform up here. We gathered them all up about an hour ago. I also sent Karen, Hank and Michelle out on an EVA to move the satellite module to our space craft. I told them to temporarily bolt it in place for the time being. Carl is also monitoring their progress. So we are waiting for the orders about sending them back any time now. They are programming the capsule for the return trip back to the U.S. from Lincoln remotely."

"OK! We are not in the space station business. I sure hope there are good instructions around here somewhere."

I looked around and asked how many have they done during my short nap. Tony laughed and said about thirty in the six hours I had slept. Wow, I had been out for six hours. It only felt like one. So I saw the last two crew members I had available were now in the process of delivering packs and supplies we brought up. They were emptying the capsule we came up in as fast as possible. We had to get everything out of there and fast. I did not see Carl so I asked who was guarding them and Tony confirmed that Carl was doing that as well. I took Tom when he returned and headed for the space station. This was a rather large place to try and search. I figured that since each of them were involved in stealing the drugs and other items that they all had them in their personal areas since there would be no reason to hide them. We went to the main area and looked for a map of some kind showing where everything was located. We finally found one on the wall next to the rear hatch of the main control room. But now that would have to wait. Carl said he just got the word to send them back as soon as we can. So we had to get them ready for their trip and soon. The capsule was being programmed to detach from the station in four hours and eight minutes. The EVA was just finishing up so that should not be a problem for the departure. I looked at my watch and marked the time minus fifteen minutes. I set the alarm. We went over to the area they were being held in and looked in on them. They were all sitting around in one spot. But there wasn't any activity so we left making sure the hatch was secure. We went to the capsule and started to help empty it. It was supposed to be a full day job but we now had about two and a half hours left. We made a chain and just dumped everything in the station since it was now ours. Doing it that way shortened the process a lot. Soon the EVA was completed and the three of them started to help move packs as well. In a little more than two hours the capsule was completely empty of everything. I looked at my watch and saw we had just over ninety minutes to get them suited up and locked in. I called for everyone to come to the main station area. Soon we were all there. I gave instructions out as to who was doing what. We found their space suits and set them up around the main room space. Then we went to the holding room and brought out two at a time. We told them to get suited up for their trip home. They refused so I told Carl and Tom to put them in the capsule without suits. I told them I really didn't care if they lived or died on the trip back to Earth. They each changed their minds and suited up and we placed them in the capsule and latched them in their seats. This went on for the other four in the same manner. Soon everyone was suited and latched in their seats. I told them the procedure for undocking and told the commander he was responsible for everyone's safety on the trip home to jail. He was a very unpleasant person. Since they had nothing with them we knew they could not have taken anything they had stolen out of the station. I looked at my watch and they had twenty-three minutes until separation from the station. I called Lincoln and advised that all six of the station crew were in the capsule and awaiting their trip back to Earth. They confirmed that everything was ready and so we waited. Finally the time had come and we locked the portal and depressurized the area. Two minutes later we heard the separation happen. Lincoln called and confirmed with us that separation occurred and advised they were in total control of the capsule from there. We watched through the window as the capsule drifted off and then saw the afterburners kick in and it drifted off out of sight. I wondered what else was in store for us. What appeared to be a great start to the mission has turned out to be a horrific day. I was not looking forward to ten months of this. We all gathered in the main station room and after talking about what just happened and how the next week was going to be a disaster without any game plan or experience on how to manage the space station. We all reminded each other that this is why we were chosen because we were the best. Everyone had to believe that right now or I was going to have a very difficult year ahead of me. We made contact with Lincoln and told them that we all want six hours of sleep before we did anything. They agreed stating it would take them some time to get all the files we needed transferred up to us. We talked about searching the station and then resuming the transfer and checking everything twice again. They told me I had three days to get the final list together or we would be on our mission without the missing supplies. We ended the conference call and we all went and found a hole to crawl into to get some sleep. It did take a while for me to slow down my brain enough to even get close to being ready for sleep. I just kept thinking about everything that needed to be done and we now had been told we had six days before the next shuttle arrived. Six days to go through everything and transfer what we needed and six days of praying that nothing went wrong with the space station systems. I looked over to the other wall and saw Tom sitting up and looking at me. I knew he was having trouble clearing his head as well. I just shook my head and then put my head in my hands and tried to drift off. The station was not a quiet environment but somehow I filtered all the extra noise out and I felt myself drifting off into dream land at last. My sleep was shallow and every time a different noise occurred I found myself waking up and gazing around looking for where the noise came from. I did that more than a few times but then I guess I finally became so exhausted that I didn't remember waking up again until I heard Tom's alarm go off but now I didn't want to open my eyes and I sure didn't want to get up and start working knowing what we had to do. Just the thought of the work we had in store for us made me tired. In the created low gravity it wasn't as bad as it could have been in zero gravity but still I knew we would be getting very exhausted very quickly as the day went on. Every crew member was slowly coming alive. Our plan for two teams was going to have to be implemented after we all got a few hours of work in as a crew. There was more work than time available at the present so sleep time was a premium at the moment. I managed to get everyone motivated and fully conscience to start the new process of what was now becoming our survival mission before we could even get started.

CHAPTER 11

WE WERE SITTING THERE TRYING TO ORGANIZE OUR THOUGHTS when I heard an alarm going off again. Knowing that Tom was in the same mind frame as I was he jumped up and started looking around to see where it was coming from. I quickly came to my senses and started to look around as well. I sat up and saw just about everyone moving about the space. There was Tony moving the fastest over to the communication center on the far wall. He stood there for a moment as there were lights flashing on and off as I approached. Then he reached out and hit a button or two and threw a switch. "GOOD EVENING LADIES AND GENTLEMEN! AND NOW FOR SOMETHING VERY DIFFERENT!"

There was a short silence and then the theme from 2001 started to come across the speaker. They played about 30 seconds of it and then it stopped.

"OK EVERYONE SHOULD BE UP BY NOW. HAVE SOME NEWS FOR YOU, ARE YOU READY?"

Tony threw the switch and answered

'YES'.

"THE CAPSULE HAS LANDED IN THE PACIFIC AND ALL HAVE BEEN RECOVERED. SONGBIRDS HAVE NEVER SUNG SO MUCH. WE KNOW WHERE MORE OF THE STUFF IS LOCATED AND THAT SHOULD MAKE YOUR FINAL LIST EASIER TO COMPLETE. YOUR INSTRUCTIONS FOR THE STATION, IF YOU

SHOULD NEED THEM, ARE LISTED IN VINCE'S DIRECTORY UNDER THE TITLE OF - HOME IMPROVEMENTS."

Everyone started to laugh including myself. The next ten minutes were lighthearted jabs back and forth before Lincoln brought it back under control.

'TALON! YOUR MISSION IF YOU SHOULD SO ACCEPT IT WILL BE TO REMOVE EVERYTHING YOU NEED TO YOUR ROCKET SHIP AND THEN DOUBLE CHECK YOUR LIST TO ENSURE IT FOR ACCURACY. THEN SEND US THE FINAL SHORTAGE AND IT WILL BE DELIVERED ON THE LAUNCH SET FOR WEDNESDAY. SO IN SIX DAYS YOU WILL ONCE AGAIN BE READY TO START OR I SHOULD SAY CONTINUE YOUR ADVENTURE.'

'LINCOLN – TALON. WE ACCEPT YOUR CHALLENGE.'

We spent time discussing the information concerning the reprogramming of all the computers aboard TALON for the new launch date. We still had to complete the transferred satellite enclosure to TALON. It had been removed from the capsule but temporarily attached to the craft. We also had to transfer the Rover to TALON. That was going to be a lot easier. We figured that would be done after the shuttle hooked up to the station. It felt like hours of talking went on back and forth before it was finally finished. We once again went back to TALON and went through everything again to make sure we didn't miss anything in our rush. After hours of doing that I told everyone to hit the sack after they found one. I was going to stay up for a while and made arrangements with Tony to start the swing shift with the crew as we had before with the two teams. We decided four hours of pack duty and four hours of other work and four hours of sleep. So I would stay up and asked for volunteers to be the first team on watch, so to say. I saw the two who volunteered coming towards me. As I figured it would be the same two from before I wasn't surprised to see Sarah and Hank. I wondered whether it was going to be Tom or Carl as the fourth. It wasn't for a while but then I saw Carl walking around with a clip board. I did the checking and listing as the others brought me packs. There wasn't any order in the number system anymore. Just bring in packs and we would put them where they belonged later. The four hours went fast. Soon we were doing other things that related to our primary jobs. I had a lot of computer time to catch up on and then I also needed to review the files they sent me. And once again four hours flew by. This time I was ready for a nap. The cycle continued for two days and then we were finally finished with the packs. We had our lists finished and made copies and then we e-mailed them to Lincoln. We then shifted the time frame from moving packs to searching the station for the stolen items and anything else of interest. What a cluster this place was. It was very disorganized and messy. We found some potential fire hazards and had to correct them as we went along. The cycle lasted two more days and during the last cycle before we finished we had received word that the launch had been delayed a day due to weather at the cape. We decided that tomorrow we would conduct the EVA to complete the installation of the satellite casing to TALON and we decided to move the rover as well. I made the three of them get extra sleep in preparation for the EVA. This EVA would take longer than the last one. They had to attach a cone to the front of it after attaching it to the underside of TALON. The set up was configured so the satellite casing was right in the middle of the booster rockets and solid fuel storage system we needed to get there and return. There were six solid fuel cylinders and two were for propulsion to get us up to speed to get there and then we had the two to get us home. There were the two smaller cylinders used for maneuvering and a small emergency load of fuel just in case. We didn't want to discuss the issues concerning what would cause its need. Everything was running smooth and like clockwork for a change but no one would acknowledge that. I found myself sitting in TALON going over the first day of our mission when we separated from the space station. I heard someone come up from behind me. I soon felt two hands rubbing the back of my neck.

"Wow! That feels great. You're hired for this trip. How about a one year contract?"

"Only if I get bonus options."

I turned to see Sarah behind me still with her hands rubbing my neck. Our eyes locked for a few moments and then I turned back around and said bonuses were not an option in government service. She stopped rubbing and stated we worked for a private agency not the government as she walked

ate. In about seven hours they will be docking and then our lives will get back to our schedule.

"I am tired and I don't want any more radical changes for a while. I hope they don't come up here with any new instructions for us. I have had enough of their changes."

He didn't say anything just nodded his head. As we were eating we heard an alarm go off in the main space. I looked at Carl and just threw up my arms. I shook my head and tried to finish eating. After a few minutes went by no one came in so I guessed I over reacted.

"I guess I need to get some sleep and get rid of this stress. I'll catch you later."

I got up and headed for the sleeping quarters. I got in the cocoon and was out like a light so fast I didn't even have time to think about it. I heard some commotion and it brought me to life. I raised my head and opened my eyes to see Hank and Tom playing what appeared to be hockey down the main aisle. I watched for a while and then looked at my watch. If I remembered correctly the shuttle was supposed to arrive in less than an hour. I slowly got out of the cocoon and went over to the unit better know as the head. After the great experience in there I watched them playing in the no atmosphere environment. They were using a nerf ball as the puck but it was flying fast when they hit it. The big deal was to actually hit it. Carl came in and broke it up telling everyone they need to get to work. He looked at me and yelled they would be docking in twenty-five minutes. I changed into my blue flight suit and headed to the station control center. I watch as Carl and Tom led them to a perfect docking. So they had arrived. I made a comment over the air so everyone including Lincoln heard it.

"And this is a moment in history. The space station and the old, which was here, with the current shuttle and the future space craft both docked at the same time. Too bad we don't have a picture." There was quiet. Every one was obviously just dwelling on the thought. It took a while but eventually the hatches were opened and in came the shuttle crew and the new station volunteers. They had to be volunteers since there was no time to have organized a regular crew change. I was sure one was being planned as I pondered it. So seven came up in the shuttle and only three were returning to Earth. We spent a few hours enjoying each others company knowing soon we also would be alone to ourselves for a long time. Once all the formal stuff was taken care of we transferred the several packs they brought for us and a special pack that was sealed. The reason I knew it was special is because all over the front were the words, SPECIAL. We laughed about it but no one knew what was in it. I did see that it came from Lincoln and Phil's name was on it as well. It had instructions that only I was to open it. We took everything to TALON and gave a quick tour to the other crew before we went back into the space station. About three hours later we performed our last EVA. It lasted five hours but even though it was slow going all went very well. Karen also took video of TALON from the outside for me. It was quite large. It appeared to be over twice the size of the shuttle in all aspects. It did have a small cargo bay but it was for use as a storage area for our supplies. So after the EVA was completed we had our conference call to Lincoln and it was set for us to depart on our journey tomorrow. We went into TALON and fired her up. Everything inside was activated to ensure everything worked before we left. After everything was on for more than a few hours we started to test each system. Some of the testing would take many hours but it would all be completed prior to separation. We were connected to the station so several times we switched to internal power before going back so we could save our batteries since our solar array was still not being used. We spend the evening socializing and helping the new station crew get acquainted with their home. We decided to spend the night there in the station. We did a lot of assisting them in getting used to the space station. We had been there only a few days but we still knew more than they did at the moment. So we showed the crew that was staying everything that we found that we felt they needed to know right away. As we explored the lab we found more things that were of concern from the previous crew. Lists were made of everything and we decided that we needed to search further. Everyone got involved and for several hours we went through all the spaces and labs and looked for anything that seemed out of place. We gathered all the things that we found out of place or unknown and listed all the items that they needed to fix or worked on after we left them. Lincoln decided to delay the returning crew by a few days to help them get the space station in order since it was really a mess. One by one my crew started to filter off and go into relaxation mode. It was now getting late in the day so we decided that we had helped enough to get them a good start of their mission to normal life up there again. We all ate dinner together and then after some more small talk my crew all hit the rack. I wasn't sure how they felt about leaving tomorrow but I was ready. I fell asleep rather quickly knowing there would be no distractions tonight. I was in a deep and sound sleep rather quickly. I was hoping for pleasant dreams to keep me there.

CHAPTER 12

MORNING CAME WITH NO ABRUPT NOISES AND NO ONE FORCING you to get up. I slowly opened my eyes to see nothing but quiet around me. It was a great feeling. I looked at my watch and saw that I had slept for almost nine hours. I got up and after the normal routine of the morning I headed for the main area of the station. Everyone was there except Tony. I ventured to the food machine and made my selection. I leaned against the side and ate. I was slowly coming around to the realization that we were going to be flying through space in a matter of hours. When I returned to the main area I was greeted by my crew and they joked about my sleeping time. Apparently they all had been up for hours. I asked Carl if everything was in order for the separation and he said Tony was going through that final list now with Lincoln. I told them that I wanted everyone in TALON by ten. I headed that way saying goodbye to the station and shuttle crew as I went. Everyone seemed excited to watch us start our mission. I couldn't blame them since I was getting that strange feeling inside as well. I started by getting the start up check list ready and the first day mission plan out. There was a great extensive library on the TALON. It consisted of about a hundred manuals on everything aboard the ship. Then there were a couple of hundred books and hundreds of DVD's and cassettes. Plus the hundreds of daily logs that spelled out the mission daily plans and left a lot of room for notes and comments. So I had the first log book in my hands. I found the first log book entry page for the mission and started writing about everything from the time we started the training to today. I was brief about the training but went into great detail starting with the added tank training forward. It didn't take me too long to get it up to the launch time. I then found the pages for the mission reports and I went to the first comment page and started writing. I decided to start with the docking at the space station. I also decided to use a little humor in the log by using the Star Ship series method of note taking. I took the pen in hand and started.

'TALON star date 20140518-1133-01.'

I skipped a line and began printing so it was very legible.

'Captain's log 01. Preparation for separation from space station.

Crew all aboard and ready.

Awaiting our orders from Lincoln Star Fleet Command.'

I sat back and laughed out loud. If nothing else this daily task was going to be humorous. Soon Tom called me to the 'bridge'. He actually told me Lincoln was ready to start the pre-whatever sequence. So I went up to the cockpit and took my seat. This was very nice. It was like the front end of an RV. Two lounger looking seats for us and then another one for Tom and then right behind were two more seats on one side. There was a small area just before the cockpit that had a seat and looked like it had a small work area with a tray that folded down. The panel in front of us was all switches and lights just like the shuttle. There were several windows in the front and a smaller one on each side so we had a view even if it was limited in size. There were hand cranks next to each window which allowed steel plates to come down on the outside of the windows to protect them. I looked around and then asked Tony where the horn was. He just looked at me. I told him I wanted to blow the horn when we left. He started to laugh and shook his head. I hooked up with CAPCON Lincoln and we started the check list process. We were about an hour into it when Carl came in and told Tony and I everything was secured and we are ready. I looked at my watch and saw we had less than forty minutes until the scheduled separation. I told Carl to get the crew prepared for separation and one hell of a booster ride. He smiled and took off. Several of the station members stopped by and we said our goodbyes once again and they departed. Carl came in later and told us the outer hatches were secured and depressurized. I confirmed that with the panel lights and reported it to Lincoln. We were now finished with all checks and just waiting. Finally Lincoln told us to separate from the station. I hit the retro rockets one pulse and we felt a small jolt as we started to drift away. The space station started to come into view from the window. We adjusted our angle and then we were told that in eight minutes we would be far enough away from the station to fire our rockets. Eight minutes did not take long to pass and when we were at the right trajectory and our path was clear of the station Tony threw the two switches that fired the rockets and glued us to our seats as the space craft started to accelerate. This was almost as bad as the lift off. We sat there pressed firmly to the back of the seats as the craft vibrated and we watched the speed indicator numbers start flying higher. Right next to that indicator was a small window the said Mach under it. The window was blank when we started but then lit up a 1 and now 10. For the next seven minutes and twenty-five seconds we were going full blast until the booster rockets exhausted their fuel. We had our eyes glued to the speed indicators.

'TALON – LINCOLN.'

'TALON.'

'THE BURN SHOULD LAST APPROXIMATELY 95 MORE SECONDS AND OUR ESTIMATE SHOULD BE MACH 60. ADVISE WHEN THE BURN IS COMPLETED.' 'ROGER.'

We looked at each other and Tony mouthed sixty. His eyes got huge and we both went back to watching the numbers fly upward. We were now at Mach 40 and we still had 30 seconds left in the estimated burn. It appeared to me they might not get to their number. Before I finished thinking about it I saw it change to 45. I looked at Tony and said,

"We are making history and no matter what happens we are in the record books."

Tony responded with a smile.

"Our names in the Guinness Book of Records for flying our asses faster than any one else before." We started to laugh as we saw it turn to 50. I looked at the clock and we were counting down from 10. Just when the countdown numbers hit zero we saw the Mach number turn to 60. Then immediately after that the engines shut off. We sat there is pure amazement and then looked at each other and Tony gave out a yell.

"Yahoooooo!"

He threw one arm in the air and looped his hand around in a circle. We were traveling through space at Mach 60. A speed never before reached in any form. Just then we heard the radio come to life.

'TALON – LINCOLN.'

"RIDE 'EM COWBOY HERE.'

There was a pause. I knew they were laughing and were trying to get themselves under control before answering.

'TALON - LINCOLN. WE HAVE A SURPRISE FOR YOU. WE FIGURED THIS DAY WOULD BE SPECIAL AND WE HAVE A REPRESENTATIVE FROM THE GUINNESS BOOK OR RECORDS HERE TO VERIFY THE RECORD OF YOUR SPEED. COULD YOU PLEASE GIVE US THE NUMBERS ON YOUR SPEED INDICATOR PLEASE.'

'ROGER WE HAVE THE FOLLOWING NUMBERS, ONE INDICATOR READS MACH 60 AND THE OTHER READS 39,287 MILES PER HOUR AND UNDER THAT 63,735 KILOMETERS PER HOUR.'

I made a short pause before I finished with an OVER.

'AND WE HAVE THE SAME NUMBERS INDICATED HERE. CONGRATULATIONS AT SETTING A NEW RECORD FOR BEING THE FAST VEHICLE IN THE WORLD AND BEING THE FASTEST PERSON TRAVELING IN SPACE. ALL YOUR NAMES WILL BE IN THE RECORD BOOK.'

'THANK YOU VERY MUCH. IT IS FUNNY THAT TONY AND I WERE JUST TALKING ABOUT THIS AND ON THE WAY HOME YOU NEED TO GET THEM BACK SO WE CAN BREAK THIS RECORD AGAIN.'

'I THINK WE CAN ARRANGE THAT. ENJOY THE RIDE. LINCOLN OUT.'

I went and got my camera and took a picture of the speed indicators. No one would believe this story. Every crew member came into the cockpit and looked at it. Karen stood there and then asked a very interesting question.

"How do we stop when we get there?"

I turned and smiled at her.

"We have this big anchor in the rear that we let out and it catches onto Mars and when we are slow enough we detach it. At the same time it will swing us so we are in orbit around Mars."

She stood there and then looked at Tony who was trying very hard not to laugh.

"I may be a blonde but I certainly am not a stupid blonde. Seriously, how do we slow down?"

"The rockets that got us to this speed are duplicated and we will fire the other rockets aimed to the rear and if the engineers know what they were doing, it will slow us down to the same speed we started at. But then it has never been tested at these speeds."

"So, basically we are hoping and praying they got it right. OK!"

She turned and walked out of the cockpit. Tony looked at me and said very low.

"There will be a lot of praying going on that day."

A lot of things started to fly through my brain. I was thinking about the retro rockets not working since they were never tested and then would it create a wobble effect to the craft. I quickly saw this was going no where but down hill so I tried very hard to get it out of my mind. It took a long time to finally stop thinking about it. The next several days were very smooth. Everything was working like clockwork. We all started our routines and were starting to get comfortable with them. I added an additional fifteen minute workout to mine. I didn't feel thirty minutes a day was enough. The experiments were started and Sarah started her once a week physical checkups on each of us to see if there were going to be any changes to our bodies during the trip. The funny feeling we all felt that first day at Mach 60 was finally going away. We settled down into the daily routine and followed the daily planning log without a hitch. I was writing my diary with stories from the training days because there weren't any items to list on a day to day basis. I was doing more exercises than scheduled mainly because I had the extra time and I was able to really go through TALON and check out all the nooks and crannies. I took notes about everything I thought needed looked at or was of interest. When I finished I posted the notes and asked everyone else to check the spaces out and give me feedback. We were now in our third week of the mission and we had our first problem. One of the computers decided to go erratic on us. It took them a day to figure it out and stabilize it. But we were never worried with such great a back up system. I was sitting in the captain's seat and Tony was in the co-pilot seat relaxing watching the black sky and watching stars and what we knew to be Mars as a nice dot out there. As we sat there Sarah came in the cockpit. She was talking to Tony about where a set of binoculars were located at. He told her where they were and as she turned to go get them I asked her what she had in mind.

"I was looking out the window in the science lab and I thought I could see what appeared to be cloud formations. There shouldn't be any clouds out here. I want to take a better look."

She walked away and Tony and I looked at each other. Nothing was said but we both thought that was a very odd statement. She was dead right on there being no atmosphere so therefore no possible cloud formations. We were still sitting there talking when Sarah came back into the cockpit.

"Tony, I need you to look out your side window and tell me what you see. Look straight out and about 10 degrees below level."

Tony looked at me and then took the binoculars and stood up and looked out the window. He was looking out there for several minutes. I could see him adjusting the depth several times and then he turned and looked at me.

"Here Vince, you take a look and see what you see."

I got up and took the binoculars from him. I leaned up to the window and put the binoculars to my eyes. I peered out the window and searched the sky left and right and then slightly up and down. When I went down I stopped at what appeared to be a slight haze. I looked at the binoculars to make sure the lenses were clean. I looked again and still saw a very faint haze that wasn't very wide but when I looked left and right it seemed to be lengthy but it faded away in the darkness. I backed away from the window and turned around.

"Ok! I did see what appeared to be a very slight haze but then it was so far out there that I think it was a delusion. Not sure it really is a haze but maybe a reflection from the ship just appearing to be way out there. Just not sure but I know there is no way it can be a cloud."

I handed Sarah the binoculars and we all discussed it for a few minutes and then she left.

"Vince, I saw it too. What are the chances the three of us seeing the same illusion?"

"Let's let it ride for now. Have Sarah add it to her research projects and log it as an experiment to be watched daily."

He nodded and left the cockpit. I went back to the window and could see nothing with the naked eye. I wondered how she had spotted it in the first place. Soon Tony came back in and relieved me for the shift change.

"Do you have to write down the day and especially the time to know if it is day or night like I find myself doing every time I go to my quarters?"

"I sure do and I even have my watch set for military 24 hours a day time. I still question myself as to whether it is day or night."

We started to laugh and I left. I went back to the lounge area which was actually a fold down table and two packs sitting near it. I saw there were four crewmembers there talking and of course one was Sarah so I knew what they were discussing. I ventured over and got a hot meal out of the machine and joined them. As I was eating they were talking about reflections and diffusion to try and explain it. I spoke up and told them that if Sarah kept a daily record all would be answered in time. They agreed that only time would either confirm the sighting or it would just go away and we would know it really wasn't there at all. Everyone was leaning in that direction as they broke up and left. Sarah stayed and sat down on the other pack.

"Have you tried the chocolate cake dessert? It is so good."

"I'll remember that next time I go over there."

"Carl told me that you can only select three times in an eight hour period. I guess they want to make sure we don't run out of food."

"Actually we decided to set that limit just for that reason. We wanted to make sure of just that. You also can not order two of the same variety at one time either."

We talked about the food for some time before I told her I needed to get some sleep and recommended she do the same. She told me she was too wired at the moment but would get there soon. I went to my space and after writing a long entry into my diary that included a comment about the haze, I went and took what they tried to call a shower and then I also tried to quiet my brain enough to sleep. I laid there and thought about the day we just had and the week that led up to it. The thoughts consumed me for a long time. I knew that I had to send a long statement about all the actions we had to take when we arrived at the space station. I got up and started to write down the events starting with the docking at the space station. After about an hour of writing I realized I was getting very tired and using up my short and valuable sleeping time. I looked over the writings I had made and made a few corrections of things I forgot to put in there. I set it all aside and went out for a quick stroll around the area to get a drink and to try again to settle down. I sat in the little area where the food goddess machine was at. I was all alone and it was very quiet. I was able to just sit there and relax to the point where I felt ready to try and get the few hours left I had to sleep. I wandered back to my quarters and again crawled back into the cocoon and closed my eyes. I laid there again trying to clear my brain so I could fall asleep. I was struggling once again with it. I finally decided to stop the racing by trying to play a round of golf in my head. I started the routine by teeing off at number one. Before I reached the third tee I was asleep. I finally found a way to silence my brain for at least a while so I could fall asleep. It was a great feeling of success.

CHAPTER 13

I FELT A NUDGING AGAINST MY SHOULDER AS I WAS COMING TO LIFE. I looked up and saw Tom gazing down at me.

"Hey boss, I just wanted to check to see if you were alive. You have been sleeping for seven hours now."

I slowly rolled out of the hammock style bed and stood up. I looked at my watch to see I was supposed to be in the cockpit ten minutes ago. I looked at Tom and said it was the deepest sleep I had been in since we started training over a year ago. I made my way to the cockpit and when I entered Tony asked me if everything was alright. I told him about the sleep and he said he was still waiting for his to happen. I told him to take an extra hour off this shift because I was well rested right now. He laughed at me and headed out. I sat there for a while waiting to completely wake up. So for the first hour there I was not fully coherent of what was going on around me. Finally I was able to get everything under control and start doing what I was supposed to. The shift just flew by and soon I saw Tony walking back into the cockpit.

"Did you take the extra hour because it seems to me that you just left here?"

"I not only took the extra hour but I am even late beyond that. I found myself reading Sarah's log about the haze she saw last night. Do you know she did a spectrum analysis on it as well? She didn't get any results but she is really getting into this vision she had."

"Did she give you the log to read?"

"No, I was in the lab while she was sleeping and just read it. So mum is the word here."

I shook my head and after we talked for about an hour we decided that we needed to do twelve hour shifts between the two of us. We agreed and passed that on to Lincoln and we were quickly denied that thought. They wanted to make sure we were always well rested just in case of a situation that required us both to be up for an extended period. So we went back to our short shifts and tried to get good quality naps. The next week went by and we were back to mission excellence. The ship was humming and there were no major problems at all. No one wanted to talk about it for fear of that dreaded jinx that came along with it. So everyone was cool and calm. I was sitting there writing in my diary when Karen and Carl came by. They both had the same issue that they wanted to discuss. It seems that some one was leaving little notes lying around the space craft. Carl handed me about ten sticky notes. I read each of them and smiled. I could not be alarmed but then they were not pleased with the note maker and wanted it stopped. Every note listed a crew member, not by name but by a feature they possessed and then made a joking comment about it. I though about it for a minute and decided I would get everyone together and put an end to it before it got too personal and then destructive in nature. So when the next shift ended I gathered everyone together and brought up the notes and showed everyone I had them and that I expected this to stop immediately before I was forced to take some action that would be detrimental to the mission. No one came forward concerning the writer but everyone agreed it needed to stop and I mentioned again that even though it was not something that was negative yet, I expected it to stop and now. The crew split off in their groups and either went to work or retired for their nap time. I took the notes back to my quarters and put them in my diary along with a few comments about them. It had also been eight days since Sarah first told us about that haze she saw and there had been no more comments about it. I knew she was doing a daily thing on it so I decided to go ask her about it. I went to her quarters and found her not there so I headed to the science lab. She was in there writing away in a journal log. I walked up behind her and made a noise so as not to scare her. She turned and looked at me.

"Haven't heard you mention the haze since that first day. Are you still researching it?"

"Yes I will keep a log and write my observations every day."

"Anything news worthy I should know about the haze since that first day?"

"I haven't been able to see it since that day so it appears you and Tony were right about it being some type of reflection from us. But I will keep looking just in case."

She looked back at her log and started writing again. I turned and started to walk away.

"Do you believe in life after death? I mean is there anything after what we know?"

She was looking at me when I turned around.

"I believe in my faith. If that faith leads me to believing there is something or some place to be after our life on Earth is concluded then I guess I believe it. I am still unsure what that belief is totally but I do know that I believe there will never be any proof of life after death. I think one will only know when that time happened. So, whether you believe in it or not is strictly a personal thing. And personally each one of us will only know the truth when it is our turn to know."

I turned back around and left the lab. As I left the space I saw she was still sitting there looking at me. I went and ate what I believed to be breakfast. There wasn't much taste to back that up though. After the great breakfast I had one of those cake selections and at least it cleared out the taste of the other meal. I went and did my daily exercise routine for about thirty minutes and then I did my routine preparing for a nap. As I was getting into my cocoon I heard a commotion a short distance away. I crawled back out of my quarters to see a three way argument going on. There was Karen, Hank and Michelle going at it verbally. I walked up to them and stepped in the middle. I didn't say anything just looked at each one in turn. It got very quiet instantly.

"We are not even 30 days into a year long mission and I have to intervene already in something that I know is going to be stupid."

Hank decided to do the talking.

"It appears that Karen is questioning Michelle concerning the posting of the notes. It was just a question that, I guess, got out of control."

"I made that clear before that I expected to see no more notes and that this was a done deal. That includes discussing it. It is over, get over it now."

I turned and walked away heading back to my quarters. I slid the curtain back and started to crawl back in when I noticed a figure out of the side of my eye behind the curtain. I peered around it to see Sarah standing there with her jump suit open down to her waist. The zippered opening was just wide enough to almost expose her breasts. She was standing there looking at me.

"You seemed very tense so I thought I might be able to help you relax some."

I took the step towards her and reached over and grabbed the zipper and pulled it up closing it.

"Is there a full moon that is affecting this mission this morning? I think you need to refocus your energy in another way. Bye Sarah!"

I gave her a smile and moved the curtain enough to let her slip out of my quarters. No one was around so she wasn't seen. After a few moments I settled down and wrote in the diary that the tension on board was starting to show its ugly head. I did not go into detail since I was hoping it would all pass. It was days like today that I had wished I had snuck a bottle of sleeping pills in my bag. I wasn't going to get much sleep this session. And I felt I was correct when my alarm went off on my watch and I was sure I had just fallen asleep fifteen minutes earlier. I got up and ventured over to the food goddess. I pressed what I hoped was coffee or the resemblance of the brew. Out came a liquid that was dark but only resembled dark hot water with no taste. I drank it and went back for my vitamins. I sat there outside my quarters for a while before I decided to head for the cockpit. I was almost there when I saw Sarah coming out of the lab. She winked at me but continued on her merry way somewhere. I was going to have trouble on this mission with her. It was becoming obvious that she was out for more than a 'hello' but I needed to keep everything here professional. I was sure she would go after one or more of the others before we were home again. I knew I was going to have to sit her down and have a heart to heart discussion sometime in the future. But for now I was going to see if she caught on by herself. I wandered into the cockpit and saw Tony discussing the haze that Sarah saw almost a week ago with Michelle. She was sitting in my seat so I stood there listening to their conversation. Soon I realized that it had been seen again.

"Did Sarah see the haze again? Is that what I am hearing here?"

"No, I saw it about three hours ago and Michelle and I have been looking at it from up here."

I looked at Tony and saw he was holding the binoculars. I motioned for him to give them to me. I took them and leaning behind his seat pressed up against the window with the eye glasses and peered out. It took me a while but then I saw the faint stream of mist or haze as we have called it. It looked like it was a long stream of cloudy air that went on for a while until it faded into the deep darkness. One could not see how long it was or if it actually had substance to it. It just appeared to be misty out there. From the great distance we could see it and there appeared to be a definite form to the haze. It looked like a vapor trail of a jet when you look up in the sky but not nearly as dense from what I could see.

"All right, so there it is again. I am beginning to think it might actually be something but I still think initially it is a reflection from us. But it is so far away I don't see how."

I backed out of the window and told Michelle I needed to start working now. She got up and gave me the seat. I went over the log and scheduled tasks for the next segment of the mission with Tony and he said that he had to be here to do some of this later before he was supposed to actually get back on duty. I looked at the time frame and agreed that had to happen so he left to catch at least four hours of rest. Michelle said she was going to go find Sarah and let her know about the haze before she went to bed. I found myself alone wondering how a mist or haze could exist in outer space. There had to be an explanation for it. I called up Lincoln on the secure channel and told them of our sighting. They also thought it was just an illusion and agreed they didn't think it possible but would confer with the space experts and get back to me later. The four hours went by very fast and we were now in course correction mode. We had to fire our retro rockets for a second to get us back on the needed course. Somehow we seemed to have drifted so very slightly off to the left of the center line we needed. We performed the burn and were back on course. We had the sun at our twenty degree point so it was giving us just enough light to see all the stars ahead of us and we had good fixes on several planets as well. Sarah had come in and taken some pictures and also was still doing her experiment of spectrum analysis on the haze. She left and soon after came back with a couple of pictures in her hand. She had this look on her face that I wasn't sure if she was in a daze or scared. I looked at her and then looked at the pictures she was holding. I reached out and took them from her. I looked at the three pictures and saw what appeared to be the haze off in the distance but there seemed to be tiny stars in the haze. I was not sure if they were stars but minute little lights barely visible. I handed them back to her and we both looked again through the binoculars and even though we could just make out the haze we saw no lights at all out there near or in it. I told her to make sure she documented this very well and I also told her that I informed Lincoln of our possible sighting of a haze in space and they are conferring with the experts to see if it is possible. She got upset with me over that. She felt it was her job to discuss this with Lincoln and was mad that I took that away from her. I apologized and said that I would not interfere again with her experiment. I asked her if Tom was involved with this since he is the scientist on the mission. She told me that she had discussed it with him but he was not interested in it and told her to knock herself out on it. When we were out of the cockpit I pulled Sarah aside and asked her if she was alright. She just looked at me not answering.

"Sarah, that little episode in my quarters yesterday. I hope you realize the implications that would have on a mission like this. I need you to be the doctor you are here to be and not a school girl looking for mister right. Do you understand what I am getting at?"

Again she stood there looking at me without speaking.

"Sarah! I would like an answer please."

"I am not a school girl looking to get laid. I am a professional doctor and scientist, and I have this mission totally in view. I wanted to give you what I thought you needed at the time, relaxation and I thought a good massage was needed. I guess your mind was elsewhere and did not see the stress I saw in your face."

She walked away from me quite quickly. I started to consider that my approach was not the proper thing to do at that moment. I decided to try and smooth things out but was interrupted when Tony called me to the cockpit. When I entered he looked at me and then turned back to the controls. 'LINCOLN – TALON, VINCE IS HERE NOW.'

'VINCE, KIRK HERE, HAVE SOME THEORIES ON THE HAZE FOR YOU.'

'AYE AYE COMMODORE KIRK, LET ME HAVE IT.'

'BESIDE THE THIN AIR UP THERE GETTING TO YOU I THINK YOU ARE SEEING A SOLAR FLARE FIELD THAT MIGHT HAVE COME FROM THE SUN AND IS DRIFTING OUT IN SPACE. I THEORIZED THAT THESE WERE POSSIBLE, SORT OF LIKE THE AURORA BOREALIS.'

'I UNDERSTAND BUT THERE IS NO MOVEMENT IN THE HAZE.'

'SECOND THEORY IS A SUN REFLECTION OFF TALON SINCE YOU ARE AT AN ANGLE FROM BEHIND THAT IS A POSSIBILITY. ANYWAY THAT'S THE BEST WE HAVE AT THE MOMENT. NOTHING WE ARE INTERESTED IN PERSUEING FURTHER.'

'ROGER!'

The conversation was over and I got the distinct message not to call them again on this issue. I told Tony this was a closed issue as far as Lincoln was concerned so anything we see out there is just between us space people. He agreed and we looked out the window again for a while. I then went and found Sarah and told her to make sure she only kept her notes for research and never to send anything to Lincoln concerning it. Then I went back to taking care of business. I did my exercising and had a snack and ventured around getting myself tired enough to take a little cat nap. It seemed that everyone was up and moving about. I got into a few conversations here and there and then I soon found myself in a conversation with everyone there. The subject came up of the satellite we were carrying on board. I told them very clearly that I still did not have any information concerning the satellite.

All I knew was that when we were told we would be launching it. After about ten minutes of this I filtered out of the conversation and headed to the storage room. I found the pack that was listed as Special and read the cover letter attached to it. It specifically listed that I open it when we were getting close to Mars. I sat there wondering how they would know if I opened it now. I looked it over and then noticed the electronic lock on one side of the container. I knew then they would have to send me the code to open this one. I then remembered that Phil had placed an envelope in my pack that was in my quarters that I still had not gone through. I entered my space and pulled out the pack and opened it. I moved a few clothes around and then saw a few of my personal pictures and things I brought with me. I started to place them around the space with Velcro and then went back to the pack. I was looking through the pack when I noticed an envelope pressed against the side of the pack. I pulled it out and tore open the end. In there were a couple of pictures of me at the party and in training. Then there was a letter that consisted of about four pages. There also was another small white envelope in there as well. I read the letter and Phil was talking about how political the training was and that there were two secret projects involved with out mission. He told me that they were both government backed and that our mission was more about these missions than actually succeeding on arriving at Mars and returning. He told me that all this information only came to be known to him days before we left for the cape. He started to investigate and snoop around after the press put out the pictures of the satellite that he had never seen before. He was writing in a mood that told me he was very angry that in his position he was kept in the dark and lied to all this time. I opened the smaller envelope to find the code for the lock on the special pack. It also included a list of codes to open hidden files in the computer. He gave me the file names and the passwords to get into them. He warned me that I needed to take care and not keep them open very long since Lincoln would see it eventually and change the passwords on me. He recommended I open and print the file and get out of it. I put the papers in my pocket and headed for the cockpit. I walked in to find Tony just standing there looking out the window with the binoculars.

"Everything alright up here?"

I startled him as he jumped back from the window.

"Oh yes! Just wasting time looking out the window."

I looked at him seeing a face that had concern on it. But I did not take it any further. I told him that I forgot to let him know that we were going to upload new programming in the morning so it was going to cut into our down time tomorrow. He acknowledged that and said he saw something in a message about it a little earlier. He looked around and produced a message about some changes they were planning for our computer system starting tomorrow. I read it and then told him I was going to try and get four hours sleep and left the cockpit. I wandered to my quarters and slowly got settled in for the nap. I was thinking about the look on his face. I didn't think he was even interested in the haze but that look was one that bothered me. It told me that he was more concerned about it than Sarah was. When you talk to her about it you get excitement. That look gave me the clear impression of concern or was it fear.

CHAPTER 14

THE NEXT FEW DAYS WENT BY WITHOUT ANY INCIDENTS AT ALL happening. I had managed to get all the secret files out of the computer system but I still had not taken the time to read or analyze them. I just printed them to paper because I was afraid they had all the passwords to every file in the computer whether common or personal and I didn't want it seen in my file system. I had taken the files and put them in my quarters in the little safe I had in there. I was waiting for the right time to get some real privacy to give them the look over. We were coming up on thirty days in space and we wanted to have a little celebration for the milestone so we found some cookies that were smuggled aboard and a case of fruit juice boxes we found in a pack of supplies. We took eight of them out and restored the rest. We put them in a container for our celebration that was going to happen two days from now. Most of us were in the main compartment just relaxing when we heard a thud like sound. It was fairly loud and appeared to definitely come from outside. I hurried to the cockpit and found Tony on the radio to Lincoln. They were discussing the noise and we started to check all the instruments to see if we had a failure of a system. We could not see any wrong readings and we checked the computer to see if there were any reports of a failure or variation in readings of any kind. We found none and Lincoln confirmed all those readings were accurate. I went over to the video recorder bank and after finding the secondary video system, I rewound it to the hour or so back to when it happened and started to review the three cameras that were on the outside of the space craft. I did not see anything directly but saw a shadow pass by one of the cameras at the same time you could hear the thud. I instantly thought it was a meteorite that had hit us. There was no way to look at the impact area without doing a space walk so we called Lincoln and reviewed the options and decided since there were no indications of any failures that at best we had a dent to the skin of the craft. No space walk was ordered and the issue was put on the back burner to be checked out when we slowed into Mars orbit. Lincoln did not want us outside at this speed unless it was imperative, and they felt this was not. I looked at my watch and saw my rest time was well over. I went in and questioned Tony as to why the radar did not activate if something came that close to us. He could not give me any reasonable answer and basically acted like he was insulted from my question. I took control of the craft and Tony went back and took a well needed sleep. He had been up for over twelve hours while this incident happened. I will be well over that when he returns to break me later. But I was wired at the present time and was not mentally ready to slow down. The next hours went by very slowly. It was like I had super hearing. I was hearing every little creak and sound. It was a very uncomfortable feeling that I did not like at all. I then remembered the system could review the radar screen as well, so I asked the computer to replay the fifteen minute interval when the sound happened. While I was sitting there watching the review I saw the radar alarm indicator go on. I looked at the screen and watched the light flashing knowing full well that the alarm should be going off as well but there was no sound to the replay. I then knew that either Tony ignored the alarm or more likely he was not in the cockpit at all to see or hear it. I was starting to get concerned about him now. The way he was acting before and now this. The time was going by real slowly and I was building up stress. I wanted to get out of here and soon. I kept watching my watch and it seemed like the minute hand just quit. We had a radar unit in the nose so I tested it several times to make sure it was operating. Finally my eight hours had expired and was I ever ready for a rest. I decided not to confront Tony just yet about this incident. I staggered back to my quarters and just crashed. I don't even remember closing my eyes I fell asleep so fast. I was lying there dreaming about something but I didn't think it was getting a neck rub. But that was what I was now dreaming of. I slowly opened my eyes and I still felt hands lightly rubbing my neck. I turned my head to see Sarah moving her hands away from me.

"It's time to get up. You were so restless I just couldn't let you be in that much stress."

I sat up and just looked at her. My neck was tight and it felt like I didn't sleep in the right position or something.

"You could see that when I was sleeping?"

"Yes, you face was cringing as if you were in pain."

We talked for a few minutes and then she left as I prepared to go to work. I got up and went and grabbed some food and headed straight to the cockpit. When I got there I put the food down and Tony and I had a conversation about yesterday. I started to eat and the discussion went to the crew. Tony was passing information about Carl and Karen being found in the lab a few days ago. And then there was the note incident when we thought it was over one was found during my sleep period. I asked where this one was found and after I heard I knew that there was a camera in that area. I told him to go and review the monitor for that area and see if it shows anyone in the area. He left and I finished eating. I just realized he diverted the subject of the meteor hit and got me side tracked. I was sitting there rubbing my neck when I felt someone move my hands and take over the rubbing. I knew it was Sarah but I was sore and it felt good so I just sat there. She rubbed for about five minutes and then stopped.

"Feeling any better boss?"

I turned to see Michelle standing behind me.

"Yes, thank you for that."

She started to talk about things being weird the last couple of days. I asked her in what way did she think it was weird. She went on to tell me that Carl was really acting funny and that she thought that Sarah was obsessed with seeing ghosts. She also told me that Tony was always roaming around even when she thought he was supposed to be in the cockpit. I listened to her and then told her I would keep an eye out for things and thanked her. She left just as Sarah came in the cockpit.

"Have you looked outside today? I think our path is getting us closer to the haze. It appears to be larger than in the past."

I told her no that I had a lot of things that were more important and that this was her project so she needed to keep good records of it. She just looked at me and then left. I settled down to work and set up the system for the next few days of commands. That took me a few hours and since I wasn't bothered I was able to complete it on time for a change. I then relaxed for about an hour and then called Sarah to the cockpit. After a few minutes she came in the cockpit. I told her to sit down and after she did I started to talk about the crew. I mentioned that I was aware of the things that were going on around here and mentioned Karen and referred to doing things other than job related. I also mentioned that some think she was spending too much time on this haze thing and not enough on mission experiments. She had her clip board with her and showed me that she was exactly on schedule with everything she was assigned to do and that if others would spend more time doing their own work they wouldn't have time to be concerned with others. She was speaking fast and obviously in a heated state. I told her that impressions would tear this mission apart if left unchecked. I asked her to be a front runner in showing professionalism. She started to settle down and I then asked her for the binoculars. As I got up to go over to the window I sensed that someone was standing just outside the cockpit door so I went to see if I was correct and looked out the curtain. Standing just outside the curtain was Karen. I looked at her and told her to come in. She said she was busy and I again told her to enter the cockpit. She went in and Sarah was next to the window looking out through it with the binoculars.

"Karen, take a seat over there. We have a situation here that is getting out of control and I will put a stop to it right now."

She sat down in my seat and looked up at me.

"First, I know you were eaves dropping on our conversation. So you heard that I know about you and Carl. It will end right now. I will not put up with interruptions to this mission. You better get your act together. Your mission assignments will be checked in a few hours by me and they better be up to date. I will not have you sneaking around trying to create a problem here. Get you act together now or your assignments will be reassigned and a report you will not like will be sent back to Lincoln. Do you understand?"

She started to cry. I waited for a few moments and she was just sitting there crying.

"Enough of this shit! You're an adult here and you are on this mission because you, at least at one time, were considered the best. Get your shit together and get back to being who you were hired to be. Now get out!"

I pointed to the entrance as she got up and left still crying. Sarah stayed glued to the window. I knew she was just trying to stay out of the way. Finally she turned and said that there was nothing new out there so she needed to get back to work as well. I told her to sit down. She did and just sat there staring straight ahead.

"Everyone on this mission is trying my patience right now. I have no patience for fraternization. It ends here today! Go and get the word out to everyone. This mission is business only. If I learn that my orders are not being followed there will be hell to pay. Now go!"

She got up and left the cockpit. It wasn't long after when Carl came in the cockpit and stood there for a moment.

"If you have something to say, say it. I expected more from you than what I am hearing. Do your job."

He never said anything but after a few more moments he left. About an hour later Tony came in the cockpit.

"Heard the law has been passed down to the crew. Let's see if they heed the warning."

"They better!"

We talked about everyone in the crew and all the rumors that I had heard and what I told Sarah to pass to the crew. Tony said that was exactly what was passed on so they got the right information. We talked about Carl and I told Tony that he needed to have a one on one with him on the side to get his head back on straight. Tony left the cockpit and was gone about an hour before he came back in and said that he had discussed things with Carl and Tom and everything will be good in the future. He relieved me and I went straight to the food machine. I was very hungry but I knew I would only get one so I picked something I knew I would like. I ate slowly trying to make myself think I was getting full. I drank a lot of water and was wishing for a beer or two when Hank came and joined me.

"I heard the world came crashing down today."

I didn't answer, just looked at him.

"Well, for what it worth, I think the word got through to those that needed to hear it."

He got up and went over to the machine and got something to eat and left the area. I finished the meal and headed for the science lab. I went in and Sarah and Karen were in there talking. I went over and told Karen I wanted her logs. She told me they were not up to date but said she was sorry for creating a problem and that everything would be corrected before the end of the week. I looked at her and then turned and left. I headed to take a shower and get rid of my stress. I had not done any exercise in four days but at the moment I wasn't in the mood. After I showered I headed for my quarters. I wrote a long entry into the diary and listed everything that had happened. I wanted to make sure I had a listing with the date for future reference if I had a problem in the future. I then remembered that I had asked Tony to review the video camera in the area where the last note was found and he had not given me any report. I went to the backup computer system room and over to the video bank of recorders. I found the one I needed and saw that the recording time was indicating a low number meaning it had been recycled not long ago. I went to the storage bank and selected the last recording session and it ended yesterday so I knew then that Tony had recycled the recorder and erased the time of the incident. The only reason that would happen was if he was the sticky note person. My mind started to add up all the things going on here and they all seemed to involve Tony in some way. I decided to keep this to myself and headed for my quarters so I could get some sleep. But my brain would not let me sleep. I was just lying there with my head racing through the events of the day. I finally got up and went to the storage bay and found a dark corner and tried to secure myself in there so I wasn't drifting around. I must have fallen asleep while I was in there thinking about things. I woke suddenly as if I had heard something but it was very quiet. I sat there for a few minutes and then looked at my watch to see that I was just a little late in getting to the cockpit. I undid myself and headed out of the space. As I was moving through the ship I saw Hank and he said everyone was looking for me. I

nodded and continued to the cockpit. I entered and told Tony I was sorry
for being late but I fell asleep in the storage area. We laughed and he said
everyone was looking for me. He had put out an APB on me for jumping
ship. After a while he told me we took another meteor hit but we saw this
one and knew it didn't do any damage. With that he left and went to bed.
After a while Carl came in and sat down. We had a conversation for about
an hour and cleared the air with his situation. He assured me he was under
control now and it would not happen again. I knew that if it happened after
one month we would be in serious trouble after five or six months. But then
I also knew I was infringing on each crew members personal choices. If they
wanted to have affairs then that was their choice. I just wanted to make sure
it did not jeopardize this mission and ultimately our lives. Over the course
of the shift every one of the crew came in to reassure me they were all on
board to make this mission a successful one. All reassured me they would
take better care of their personal behavior. I sat back and day dreamed for a
while thinking about how I left home and the possible situation I was in. I
had a strong feeling I was not going to have someone to go home to. I never
saw a problem coming but that last day or two before we left I definitely
felt Susan was not with me on my choices. She had once a year ago voiced
her concern about this mission and how she didn't know whether she was
strong enough to manage a year without knowing how I was. But I blew that
off as just a thought and not actually a strong feeling of action. But when I
left the house the other day I knew something was not right and then when
I was told she had left the house to go spend time with her family I had the
deep feeling that it was for good. So I did not want any of my emotions to
over come my desire to have a good mission. This mission was my fate and
I intended to make it a success. Tony came in and relieved me and I went
straight to my diary and wrote three pages concerning my thoughts and the
events of the day. I was in a very relaxed state at the present time. I drifted
off to sleep without eating. After another calm day we arrived at the thirty
day mark and along with the normal Lincoln congratulations and some in
the crew talking to a loved one back on Earth for about ten minutes each,
we gathered around to celebrate with cookies and juice. It was nice to have
the opportunity to talk to the family. I managed to get my brother on the

line but no one knew where Susan was so there was no conversation with her. It was funny that when I had her sister on the line she didn't know her whereabouts. I felt that was not the truth but I accepted the answer anyway. I left the crew as they were cheerfully having a good time and went to the cockpit. I sat there alone for a good twenty minutes just pondering what my life would be like when we all returned home. I found myself going places I did not want to visit. I was falling into a depressed state and I needed to get out of it and now. I knew that these thoughts would linger in my brain for days repeating themselves over and over unless I had something dramatic to clear them out. I needed that change but I was not getting it. I got up and left the cockpit and went to the food machine. I looked over all the selections. I noticed that a lot of them had changed. I saw on the list that someone had refilled the unit and we actually had different choices. I selected something that said it was pot roast. After a few minutes out came this steaming tray with what looked like mashed potatoes with a meat and gravy topping. There was a very small section of peas with it also. I got a cup of water and waited for it to cool down some before I took that first bite. When it came I thought about how pot roast should taste and then put that completely out of my mind as I ate the selection that sat in front of me. It was alright but one knew that it lacked the real food taste. We all knew and were told the meals were designed to sustain us and had a lot of vitamins and minerals added to it that would change the taste of most of the meals. So I dreamt of a home cooked pot roast and slowly finished the tray. I ventured back to the cockpit and after a few more hours Tony came in and stated,

'one down and eleven more to go'.

I nodded and we both sat there for a while without speaking before I left and headed for bed and ended a day that was full of both good and bad emotions.

CHAPTER 15

THE NEXT SEVERAL WEEKS JUST FLEW BY AND THE DAILY ROUTINE was the normal for just about everyone. The crew was more on the quiet side still trying to heed to my warning of last month. But everyone was in a cheerful working mode most of the time. There were a few minor incidents that created tension but none of it ever lasted for than a few hours. We had a few more problems with the space craft and it seemed that each week that passed created more and more frequency of issues coming up. I was sitting there in the cockpit putting the daily mission adjustments and orders into the computer when two lights on the overhead panel started to blink. I looked up and noticed they were both indicating a problem with the evaporator system on the starboard side. We had two systems so the other one was working just fine but this second one now indicated a problem. I called for Tom to come up to the cockpit. He was the systems man for what we called the health and welfare equipment. When he arrived I pointed to the flashing lights and told him it was the starboard evaporator. He acknowledged the problem and left. It was over four hours later and the lights were still flashing. Lincoln had called several times with solutions but so far none of them worked. Soon Tony came in and after I briefed him on everything that was happening I left to go look at the evaporator myself. I was there with Tom and it appeared to be running and it was making water. There did not seem to be anything wrong. I decided to leave it be and I told Tony to reset the switches on the evap. He did and told me they did not come back on in the flashing mode. They were lit full

111

time now. I told him to just keep monitoring them from time to time and keep a log entry of it. I told Tom to check on the system every hour to make sure it was still working. Lincoln was still trying to resolve it from their end as well. I went and took a shower and when I entered my quarters I found a note on my small desk.

'Need to talk to you. Can it be soon, signed Sarah.'

I left the space and moved down the hallway to her area. She was not there so I left her a note to stop by when ever she had time. I went back to my area and crawled into the cocoon and was lying there drifting off when she came to the opening and called my name. I told her to come in. She entered and slid the curtain mostly closed. She stood next to me as I lie there fighting the sleep back.

"I just needed to talk to someone about what happened to me before."

She paused and I quickly said

'before!'

She looked at me as I saw a tear in her eye starting to form.

"We all made phone calls as you know. I was happy to have that chance and was looking forward to talking to him but he cut me off after less than a minute of talking saying he was busy and needed to go. I knew before I left that he wanted to end our marriage but I know now that it is over. I could hear another voice in the background so I knew he was somewhere other than work and with someone else."

She then broke down and was trying to keep it quiet but she still was crying. I got out of the cocoon and stood up next to her. I put my one arm around her shoulder and told her that I understood what she was going through and she needed to be strong about it. That nothing was going to change while we were on this mission. Worrying about it will create more problems and from out here she could not resolve anything. The reality of the situation was if it was over then she would know it when she returned. Time can change people and things might be resolved on their own by the time we returned. She leaned into my shoulder and told me that she understood that she needed to be just concerned with work but that she would have trouble not thinking about what happened before she left and then the call. I did not want to pry into what happened before we left but she started to tell me anyway. She indicated that for about two months before we left her husband was coming home late on a lot of days. He also was spending more money than usual. She suspected he had a girl friend on the side so she confronted him and he got mean and on a few occasions it became abusive. One day she saw him drive by as she was on her way home early and she thought she saw someone else in the car crouching down. When she got home she knew someone was there because there was a perfume smell in their bedroom that did not belong to her. Again she started to cry.

"I told him I knew he was cheating on me and he told me I was so wrapped up in my job that I couldn't know the sun from the moon. He also told me that while I would be on this trip what was he supposed to do, just sit around at home waiting by the door for me to come home."

She cried again and this time a little harder.

"I know my marriage is over now. But I needed someone to be able to talk to and tell things to. I need a friend who will be there for me."

I didn't answer her but I knew she could not be left alone all the time on this mission now. I had to decide how to deal with this and soon. I told her that she was welcome to come and talk anytime she needed to. I also reminded her that this was a small crew so her actions would not be unnoticed. She needed to be discrete about what she did and said in public areas. She agreed and thanked me wiping the tears from her face. I told her to go wash up and I would meet her by the food machine in about ten minutes. She nodded and left. I stood there for a while and after acknowledging that I was not going to get much sleep this time again, I headed out for the food area. When I arrived there I saw Hank and Michelle nearby talking. I went over to the machine and made a selection from the snack side. I stood there eating it when Sarah came strolling up. When she went to the machine Michelle and Hank approached as well. I decided to make it look accidental that we all were there together.

"Is this get together day at the food store?"

"I thought it was just me that seemed hungry today more than usual."

Michelle spoke up first. No one else decided to chime in.

"So, Sarah, how is the haze viewing coming along. I haven't heard an update for about a week now."

She looked at me while she was eating before answering.

"Everything still is in the unknown stage. It is still out there but we still have not determined if it is real or just a reflection from us."

Then Hank decided to join in.

"I have looked a few times but I just don't seem to see it."

"Oh it's there alright!"

Michelle said with a little excitement in her voice.

"I have seen it a couple of times. You really need binoculars to see it good."

I decided to make this a game.

"I have a wager on this one. I will offer to the first person who can verify it to be real the right to be captain for a day and the right to have one thing, real or not, made policy or a rule on the record."

"Now that's something I would love to win, then we would have theme days put into effect. I can think of a few I would love to have around here."

"I am sure nudist day would be one of them."

Michelle sang out and started to laugh.

"I take it you have been caught prancing around in the buff?"

I looked at Hank as I said the words.

"No, not really. I was in my area and the curtain was partially open when someone was standing outside it playing peeping tom, or should I say peeping tomette."

We all laughed and the conversation went on for a while longer. Then I excused myself and asked Sarah to show me her record log on the haze. She agreed and told me it was in the science lab. We proceeded over to the lab and the others were still there talking. We entered the lab and I stopped.

"How are you feeling now, I hope better."

"I will be alright. I just need to keep busy and not think very much about home."

"We all need to do that. This mission is not an easy one. We all knew that in the meetings and the psychiatrist made that clear in the counseling sessions, remember."

She nodded and walked up to me and planted a kiss on me. She didn't hold it very long but she planted it full on the lips. I was a little shocked but I did not back off and I did not return the kiss fearing implications.

"I needed to do that to show you my thanks for what you are doing to help me."

"I would have thought there might have been another way to show that but that's alright."

"I have another way to show that but then we don't want to start any gossip."

"Enough now, we will not be going down that road."

She went over and picked up the log book and was showing it to me when Hank came in the lab. I noticed that she was giving great detail to the size and appearance every day she observed it. Hank came up and looked over my shoulder and after a moment stated.

"So what if this turns out to be something real, like a vapor trail of an alien space craft?"

I looked at him and shook my head.

"You need to understand the scope of this sighting. If it is real then it defies the laws of science. There can not be a vapor trail in no gravity space. So if we have a real mist or whatever it is, then we have something that is not there by accident."

His face got very serious.

"So you are saying that if it is real we are not alone out here right now."

"I am not saying anything of the sorts. I want to know what it is before I will venture as to where it came from or why it is here."

We all carried on the conversation a while longer and then I told everyone I needed some sleep since I had to be back in the cockpit in six hours. I left and went to bed. It seemed like minutes had just passed when I was awaken by the sound of my watch alarm going off. I slowly crawled out of the space and made my way to freshen up some. As I got there I found it to be busy. We had two stations but we reserved the other for just the women so I really didn't want to impose. I waited for a while and finally Tom came strolling out and I went in. It didn't take me very long to finish up and I was off to the bridge to play again. When I arrived I found Tony leaning back with his head cocked to one side and sound asleep. I went back out and went and got something to drink and met Michelle and Karen having a chat. I just waved to them and they acknowledged me and skirted off in separate directions. I filled a cup with water and went over to check on the evaporator. When I arrived I found it not running at all. It had finally shut down. I made my way back to the cockpit and made some noise this time as I entered. Tony sat up straight as I moved into my seat.

"So when did the evaporator finally stop working?"

He looked at me with a look that told me he had no idea it had stopped.

"I didn't know it had stopped."

"I just passed by it and the whole system is off. And I see that the switches are red so I know it has been turned off."

"I will look into it before I go to bed. Tom probably forgot to tell me, that's all."

"There seems to be a lot of forgetting to tell people things around here lately."

He didn't answer me on that one but just passed on the orders that Lincoln had left for later and he left the cockpit. I went over all the work that was lined up for today and saw that the evaporator was set for a complete recycle. Lincoln must have shut it down electronically from there. I noticed a yellow light was glowing over on Tony's side of the panel. I got up and moved over there to get a better look at it. I saw it was the trash compactor indicator light showing it was full. I leaned over and pressed the button and held it in for three seconds and then released it. The light turned off and then blinked three times and off again. I knew that the trash had just been flushed out into space and the pressurized system had reset itself. At least that worked right went through my mind. I started to perform the duties of the day and updated all the computer entries required. When I got to the bottom of the page I read the bottom line. It was a note that today was the end of the seven week mark in the mission. I was now five hours into my shift and again I was amazed that no one had bothered me for five hours. I thought about it for a few minutes and then I heard someone come in the space. I immediately blamed myself for causing this to happen by thinking about it. I turned around to see Sarah there with binoculars and a camera.

She went straight to the window and planted herself up against it peering out. After a few minutes I finally heard her mumbling.

"It's getting closer. It is now very visible and I can see the haze more clearly."

She put the camera up to the binocular lens and took a few pictures. She went back to peering through the binoculars still talking about how clear she could see it now. I got up and moved over behind her.

"Let me get a look at this thing."

I took the binoculars and looked out the window. She was right. I could see definite structure in the formation of the haze. There was definitely a top and a bottom and it was more defined than what appeared before. I moved away giving her the binoculars back.

"Make sure you make a good entry today. This needs to be recorded especially the definition of its formation."

I stood there gazing towards the window. Sarah left the cockpit and I returned to my seat. Soon after that Tom came in the cockpit.

"Vince, the evaporator has been turned off. Did you do it?"

"No, I was waiting to ask you about that."

"No, it wasn't me. Who would have turned it off?"

"Probably Lincoln, they have control of everything we do, remember."

He nodded in agreement and left. It wasn't very long again before Sarah came hurriedly back into the cockpit.

"You have to see this. This is amazing! It is real! It is a medium from one place to another. I can't believe we have found something one only dreams about."

I broke into her fast talking.

"What are you talking about, a medium."

She handed me a few pictures.

"You looked out the window. What did you see and what did you not see?"

I looked at her like she was crazy and then I looked at the first picture. There in the picture was the slightest hint of the haze. But what was very visible were dozens of what appeared to be tiny lights. They were dull and they also appeared a little blurred. With my knowledge I knew that either she moved the camera when she took the picture or the lights were moving. I looked at the rest of the pictures and they were all the same. I then looked at a chart and a graph she handed me. It was the spectrum analysis report. There were variations in the colors and there were clear indications we had depth perception out there. I looked at her and got up. I went to the window and looked out it. I could see nothing with the naked eye. I took the binoculars from her and looked again. There was the haze but there were no lights visible through the binoculars. I backed out and looked at her for a moment.

"You do realize we have just crossed over the line here. Lincoln will never believe what we would tell them so I do not want to broadcast this just yet. Maybe in the coming days or weeks we will get more data to support what you have here."

"I can't believe it. We have a … … OH! I don't know what we have. I just know we have it."

She was jumping up and down or trying to in the zero gravity.

"Document the hell out of this. I need to know exactly what you have. I want to try and figure this out before we go public."

She took everything and left, singing a song as she went. I went to the window again and looked out it.

"Whatever you are, I sure hope you are friendly and kind to our ship."

I caught myself as I was speaking out loud. It wasn't anyone. It was just a formation that seemed to have stars trapped within its boundaries. So that is what I needed to be concerned with. If we eventually start to get closer and cross paths with it I needed to know what will happen. Will we be sucked into its hold and be trapped forever? Just what is it made of and why can't we see the stars or the lights with the binoculars. They are there but we can't see them even with the naked eye. Was it a frequency issue that was out of our visual range or just an illusion? The visual range thing had to be the answer. It wasn't much longer when Tony came strolling in. I told him everything about the haze and said I would send Sarah in to show him the pictures. He showed very little emotion. I think he thought I was crazy. I knew as soon as he looked out there and then looked at the pictures he would be in the same state of confusion as I was. I left and went to the lab.

Sarah was in there writing away. I asked her to take the binoculars and the pictures and go show Tony what you have. She was still very excited and just gathered everything up and scurried as fast as she could move to the cockpit. I went and sat at the lab desk and started to read her notes. There were many pages written just today on her findings. She was putting in theories about what she though as well. I needed to caution her on that. It might not go well back on Earth at the end of the mission if there was no physical proof to support her theories. Her credibility would be in jeopardy. About forty-five minutes later she came back to the lab.

"Tony thinks it still is just a mirage. He doesn't get it."

"Let it rest for now. You need to write facts here."

I pointed to the log entries.

"Do not put in your theories as to what it might be just yet. We want to maintain our credibility here."

She thought about what I just said and agreed and said she would rewrite that last page. While I was in there I sat down at her computer and sent a message to Lincoln concerning the evaporator. I wanted to know why they didn't inform us that they were shutting it down. I sat there and talked to Sarah for a while and then received a response from Lincoln. They indicated they did not shut it down from their end. The switches were turned of from our end manually according to their indicators. I told them I was not aware of who did it but would look into it. I left and sought out Carl. When I found him I asked him about the evap and he told me that he did not even go in the space all watch so it wasn't him. I went to the space and stood there with Carl and looked at the control panel. The switches were in the off position so they had to have been thrown manually. I told Carl to come with me and we went to the other side and I pulled out the surveillance camera machine for this space. Once again the counter was way off from the others. All the recordings were changed at the same time so the numbers should be close to each other. This camera system was hundreds off. Someone had reset the system here again like the other one from before. I didn't say anything to Carl but I asked him not to talk about this to anyone except me because I needed to find out what was happening here. He looked at me and reached out and grabbed my arm.

"You think it is Anthony, don't you?"

"I don't think it is anyone right at this moment. Why would you ask that?"

"Because he has been acting very strange lately. Every time I see him he moves off in another direction to avoid me. I thought you guys were supposed to stay in the cockpit most of the time. He wanders a lot."

I patted him on the shoulder and thanked him for that information but I was sure there was a simple explanation for all this. We left the space and as I was walking towards the cockpit I saw Tony standing just outside the entrance to it. As soon as he saw me he went back inside. I decided to have a talk with him. I entered the cockpit and sat down in my seat.

"Tony, there have been a lot of things lately that are not adding up. The switches to the evap, the alarms going off in the cockpit and you not hearing them, things like that. Is everything alright with you? Do we need to talk just you and me, friend to friend?"

"There is nothing wrong with me. I am just trying to do the best I can on this mission. There is too much work for just one person and I am just tired, that's all."

"What do you mean for just one person? We are a team here. We share the work load and I certainly do not find myself over worked."

"If you're not here to relieve me then I need to get some work done. If you don't mind."

"You were getting ready to leave the cockpit when I saw you so your priorities are in the wrong place. If you are stressed then you need to inform me that you no longer can perform you're job and I will deal with it."

He sat there looking at me and then seemed to get himself under some sore of control.

"I am alright! I just need to get more sleep. Now get out of here."

I got up and left the cockpit and roamed around for a while watching the cockpit entrance. After about an hour I was very tired and decided to call it quits. I didn't even want to eat right now. I just wanted to dream about the 'what ifs' and drift off to sleep. And so I did, and quickly.

CHAPTER 16

I WOKE TO THE NOISE OF CLANGING. SOME ONE WAS BANGING AGAINST metal. I quickly got up and headed towards the sound. When I entered the engineering space I saw Tom with a wrench in his hand and standing there next to the evaporator.

"What the hell are you doing?"

"I am trying to get this thing opened. They want me to replace a sensor under this panel but I can't find the wrench that fits it so I was trying other methods."

"Enough of this! Get the right tool before you ruin the bolts and then we can't get it off at all. Use your fucking head. If we have no evaporator we have no water. Think!"

I walked away still trying to shake the sleep off that was still a fog in my brain. I went and found Hank and told him to go and assist Tom in the repair of the evaporator. I wanted it done right not jury rigged. He got the message loud and clear. I looked at my watch to see I still had over an hour before I needed to go to work. But now I was up and not in a good mood. I saw Carl and Sarah wandering around and questioned why she was still awake. I lectured them on the need for sleep and they crept off to get away from me. I wandered to the cockpit and told Tony what was going on and asked where the orders came from to work on the evap. He told me Lincoln sent up instructions on what to fix in it so he gave them to Tom. I left the cockpit and went and found someplace to hide for a while. The storage area seemed to me to be the best secluded place on board. I went in there and made my way to the back corner again and attached myself to the wall clamp and tried to rest and calm down. It was only a matter of a few minutes when I heard and saw the door opening to the storage space. In came Karen and Carl. Carl was leading her by the hand. They closed the door and started to embrace each other.

"I would think one might check out the space before they made asses out of themselves."

I blurted it out loudly. They jumped and Karen hurriedly left the space. Carl stood there for a few minutes and just looked at me.

"I guess my warning on inappropriate actions a few weeks ago didn't hit home very well."

"I heard your remarks but I really don't see where you have the right to interfere in people's personal lives."

"I am not interested in your personal life. I am interest in not having my crew members distracted from doing their job clearly. Now get out and get to work."

He stood there like he really wanted to continue to argue his point but then he turned and left the space leaving the hatch door open. I went and retrieved a meal and some water and ate. After that I went to the exercise area and worked out for over an hour. Then I showered and went to the bridge to work. Tony told me a few of the crew had been by to voice their opinions on my grumpiness this day. I told him about Carl and that I was finished with the lectures. Each one would be dealt with if any mistakes or mission assignments were missed or ignored. I was planning on putting out a review schedule for each of them. Tony passed on the needed information and he left. I started performing the daily updates and corrections and then after that was completed I wrote a memo on the computer bulletin board telling them all that on every Friday there would be a full review of their work for the week. That I expected to see every assignment completed and in full compliance with procedures and schedules. I would not accept shoddy work or excuses. I figured that would create a storm when they got around to reading it. I did not see or hear from any of the crew for the remainder of my shift. In fact it took several days before I heard a comment on the message that was put out there for them. It was a Thursday by my recollections so I was planning the inspection for tomorrow and figured they all were hurriedly trying to catch up and get all their work finished in time. I printed out the work and experiment schedules for everyone and put them in my quarters waiting for tomorrow. I did get a notice from Tom that the evaporator sensor was finally replaced and they were ready to turn it on and test it. I left word that Lincoln needed to be told that and it was up to them to conduct that test with him. I was wandering around when I decided I just needed to get some sleep. I headed for my quarters and when I entered it I found a note on my desk. I picked it up and opened it. It was a hand written coupon that read,

'Massages to relieve stress. First one - FREE. Appointment required. Sarah.'

I looked around the outside area and saw no one. I wandered over to the science lab and entered. In there was Sarah, Tom, Hank, Michelle and Karen.

"Is this the new crew's lounge?"

They all looked at me but no one said anything.

"Doctor! I need to make an appointment. I have a problem with my arm and need it checked. Let me know when you have time to be the doctor."

I turned and left the lab. As I was walking away I heard her voice call out.

"Be in the clinic in fifteen minutes."

I raised my arm to acknowledge her and kept walking. I went to my quarters and picked up the coupon and put it in my pocket and headed for the small clinic. I went in and looked around. It had locked shelves of medicine and a stainless steel table with lights over it and a small desk and chair. I laughed since there was no gravity how were these things supposed to be used. In one corner was a large cabinet. I went over to look in it but found it was locked also.

"Everything in here is locked."

I turned to see Sarah just inside the door. I made my way over to her and reached in and pulled out the coupon.

"I think the crew feels I need this."

I handed it to her.

"You have not been yourself this last week. Come over here and take off the jumpsuit and lay down on the table."

I watched her arrange some straps attached to the table.

"How about locking the door?"

I looked at her and she just stood there for a few moments and then reached over and locked the door. I removed my suit and was standing there nude. She stood there looking at me. She eyes went up and down several times.

"Are we missing a piece of clothing here?"

"No, I never wear underwear. I just never have since I was about twenty-two."

She placed a large towel on the steel table as I crawled up on it and she strapped me down.

"I think I am at a disadvantage here."

"I know you are."

She went and got a bottle out of a cabinet and came back.

"Relax, I am not going to take advantage of you. Not today anyway."

She was smiling at me as she started to pour the liquid on my back. After about ten minutes on her massaging my shoulders and upper back I was feeling very relaxed. I reached out and let my hand touch her leg as she stood next to the table.

"Those weighted shoes really make a difference up here in space, don't they?"

She replied yes and I placed the open part of my hand on her leg and slowly started to move it up and down about two inches each way.

"I think my back is relaxed now. How about you? Do you think so?"

So loosened the strap and told me to turn over. When I did she tightened it just a little. I reached up and took hold of the zipper to her jumpsuit and pulled it down to her waist. She leaned over and planted a kiss on me that I returned this time. I ran my finger up and down in between her breasts very lightly. She was not ending the kiss but started to press harder to my lips. I finally broke it off and moved her shoulder back from me.

"Maybe you're right. This is not the right time yet. I don't know what I really am doing here."

She reached and opened her jumpsuit and slid it off her shoulders to where it was just loose at her waist. I could see her breast peering through the material of her bra since it was almost sheer. I looked at them and could only think how perfect they were. I was not a large breast man and these were absolutely the perfect size for my liking. I reached up and cupped one of her breasts with my hand and she leaned again and kissed me hard. After a few minutes I broke the kiss off again. I told her to unstrap me. She reached down and released the strap. I started to drift upwards and she held me down. I tried to sit but she had me pinned to the table. I had moved my hand away from her trying to stabilize myself. After a minute of this I whispered to her.

"I think we need to pick this up on another day. Like maybe tomorrow. I want to be able to enjoy the moment and we have been in here too long today already. I am sure there is someone out there waiting to see when I come out."

She moved back and released me. I reached out and pulled her in closer. She put her hand on my chest and said tomorrow. We both dressed back in our suits and she went over and unlocked the door. After I checked to make sure I didn't have any lipstick or anything else on me I opened the door and exited. Standing across the way were Michelle and Hank. I walked over to them and stopped right in front of them.

"Well, did I meet your expectation on time. My shoulder is feeling much better but I must have pulled a muscle since the pain is still there. Any way I hope I wasn't in there more than normal, I would hate to have the rumors suggest something else happened. You little kids need to be worried more about you're reviews tomorrow."

I walked away as Sarah came out of the clinic and stopped and looked at all of us. She stood there glaring at them and they started to move away when she spoke up very clearly.

"You are all worse than sixteen year olds at the mall. Grow up you assholes."

Hank turned and pointed a finger at her but didn't say anything. He just left the bay. I turned towards her and smiled as I went to my quarters and went to bed. My alarm went off and I stretched and climbed out of the cocoon. I drifted over to the desk and wrote the events of the day since I didn't take time to do it yesterday. The day went smooth and the evap was fixed and put back in service. Nothing was said about my doctors visit but then I think I made it clear to Hank and Michelle I would not tolerate gossip from them. They knew if rumors were spread they had to come back to them. So I did not expect to hear anything, at least I hoped not. The day went quickly since we were busy getting ready for another course change tomorrow. We seem to be drifting off to the left of center again and Lincoln could not figure out how or why. This was going to be the second course fix since we started the trip. I got a message to Sarah delaying our rendezvous for a day or two due to the mission course change. I needed to be sharp on this one. The next day came and everything went good with the change. We had some more glitches with the computer over the next few days and then there was the noise that sounded like wind moving past a door that leaked air. It was strange but we had heard it several times now over the last week. The day came when we went past the two month mark. We did not celebrate this milestone but rather started to get heavy into the science experiments and our work load had almost doubled. Mars now was appearing in our window the size of an apple. We were just about half way there and with the increased work load there wasn't much time for anything else. I kept complaining about my shoulder to keep up the appearance I needed it worked on but other than an occasional mention of it I never made it back to her and the clinic. She was also very busy with her experiments and then there was the haze. It was getting closer to us every week. From the angle we could see that as we approached Mars it was approaching us. We still could not see it with the bare eye but it was very clear in the binoculars and still no visual sighting of the lights without pictures. It was very strange and from time to time we had little conversations about what it might be. There were more unknowns about it than we could list. Then one day as I was in the seat doing the computer update I was distracted by what I thought was a flash of light that went across the window. I stopped doing what I was doing and looked at the window in front of me. I sat there looking straight ahead waiting for it to happen again. It happened so fast I wasn't sure if it was real or a just an illusion. I thought about it for a while and determined that if I had seen it that it was inside the cockpit not outside the window. That was the most disturbing part of my sense of seeing the light. How could it have been inside? A few minutes later Tony came in the cockpit and made a statement that floored me.

"Michelle and Sarah were gazing out the window in the science lab and thought they saw a flash of light go by the space craft. I didn't give them any credence to it but I thought I saw a flash a few days ago while sitting right here in the cockpit. I just wanted to tell someone about it."

I looked at Tony and told him that just a while ago I also saw that flash of light. We talked about it for a few minutes and then decided not to confirm it to anyone just yet. As we were getting ready to finish the shift change Sarah came in the cockpit very excited.

"You guys need to look at these. This is amazing. I think we finally have proof that haze out there is moving."

I looked at her as Tony took the pictures from here. He looked at them and then handed them to me. I looked at each on and noticed they all showed the lights with the smallest hint of a tail on each of them. That could only mean they had movement to them.

"Next week we will be out here three months. I think it is time to notify Lincoln about this. This time we will send them the pictures and some of your data."

She got very excited again and said she would transfer the pictures to a computer file and get everything ready for when I was ready to rock their world. She left and I soon followed her out the hatch. I was not gone more than a minute when Tony called me back. When I entered he was sitting there in sort of a state of hypnosis.

"Tony! You OK!"

"It was here! It came in the cockpit and stayed for about two seconds and then left. It was here!"

"What was here?"

"The light!"

I looked at him and he was sitting there like in a state of shock still.

"Ok! Tell me what happened. Everything!"

He turned his head and looked at me.

"The light came in the side behind me and moved over to above your seat and stopped and then went back out the window behind me. Two maybe three seconds. It stopped over there Vince. It stopped."

I moved over to my seat and sat down.

"If I go and get a few things will you be alright?"

He looked at me and said yes of course. I told him I was going to go and get a camera and set up surveillance in the cockpit to maybe catch it the next time it happened. He said he hoped it did happen again. He wanted to be ready the next time instead of it surprising him. I left and went and retrieved a camera and a DVR system and brought them to the cockpit and down in the corner I set it up. I attached the camera up in the corner behind my seat looking downward covering the whole area. I started the recorder. I knew it would record 120 hours before we had to reset it. I was hoping it would happen again to support our report back to Lincoln on this haze. I was sure it had to be connected to the lights we could see in the pictures inside the haze. I made sure he was alright before I retired to get some sleep. I didn't get much sleep thinking about what had happened to him. My mind would not allow me to clear it out of my thoughts. I guess eventually the exhaustion finally took over. The next couple weeks went by without any incident of lights. We were now past the three month mark and the work load was getting larger and larger every day. We still had not told Lincoln about the haze and all our experiences with the lights but knew we had to do it soon. Every day we watched Mars get larger and larger in the front window. The mission book now had sections in it that were larger than all the previous months work issues. We were all secretly giving thanks for the crafts non-issues on this trip so far. No one wanted to say it but everyone was waiting for the big failure to hit. The crew had their experiments in full bloom now and we were growing tomatoes and lettuce and a wide variety of things. We planned on using them to make a special meal real soon to check the flavor and texture of these experiments. The crew was working very harmoniously lately. There was no idle time to get into mischief so we had no secret rendezvous episodes lately. At least none that I was aware of. I know that if I hadn't increased my work load I was headed for one of those events as well. I came close that day a month ago but I have managed to get myself under control again. A few more days went by and Sarah came to us with a bunch of new pictures. She told us that the haze was now only about two hundred feet to our right and even though because of the vast darkness of space she could see it with the naked eye quite clearly meaning it was well developed and formed. It definitely had mass and yet it had a transparency about it. We still could not see lights with the naked eye but the pictures were getting better and better showing their presence. The ones she just handed me clearly now show the lights with tails. Meaning they were moving and not slowly. The streaming tails were getting longer as we got closer and could see them more clearly. In one of the pictures the main body of the light itself seemed to have a form to it. It wasn't clear enough to make out but there were shadows in the light itself indicating forms of layering. I told her to make sure these were part of the package she prepared for Lincoln and she told me that was already done. I told her she was doing great work and soon she would be able to claim the haze as a discovery and name it. That apparently never crossed her mind and it made her giddy. She left and we talked about the haze for a while before I gave Tony the con and went to get some rest. He seemed different now than in the past month. I was sure before that he was creating problems for us but now he was more focused on work than before. I was hoping that he was over his depressed state. I had a feeling it had to do with missing his wife and kids and the loneliness of space. But I was happy to see the change in him. He still was keeping to himself and not really associating with anyone in the crew. That still was not like him but I was satisfied for the time being for the small change I did see in him. I walked around for a few minutes just looking around the craft. I got a bit to eat and then wandered over to the mission prep room. I looked at all the packs and read the labels on some of them. In a few weeks we will be opening these and the real work then will begin. I turned and left and headed for my quarters and then wrote a few pages in the diary. I wrote a few pages and a lot of it was about Tony and his issues and the change I was seeing in him. When I was happy with what I wrote I eased into the cocoon and slowly drifted heading for sleep. My mind still wanted to dream about

Mars but I was trying to fight the thoughts and relax. It was one of those times that nothing I did slowed down the brain functions. I remembered the last time and started to play golf in my brain as I did that last time. I made it a lot farther into the game this time. But I guess I finally did just drift off into sleep.

CHAPTER 17

I COULD HEAR TONY ON THE P.A. CALLING PEOPLES NAMES OUT. I hurriedly got up and headed for the cockpit. When I arrived he told he to sit down and he would fill me in on what is happening. As I strapped myself in I could see the radar screen had several targets being marked on it.

"I do believe we just entered a meteor or asteroid belt. One flew past the nose and it was a big one. Now we are seeing them on radar and it looks like we might be on a course to play tag with at least one more of them."

I quickly started to look over all the computer data that was coming in. Lincoln and Tony were talking and calculating trajectories. The computer plotter was showing a crossing of two of the rocks coming up pretty soon. It started to run a plot on the time of the intersection. After a few seconds it indicated the first on would miss us by what it said was 600 feet. Then it showed the second one as crossing just behind us less than 20 feet. That was a pucker factor warning. We ran it again and the same results came back. We had about two minutes for the first crossing and then seven minutes for the second crossing. I got on the P.A. and warned everyone to get to their secure seats as soon as possible. We talked and decided to trust the computers for the first one. When it passed we would know what we had to do for the second one. We sat there and waited. It was very stressful just sitting there knowing that there was very little that you could actually do. Then we saw it out of the left window. It was rather big and it was tumbling towards us. Tony calculated that it was about twice the size of us. We watched it cross in front of us and then we felt the slight turbulence that it created. We weren't rocking and pitching but with the slightest sway and it lasted about ten seconds. The computer calculations were good, very good. We figured it was about 600 feet in front of us when it passed. So now we knew that the second one was going to be too close for comfort. We told Lincoln and they agreed we needed to make the distance greater between us. The suggestion was to do a ten second burn of our propulsion engines. They recommended that since we needed the most thrust as quickly as possible. So we did the calculations and agreed that in two minutes to fire the engines. Tony and I knew that using some of the fuel in these engines meant we would not obtain the speed we wanted to get back home on schedule later. That meant the trip home now would be quite a bit longer. But our immediate concern was to live. Soon the time came and we threw the switches and the engines fired. Soon we were feeling the G-force and the speed indicator was moving higher. We shut down the engines after ten seconds and saw we were now just under Mach 62. It was incredible that we now are going even faster than before. I put in the new data and set the computer to task checking the crossing points again. After a few moments it came back and said the crossing trajectory was going to be about 2600 feet behind us. That made us all feel an awful lot better. I told the crew what was going on and that we now were out of immediate danger. When the time came for the pass we waited to feel the turbulence like we felt from the first one. This time there was none from behind but we felt a slight waiver for a second which felt very different. It wasn't very much at all but we still felt uneasy when it happened. For the next two hours we watched the rocks on radar and plotted those that we thought needed to be watched. We were both up and in the cockpit for close to twenty hours before Lincoln told us they had calculated that we had completely passed through the belt. They also told us that our flight path had been altered from the engine burn even though it was slight but we needed to make a few corrections. We fired a few retro rockets several times and Lincoln determined that was close enough for now to get us close to our target point when we approached Mars. I looked over at Tony.

"Tony, I do believe we just created an Oh Shit scenario."

"What do you mean by that?"

"I mean we just increased our speed to basically Mach 62 and the main reverse engines were designed to equally match the initial burn so therefore we do not have the same amount of fuel to slow us down anymore."

He looked at me and lowered his head. When he raised his head again he started nodding.

"You're right about that. We will have to get Lincoln to do some real work here to fix this."

He turned and threw some switches and then called Lincoln.

'LINCOLN – TALON.'

'LINCOLN.'

'WE HAVE A SITUATION HERE THAT NEEDS YOUR GROUND CREW TO FIGURE OUT. WE JUST INCREASED OUR SPEED TO MACH 62 AND THE REVERSE BURN, IF IT HAS THE SAME FUEL AS THE INITIAL BURN, WILL NOT BE ABLE TO SLOW US DOWN TO OUR INITIAL SPEED.'

There was a long pause.

'WE ARE AWARE OF THAT AND WE ARE REVIEWING EVERYTHING AND WILL GET BACK TO YOU AS SOON AS WE HAVE A SOLUTION.'

'ROGER.'

Tom and I started immediately running computer simulations to see what the results were. We were not happy with the results the computer was giving us. Every one showed us over shooting the Mars orbital path. Even when we started the burn early we were going to fast to stay in Mars orbit. I told Tony that I needed to do some computer work to try and figure this out so he needed to try and get some sleep. He told me there was no way to sleep but he said he would go and try. As he was leaving I asked him to send in anyone that he passed. I just wanted someone to get something for me. After a while Sarah came strolling in the cockpit. I asked her if she would please get me some food and water since I could not leave the bridge. She asked me how bad was it and I told her that what we had to do to keep from being destroyed by the asteroid has put us in a situation that will take some time to fix. She told me that the crew was discussing what might have happened and they were all confident in me and Tony. I gave her my food card and she left. I sat there for a few moments and wondered if they really knew what had happened if they would still be so confident. The computer finished the program I ran and on the screen were the words,

'INSUFFICIENT FUEL TO MAINTAIN ELIPTICAL ORBIT.'

I sat there for the longest time just trying to think of another way to reduce the speed but all my thoughts were coming up with blanks. I did not hear Sarah come back in.

"What does that mean insufficient fuel? Just what happened up here that created this message?"

"It is a message to a program I ran to check out different scenarios. It is not something that is happening. Just a scenario I ran."

I reached over and cleared the screen. She started to ask me questions but I did not answer her. Her voice was starting to get shaky.

"Sarah, you are a scientist. I am the Captain and I assure you that we are not in any danger right now. We are going a little too fast and have to slow down some before we get to Mars. We are just trying to determine the best way to do that. I am not concerned about it, so you should not be either."

She looked at me and then up and out the window as to stare at Mars which was very large now in the forward window. It was like looking up at the moon from Earth. Then all of a sudden I heard her gasp. I looked over at her to see her eyes expand wide open.

"Look, the haze is right there."

I looked out the right front window and there it was like it was right beside us and we were traveling directly alongside it. She went up to the side window and peered out.

"I can see them! I can see them!"

"You can see who?"

"Not who, the stars, I can see them with my own eyes."

I made my way over to the window and looked out. I could see what appeared like looking through thin clouds and there they were, lights moving past the window at a nice pace but not so fast you couldn't make them out. I tried to focus on a couple of them as they went past. I could swear that I saw a figure formation inside the bright glow. I stepped back and told her to get the camera. She took off out of the cockpit. I kept looking out the window and watching the lights go by. There were streams of light trailing from the main glow. I watched them for a good five minutes waiting for Sarah to return. When she came back I let her get into the window and she started to take pictures. After she took about seven all of a sudden there was a glow inside the cockpit. There was a light in our space. It hovered over my seat as we turned and watched it. It hovered there for about two seconds and then left out the front window going straight through it as if it did not exist. I called Tony to the bridge over the intercom. It took him only a couple of minutes to get there. When he arrived I pointed to the side window and Sarah moved so he could get in there and look out. He stood there for a few minutes and then turned towards us.

"The haze is right here. Too bad we can't reach out and get a sample."

Sarah jumped up and took off out the entrance to the cockpit.

"Those lights are pretty bright now so I was surprised we could not see them before now."

"What lights?"

"The lights we only could see in the pictures. We can see them now with our bare eyes."

He looked out the window again.

"I can't see any lights. All I see are thin cloud like formations. No lights."

I moved over to the window again and peered out. I definitely saw the lights. I stepped back away from the window and looked at Tony.

"We have an unusual problem here. I can definitely see the lights with my eyes. You can't see the lights at all. This is going to make it even harder to explain to Lincoln when we pass this information on to them."

He looked at me and went back to the window. After about a minute he turned and again stated he could not see any lights at all. So I started to change the subject to our speed. He asked if Lincoln had called with a suggestion and I told him no. I told him I have thought of two ways to do it but both were rejected when I put them through computer analysis. I told him the only way I saw us being able to slow down to the right speed was to use some of the reverse burner fuel dedicated for the trip home. That meant we could not travel as fast going home only as fast as we calculated we had stopping fuel for. I mentioned that we did have the spare fuel rockets but that Lincoln insists they are for emergency use only. We both agreed that this put us in that category but Lincoln did not agree to that yet. He asked me what the bottom line was. I told him I thought it would mean an extra ten to twelve weeks to get home. He looked at me and didn't say anything. He didn't have to because we both knew that was stretching our food and other life permitting sources to their limits. We have built into the system an eight week extra supply of food and oxygen. We weren't sure about everything else. After about an hour Sarah came back in and told us she was able to get several samples of the atmosphere inside the haze. She told me everyone was soon coming up to look and see it and she needed to go analyze the air. I kept thinking what is she doing, there is no air out here in space. But I didn't say a word, I just let her leave in her happy state. One by one the rest of the crew made their way into the cockpit and then up to the window. I kept a written record of each of their responses. I did not tell them what to look for just wrote down what they said. Carl only saw the haze, never saw lights like Tony. The same went for Karen. But then Michelle went to the window and immediately started to talk about all the lights going past. Tony looked at me just staring waiting for me to say something. I did not say a word. Then Tom came in and he made the comment that the lights were very impressive as they streamed past the window. Then the last one, Hank came in and after looking out the window for over a minute only questioned how there could be clouds in outer space. There was no mention of seeing lights. After they all left Tony went back to the window and looked out it for a long time before coming back down to his seat.

"Why can some of us see only the cloudy formation and other like you see lights inside the clouds? I just don't understand that at all."

I agreed with him. We had enough of a problem trying to figure out why there is a cloud formation out here let alone there are lights associated with it that are only visible to some of us. A short time later Lincoln called and said they were still working on the speed issue but also wanted us to check several sensors that were located on the right side of the craft that were measuring the outside elements. They indicated they were getting strange readings from the right side sensors only. Tony and I looked at each other and Tony asked them to clarify what they meant by strange readings. They said their speed indicator sensor was fluctuating up and down and not giving a constant speed. Then the indicator that should not be giving any reading until we arrived in Mars atmosphere was indicating almost normal Earth atmosphere readings. So they knew there was a problem with the sensor. I threw my switches and responded to Lincoln.

'LINCOLN – MARIANI HERE.'

'GO AHEAD VINCE.'

'I AM SENDING YOU A FILE THAT NEEDS TO GET TO YOUR SCIENTIFIC BRAINS. I THINK THEY WILL BE QUITE INTERESTED IN WHAT I AM SENDING AND YOU MIGHT GET YOUR ANSWERS ALSO. WILL EXPLAIN AFTER YOU REVIEW THE FILES.'

'OK, WILL BE WAITING FOR THEM. IN THE MEAN TIME CHECK THE SENSORS.'

'ROGER.'

I called Sarah into the cockpit. After she arrived I told her to add all the new stuff to the files and then send everything to Lincoln. To make sure she had a cover letter on it indicating that she was the discoverer of the haze and wanted full credit for it. She looked at me and gave out a cowboy yell and left. Tony and I sat there and tried to analyze what was going on around us. It was hard to try and keep our minds on the problem we were having concerning how fast we were going when we had this unknown entity along side the craft that was completely without reason. We were working hard on the speed issue when Sarah called from the lab and asked if I could come there right away. I told her I would be there as soon as I could but it might be a while. She again stated it needed to be very soon. I told Tony that she must have just analyzed the air sample and found out what Lincoln told us about being just like the Earths atmosphere. He agreed and told me to go take care of it. Our speed issue will still be here when I returned. I got up and left the bridge. As I was making my way to the science lab I saw Tom coming out of the lab carrying a bag. As he approached he started talking.

"You are not going to believe what she is going to tell you, god, I don't believe it, so how can you believe it."

He kept on talking to himself as he went past. I entered the lab and she turned and told me to get over to where she was at.

"You're not going to believe me but I have the results right here."

She was gleaming from ear to ear.

"I think I know what you are going to tell me."

"Did Tom tell you already, damn him."

"No, he didn't say anything. I just know why you are so excited."

"Then you know it is the air sample I am referring to, don't you?"

"Yes, Lincoln called and told us we have a faulty sensor on the right side of the craft. When you called I knew the sensor isn't faulty and you are going to confirm what Lincoln thinks is faulty equipment."

She started to gleam again.

"It's air. It's real air. The readings are the same as if we were on Earth. I don't know how or why but that is real air out there and it is only in the haze formation."

"Have you sent the files down to Lincoln yet?"

"Yes, about ten minutes ago so they should be getting them in a little while."

"Then you need to send another file with these results included in there."

"I added the test results to the file I already sent. The test results came back just as I was finishing putting together the files to send so I added them before I sent them."

"They are going to shit themselves when they read all this."

She came up to me and threw her arms around me and planted a kiss on me. I wanted to continue it but I broke it off looking back at the door.

"Don't need to get caught."

She stepped away from me and just kept smiling.

"I want to name this now. I want Lincoln to put out a press release with me as the discoverer and give them a name for it."

"I will let them know about that when they call. I better get back because they will be calling soon."

"Tell then I discovered it and I want it named 'ARWEN'S HAZE' or better yet 'ARWEN'S SPACE RIVER OF LIGHT.'"

I looked at her and questioned why Arwen. She told me that was who she always wanted to be when she grew up. She loved the movie so much that she wanted to be Arwen, so that's what she wanted it named. I told her I would pass it on and I left the lab heading back to the cockpit. When I arrived in the cockpit I heard Tony talking to Lincoln. I slipped into my seat and listened.

'WE RECEIVED YOUR FILE AND THE COMMAND WISHES TO KNOW WHY WE WERE NOT INFORMED PRIOR TO THIS INCIDENT.'

I put on my headset and threw the switch to go live.

'THIS IN VINCE, IF YOU RECALL THREE MONTHS AGO I INFORMED YOU WE WERE SEEING A HAZE OUT OUR WINDOW AND WAS ADVISED TO DISREGARD AND NOT BRING IT UP AGAIN.'

There was a pause and then finally command responded.

'OK VINCE, SO NOW WE HAVE SOMETHING OUT THERE AND YOU ARE TELLING ME IT HAS ATMOSPHERE.'

'I'M NOT TELLING YOU, THE MEASUREMENTS TAKEN ARE TELLING ALL OF US. OUR DOCTOR AND SCIENTIST SARAH HAS BEEN MONITORING THIS FROM DAY ONE. IT IS HER DISCOVERY SO SHE WILL GET FULL CREDIT FOR THIS, UNDERSTOOD.'

Again another long pause before they responded.

'SARAH WILL GET FULL CREDIT. WE NEED EVERYTHING YOU HAVE ON THIS.'

'SHE SENT YOU EVERYTHING WE HAVE. SHE WISHES TO NAME IT – ARWEN'S HAZE OR ARWEN'S SPACE RIVER OF LIGHT-, DO YOU COPY.'

'ROGER WE COPIED IT. NOW WE WILL GET THE RIGHT PEOPLE ON THIS AS SOON AS POSSIBLE AND FOR THE TIME BEING THIS IS CLASSIFIED. NOT TO BE DISCUSSED ON THE OPEN NET.'

'ROGER, UNDERSTAND.'

'NOW WE HAVE A SERIOUS PROBLEM AND THE BEST WE CAN DETERMINE IS THERE IS NO WAY TO SLOW YOU DOWN TO THE REQUIRED SPEED WITHOUT USING EXTRA FUEL FROM THE OTHER ROCKETS. THAT LEAVES US WITH A MORE SERIOUS PROBLEM. IT RESTRICTS THE RETURN TRIP SPEED.'

'ROGER, WE ALREADY HAD THAT AS THE ONLY RESOURCE WE HAD AND WE UNDERSTAND THE CONSEQUENCES.'

'THEN WE NEED TO MAKE SURE WE CONFIGURE THE BURNS TO GET INTO MARS ORBIT AND WE WILL THEN DEAL WITH EVERYTHING ELSE. IT IS VITAL WE GET YOU INTO ORBIT THERE BEFORE ANYTHING ELSE IS RESOLVED, CONCUR?'

'ROGER CONCUR.'

'OK WE WILL DO THE CONFIGURING AND PROGRAM THE COMPUTERS. LINCOLN OUT.'

I turned to Tony and told him I got the feeling they were just a little peeved about the haze. We laughed about it for a while and then started to think out loud about how this mission would be a disaster if we could not get slowed down and get into Mars orbit. Just as we finished talking one of those lights came into the cockpit again. It hung around for about two seconds again and then left.

"This light is starting to bug me."

Tony looked at me and then looked at the window.

"How can I see the light when it came in here but can't see any lights out there?"

That was just another question that no one could give an answer to. There were nothing but questions here and no possible way to get answers. Tony told me to get out of there and get some rest. We both knew neither of us were going to get any sleep but we were trying to rest as much as possible. I passed everything I had on to him and left the bridge. I headed out the hatch and went and grabbed some food. I was eating when Michelle came and started a conversation about the lights. She didn't understand why some of the crew could not see the lights. I told her I didn't have any answers to these questions. I knew as much as she did. She told me she was praying that all this was a good thing and they weren't evil aliens. I looked at her and reassured her that I didn't believe they were aliens at all. She got up and left and I headed for the science lab. I was thinking as I made my way over there about what she said. The thought of aliens never crossed my mind. I didn't want to believe that was the case at all. I decided that was not going to be any part of my vocabulary on this issue. I entered the lab and Sarah was still there doing experiments.

"Did Tom get samples yet?"

"Yes he has already analyzed them and the results were the same as mine. He has gone to get some sleep."

I was still near the door to the lab so I turned and locked the door.

"Why captain, I think you have me in a very awkward position?"

"Not yet I don't."

I moved over to where she was and then remembered the cameras. I told her the camera where rolling and needed to be turned off. She said she would take care of that later as she put her arms around my neck and we kissed for a long time. We did a little talking in between sessions of kissing. I told her I was very tired but wanted to apologize to her for my actions. We talked about our marriages and that we both felt they were over. She went over to her desk and pulled out a crumpled piece of paper. When she brought it back I knew it was my letter that Phil gave to me. She told me she took it from my desk at the cape and knew my situation was the same as hers. The conversation went to how we would deal with the crew if they found out and we decided that we just had to make sure they did not. So we set up a meeting for tomorrow after our shift was over. I gave her another kiss and I left the lab leaving the door unlocked. I wandered over towards the water machine and after a long drink I went and took a shower and then headed for my quarters. It took me a long time to write the events of the day in my diary. I spent pages writing about the lights and the haze and I started to even write theories about what I though about everything. I gave my impressions of how each crew member was taking this and I listed the plans for the next few days to make sure the crew was going to be psychologically sound to deal with whatever was going to happen now that we had our first real problem. I knew most of them did not know about our fuel situation yet but they would very soon. I had to determine how to handle each of them separately. I was tired but for some reason I thought that now was the right time to look over the papers that Phil set up in the envelopes. I opened the safe and pulled them out. I started to read them and they were all about the satellite and its mission. It went on to explain the purpose of the satellite and then it went into detail about its capabilities. I knew then that if I knew this information I would have refused to take it on the mission. I finished reading the papers and put them back in the safe and locked it up. Once I finished I crawled into the cocoon and laid there for a very long time trying to relax and hoping to get some sleep. I finally started to think about Sarah and I didn't remember anything else as I drifted off.

CHAPTER 18

I WOKE UP SUDDENLY AND REALIZED THAT TOM WAS SHAKING ME. I was startled as I opened my eye and looked up at him.

"Tony needs you in the cockpit like yesterday."

I got out of the cocoon and got into clean clothes and headed for the cockpit. I entered and Tony told me to sit down. I went over and sat down and looked at him.

"Look out the front window."

I turned and looked out the window and saw we were now inside the haze. I called Sarah to the bridge over the intercom.

"When did this happen?"

"About twenty minutes ago. It moved over us, it had to since we certainly didn't change course."

We sat there looking out the front windows. I could see the lights streaking by the windows. Some were going a little faster than others, and some were just drifting by. They were larger now and I could see they had mass to them. It was all very diffused so all I could tell was there was mass in the light and it got thinner as it went down into the tail. After a while Sarah came into the cockpit and she froze instantly looking out the front windows.

"My god they are people."

I instantly turned and looked out the window. I saw no people only lights and haze.

"What are you seeing out there, I don't see people?"

"The lights they all have figures and a hazy vision of faces. I can see the make up of faces."

I still was looking out there and did not see this.

"Can you take some pictures?"

She nodded and left. Tony was still looking out the window and never moved.

"Vince, I am still baffled as to why each of us sees different things. I still can only see the hazy clouds out there. No lights and definitely no people."

I was watching the lights move away from us since they were traveling at a faster speed than we were. That alone baffled me. Every once in a while a light would seem to slow down right in front of the window and then resume whatever speed it was traveling at.

"This is amazing no matter what we see. I wish they could hear us and we could see and hear them?"

"Tony, I didn't think you believed in ghosts and things like this?"

"In theory no I do not believe, but this isn't theory any more. This is for real and I am here and so is what ever it is."

Just then the radio broke the silence.

'TALON – LINCOLN MISSION CONTROL.'

'TALON HERE.'

'WE JUST CONFIRMED THAT ALL OUTSIDE INDICATORS ARE NOW READING THE SAME ATMOSPHERIC CHANGES AS WE INDICATED BEFORE. HAS THERE BEEN A CHANGE OUT THERE THAT WOULD CAUSE THIS?'

'LINCOLN WE ARE RIGHT NOW IN THE MIDDLE OF THE HAZE. A LITTLE WHILE AGO IT MOVED OVER US AND WE ARE COMPLETELY SURROUNDED BY IT. IT STILL IS TRAVELING FASTER THAN WE ARE BUT LOOKING AT OUR SPEED INDICATOR IT IS NOT AFFECTING OUR CURRENT SPEED.'

'ROGER CONFIRM. WE HAVE NOT BEEN ABLE TO COME UP WITH A FIX TO SLOW YOU DOWN OTHER THAT THE USE OF THE MAIN REVERSE ROCKETS.'

'ROGER, SURE WISH WE KNEW WHAT THIS WAS AND MAYBE WE COULD ASK THEM FOR HELP.'

I tried to make a joke but I guess Lincoln was not in the cheerful mood. There was no reply but during the conversation several lights were sort of hovering in front of our windows. Eventually Lincoln called back.

'TALON – LINCOLN CONTROL.'

'TALON HERE.'

'OK, WE HAVE DECIDED THAT WE WILL WAIT AND DO THE NORMAL REVERSE ENGINE BURN JUST PRIOR TO YOUR ARRIVAL TO MARS ORBIT. THEN WE WILL DO ANOTHER BURN FROM THE OTHER REVERSE ENGINES FOR THE NEEDED TIME TO PUT US IN MARS ORBIT. WE WILL RECALCULATE THE RETURN DURING OUR MARS MISSION. DO YOU CONCUR?'

'WE CONCUR.'

That was it. The decision was made and our return to Earth was now a major issue for our survival.

"I guess we do not need to think about whether we will live or die out here in space but just get the mission done and make it a success. At least then we will be heroes, even if we are dead ones."

I looked at Tony while he was speaking.

"I thing we all will come up with something to get us back before we run out of supplies. They still have the emergency fuel reserve that I know they will use when needed."

"Its not the supplies that worries me its oxygen to breathe on the trip home that we don't have enough of it left in our tanks."

He got up and left the cockpit. I knew he was real upset at the moment. I thought about what he just said about the oxygen and decided that it didn't matter at the moment. All the problems will be on the ride home. I sat there for the next two hours running computer analysis runs for as many different scenarios as I could think of and none got us home safely. Sarah had taken her pictures and now came back with the results. She was smiling at me when she handed me the prints. There in front of me were ten pictures and every one of them had visions of faces and or body images within the light streams. I looked at them over and over. It even seemed that in two of them they were looking at us through the windows. Sarah started to talk about her theories as to what they were. She spurted out theory after theory.

Then all of a sudden she gave one that just ran chills up my spine because I immediately thought of the possibility that she could actually be right. But I hesitated and really had to think about this long and hard. I asked her not to spread her theories around just yet. We needed to think about them for a while first. I told her to send these pictures to Lincoln as soon as possible and she reminded me that her job wasn't too hard to not have done that already. I reminded her that she should not do things before she received permission from the captain. I had initial thoughts not to send these images to Lincoln just yet but then I had no choice in the matter anymore. She understood where I was coming from and agreed not to send anything without my authorization again. We were still sitting there talking when Tony came back in and while we were all talking he stopped talking in mid speech. He stood there staring straight ahead. We were both turned towards him so I turned and looked out the window. There were a lot of lights right in front of the windows. A very high number of lights and it seemed that the number was growing. Sarah said very softly the faces were looking in at us. I looked at her and then at Tony. Tony was standing there with a very strange look on his face.

"Tony, are you alright?"

"I see them. There are people out there. This can't be really happening."

I turned and looked and I still did not see the images but the windows were completely lit up from all the lights out there.

"Vince, look at the speed indicator."

Tony was pointing at the indicator. I looked at it and I just could not believe what I was seeing. Sarah started to clap and she got very excited.

"They know we are in trouble and they can hear us. They are helping us."

She was talking very fast and if she could jump she would be jumping from her actions. I looked at the indicator and watched as it was very slowly decreasing in speed. I reached over and put on the headset and threw the switches.

'LINCOLN – TALON.'

There was no response. I called again and again no response. Then Sarah made a comment that they must be not allowing us to tell Earth they are helping us. I watched and over the next hour and a half we slowed down to the speed that we were supposed to be traveling at, exactly Mach 60. As soon as we reached that speed the lights started to drift off again. The lights became less and less until the view was as it was before with a few lights at a time streaking past the craft. Then as if there had been no loss of time the radio went off.

'TALON – LINCOLN, GO AHEAD VINCE.'

I looked at Tony and then Sarah who was still giddy and clapping.

'LINCOLN WE HAVE TO REPORT AN INCIDENT. COULD YOU PLEASE CHECK YOUR SPEED INDICATORS.'

There was a pause for a good while before they responded.

'TALON, WE SEE IT BUT WE DO NOT UNDERSTAND, OVER.'

'I CAN NOT EXPLAIN AT THE MOMENT BUT WILL SEND YOU A MESSAGE IN THE NEXT FILE TRANSMITTAL IF THAT IS OK.'

'ROGER WE LOOK FORWARD TO RECEIVING THAT ONE. I GUESS WE HAVE TO REVIEW THE BURN AGAIN.'

'ROGER I DO BELIEVE WE ARE BACK TO NORMAL.'

'WELL, NOT SURE ABOUT NORMAL, BUT, ROGER.'

They went dead and we sat there just completely baffled as to what happened. We talked about it for a long time but no one was willing to call it a miracle or even admit that we were not in control at all during that time. We all tried to get back to normal business but no one could. Some of us had been up for going on fifteen hours now and we did not want to leave the cockpit. There was a concern that since this incident occurred that with us being inside the haze we were not in control at all. None of us wanted to leave for fear that something might happen. Something we were not willing to accept. We did not know how they knew we were in trouble but they did. We did not know how they managed to arrange the situation that slowed us down but they did. And finally we did not know their intensions going forward and that scared us. All except for Sarah. She was beaming from ear to ear and would accept anything that was done as faith and with complete love of the situation. I told her she needed to write a book in her log on this one and to make sure she did not forget anything. I also told her to list any theories she wanted to in this chapter. She took some more pictures and was in the window talking to the lights for a while before she took off to the lab and her journal. We called and told Tom to get some sleep because we needed him to be in the cockpit for a few hours later. He agreed and hit the sack. I told Tony that I was going to write a log entry for a while and for him to hit the sack as well. He told me he would try but if he couldn't he would be back soon. I wrote the file and entered it into the computer and then sent a copy of it to Lincoln. It covered everything that happened right down to the T. I was running on fumes when I finally finished with everything I needed to do. I was creating separate folders and putting multiple copies all over the place to make sure we didn't lose any data. As I leaned back I realized it was now over twenty hours since I had some sleep and it was a very shortened version of it at that. Sarah came into the cockpit and went over and sat down in the co-pilot seat.

"Do you know how long we have been up now?"

"Yes and I am loving it, so I don't care if I am tired. Just look at that. This is way beyond cool. This is living a dream that you know would never come true and yet here it is. If only we knew why and where they are coming from and going to."

"You talk as if they were alive. There is a problem here and this is that they are visions. Sort of ghosts drifting in space. You're right in that we don't know where they came from or where they are headed but your last theory you mentioned earlier about them being the recently departed souls from Earth ascending into heaven might not be too far from what is happening here. Since I can't see them, I need to know if you see male and female and dare I ask if they have wings."

"Yes I can tell that the face visions I do see are both male and female and they seem to have distinct characteristics that look like different ages too. But I am not sure about that. SO, what if I am right and this is the pathway to wherever after you die. Do you know what this means. We can tract their path to the next world where ever that is."

She started to type on the computer and was going a mile a minute when all of a sudden there was a light in the cockpit. Before I could say or do anything there were two. Sarah looked up and slowly waved to them. I knew see was seeing visions but I was not.

"Excuse me, but I can not see you. Can you explain somehow why I can't see you?"

I caught myself blurting it out loud. Sarah was closing her eyes and reaching out her hands.

"Oh no, you can't be serious here. Sarah, do not try and interact here."

I was getting excited thinking something very wrong was going to take place right in front of me. I was watching the lights and they never moved but she started to nod her head and then she opened her eyes and looked down at me and then back up. She said nothing but it appeared she was communicating with the lights. I could not handle this. I started to get up out of the seat. Immediately the lights moved to a farther distance from me than before.

"Vince, stay where you are! You will be alright and they will stay but you need to sit back down."

"What the hell is going on here Sarah. Tell me you are not talking to them."

"No but I am sensing what they are telling me and I can feel the words forming in my brain. They can understand us and they used their energy to help us since we didn't know how to help ourselves. Is that making sense to you? They feel our love and just wanted to be a part of it one last time. So, you know, I think that I am talking to them after all."

All of a sudden the cloudy vision of the light started to form figure visions in front of me. I now was seeing them for the first time. Sarah was still sitting there and now with her eyes closed again. After about a minute of this the forms drifted out through the skin of the craft and were gone. Sarah opened her eyes and looked at me.

"Vince, I think I was right. I think they are transitioning to what ever is the next world. I thought the question about where they were going and got nothing back except I saw what looked like a planet and lots of stars. Lost my thoughts Vince, I can't think of anything right now."

Just then the computer screen came on and on the screen was a whole series of mathematical equations. I looked at the screen and saw at the bottom of the page it was listed as page 1 of 264. I immediately hit a few keys and saved it to a file. I also noticed that several of the lights on the overhead were flashing. I looked at them and saw they were all sensors and reset them all. I looked at her and asked who would ever believe us if we tried to tell them what just happened. We were in there for over an hour trying to reason with the events that took place and could not. We wrote in the log the story we just experienced and saved it. We were not going to send this one back to Lincoln. While we were still talking in came Hank and Michelle to the cockpit.

"You two are joined at the hip. I never see one without the other. But, you know, that's alright. I have decided after what we have witnessed so far on this trip that nothing that doesn't jeopardize the mission will be questioned by me every again. So what can I do for you two?"

Hank looked at me and then at Michelle before getting back to me and speaking up.

"I appreciate what you just said but you need to check the equipment status in the computer. I think you need to run a few tests on the equipment to look for sensor failures."

I turned and pulled up the equipment status screen. There were several pieces of equipment that were listing as being at 100% full. I started to run an analysis of each one individually and they all came back as accurate. I told Hank about the sensors tripping and me having to reset them. Then I told him to go to the rear system control panel and check the gauges there. He told me already did and they all indicated full. He then hit me with the big shocker of the conversation.

"Now look at the fuel indicators for the main propulsion rockets."

I sat there and just looked at him.

"You're going to tell me they are full also aren't you?"

He stood there and just looked at me.

"How can that possibly be correct. There is no way humanly possible to add solid fuel in the rocket booster engines."

When I checked the fuel indicator it was showing 50%. That is where it was before we made that short burn to get out of the way of the asteroid.

"I'm glad you said it not me."

I looked at him with a puzzled look so I guess he explained it a little better for me as he repeated the words,

"Humanly possible!"

"So somehow the gauges are saying we didn't use any fuel for the fuel burn and that somehow all the oxygen tanks completely refilled themselves."

We all talked about the facts and agreed that since there was no way to prove there was more oxygen and fuel we had better plan on going with the plan we had already being put in place. We were going to tell that to Lincoln the next time we talked to them. Tony came in and after a major discussion as to what occurred while he was gone we passed on the logs and everyone was ready to change over the shift when Sarah spoke up.

"Has anyone looked at the windows lately?"

I turned and looked at the windows. There was no haze, no nothing. Sarah and Tony went to the windows and up close looked out peering into the darkness.

"There is nothing that I can see on the right side here,' came from Tony. Sarah agreed that there was nothing in front of us either. The haze and all the lights were gone. Then Sarah told us to wait a minute as she moved to the left window.

"It's over here. It is out there, quite a ways out there."

I moved to the window and saw it about a hundred feet away. Again I only saw the haze and no lights. Sarah confirmed she saw no lights as well anymore. We all discussed this again and decided we had been on a course that passed through the path of whatever this was since we still were not positive of what we saw. We did believe in the theory that Sarah had and everyone including Tony agreed it was the best option to accept. So in the logs it went down as being most likely a pathway to another dimension after life on Earth was concluded. That alone was going to create quite a stir and debate when we return. But none of us had a better explanation at the time to explain the things that had happened that in all intensive purposes, were going to save our lives. Tony took over and Hank stayed in the cockpit when the rest of us left to go crash. I had a lot to write in my diary this day but it was going to have to wait. I didn't think I could stay awake that long. We all were totally exhausted and needed a lot more than seven hours of sleep but that is what we knew we would have to settle for. I told Sarah as we walked reservations had to be changed and she agreed without hesitation. I hadn't eaten in a very long time but didn't want to take the time to do that either. I went into my quarters and started to get ready to crash when I saw a note on my small desk. I opened the paper and saw a hand written note from Tony.

'I know you and everyone else believes we have seen visions of hope and believed you saw our destiny. I didn't see that at all. When I was able to see the couple of visions all I saw were dark shadows of outlines that to me looked like skulls. I do not feel the sense of helpfulness you share. I thing everything that happened is an illusion and nothing has changed. We will die out here if we believe in these illusions.'

I wanted to go back to the cockpit and talk to Tony about this but I figured since the haze was gone for now it could wait till later. I made the determination that without the haze still looming over us he would be a calmer individual for the time being. I crawled into my cocoon and was instantly out drifting far away.

CHAPTER 19

THE NEXT FEW DAYS WENT BY WITHOUT ANYTHING OUT OF THE ordinary happening. We were still talking about our experiences and Lincoln was not talking about it at all. They sent us an order not to discuss it on the open frequency at all. Every test that both of us conducted indicated the current readings were correct. I sent Lincoln a message that we as the crew wanted to trust the readings and not come out of the orbit burn early as the new schedule planned. Lincoln declined to change the burn programming stating that we still could make the correct orbit even if we had the corrected burn time. It would delay the orbit by two days. To them that was acceptable. It was now only eleven days until we were going to start our accent into the Mars orbit so we were quite busy still checking and rechecking all the data and the checklist was getting worn out from all the practice sessions we had performed. I had completed everything about an hour prior to being relieved for my session when Michelle came into the cockpit to talk to me.

"Captain, you know that Hank and I have being hanging around a lot together lately. We know this is not proper but I need to know from you if there is going to be a problem. I mean I don't want our friendship to become a public gossip thing when we get back."

"I do not like the outward looks but I made a decision weeks ago that if it did not interfere with this mission I would have nothing to say one way or the other. That will apply during this mission and after we return from it. Your actions when we return will be all that is know to the community.

There is no record on paper of any personal issues and it will stay that way. Now I can only speak for myself as Captain. I do not pry into the writings or the lives of the rest of the crew."

She understood that and thanked me for reassuring her that at least officially nothing was in writing. She left and I went back to relaxing until Tony arrived. He came in and wasn't looking too good. I asked him if he was alright and he said that his stomach was acting up and Michelle had given him some stuff to settle it down but it hasn't worked yet. We had our discussion earlier about his note and he assured me that his feelings would not interfere with this mission. But I could see in his face that he was not the same Tony I had spent many years with. I had concerns inside but I kept them there. I offered to stay a while and let him go and rest but he chose to stay so I headed out. I roamed around for a while to see who was around and I could not find anyone. So I slid into the science lab door. I thought I would catch up on a reservation I had made but when I entered I was confronted by four crew members being in there. I went over to the lab table to see what they were looking at. Sarah and Carl were busy doing tests on something.

"What is the main attraction here?"

"We are testing some of the haze matter we were able to capture a few weeks ago."

Carl seemed excited about this. I just stood there and watched for a few minutes and then told them to enjoy the results and I turned and left. I caught the eye of Sarah as I started to leave and the sudden change in her facial features told me she just got why I had come into the lab. I glanced at her and waved saying it was time for some sleep. She just looked at me until I cleared the doorway and was out of sight. I went and showered and then after filling in my diary I got in the cocoon and tried to sleep. For some reason I just could not relax enough to drift off. My mind was racing from the haze to what could have been happening in the lab to Tony. I laid there and just decided rest was better than nothing so I was content to stay right where I was. I must have fallen asleep because the next thing I remember was being awakened by my alarm going off. I just laid there and really did not want to get up but eventually rolled out and got ready for another session. When I arrived in the cockpit I found Tom at the helm doing some computer work.

"Where is Tony? I know he wasn't feeling well last night, did he get sick?"

"Yes and he asked me to cover instead of waking you. He is having real trouble with his stomach."

"Did he go back to Michelle for something else to help him?"

"Don't know, he was heading for bed when I relieved him."

We covered everything that happened overnight and I took over. I asked him what the alarm was that I had just heard and he told me it was a hatch seal in the storage compartment but Hank checked it and found nothing out of the normal and reset it. I was doing my normal routine when Lincoln called and advised they were updating the computers with all the new de-orbit programming and didn't want us to interfere with the download. Communications now was almost a ninety second delay. So talking to them what felt like real time to us was actually sent ninety seconds ago. That was hard to get used to. The systems were being updated and over the next couple of days we were putting in long hours testing the systems to make sure they were right. Finally we had three days left to go before we started our burn to go into Mars orbit. Mars was very large now in our window. We could not see much more than the planet covering most of the view out our window. Sarah had reported that the haze was no longer anywhere in view so she was content to finish all the experiments she had left to do prior to our arrival into orbit. Some of the tests we found ourselves doing dealt with the satellite we were carrying. Most of us had completely forgotten about it. But now it was becoming part of the daily routine. Lincoln still had us doing our burn almost ten minutes early to make sure we had time to do another burn if the numbers were wrong. We knew it was rather late in the program to make changes now so we quit confronting Lincoln about it. The next day we did our last mock burn and we went into rest mode. Lincoln ended all tests and told us to get as much sleep as we could. Tony and I decided on ten hour shifts since we only had 12 hours left before the burn. We threw Tom in there for a four hour session so we would both be fresh in 12 hours. Since he was still not acting like himself, he took off and went to bed. I ordered the crew to do the same. Everyone was to have at least 10 hours of sleep during the last 12 hrs before the burn. We were preparing to have a long day when we went to orbit just in case we had problems. My shift went very fast and soon I found Tom coming in to relieve me. I went over the little bit of instructions we had for the time being. I left the cockpit and went straight to the science lab. I entered and found no one there. I went to the food station and got a bite to eat. As I was eating I saw Sarah and Carl walk past and head for the lab. I finished my meal and thought about going back to the lab but decided to just call it a day. I went and took a shower and headed for my quarters. When I entered I saw Sarah standing in the corner where she could not be seen from outside. She was standing there wearing only a towel that was wrapped around her waist. I pulled the curtains closed and started to take off my suit. When I was standing there in the buff she dropped the towel. We knew this was going to be difficult in such a small space but we were determined to give it our best. There were no words spoken and it took us quite a while to accomplish our private mission. Afterwards we were leaning against each other and the wall. I started to chuckle looking down to see both of us still in our gravity boots. She was still in the snuggling mood and we caressed for a while before we got dressed. I poked my head out the curtain and looked around for a few moments before I let her slide out and watched her head for her quarters down the way. She looked back at me as she entered and blew me a kiss. I went back inside and after writing a little bit in the diary I crawled into the cocoon and instantly fell asleep. I woke up and laid there thinking of the great dream I had and wanted to go back to sleep to have it continue. As I laid there I thought about Sarah and I wanted more. I knew that the session was probably going to be the only one of its kind for a long time. I looked at my watch and saw I still had about an hour before I needed to be in the cockpit. I wandered over to Sarah's quarters and peered in around the curtain. She was not in there. I went to the lab and she was in there working. I walked up to her and told her I have not been so relaxed since we started training almost three years ago. She smiled and said it was a wonderful night. We talked for a while and then I told her that in about two hours everyone needed to be in suits and strapped in so not to get too into what she was playing with. She acknowledged it and I left for the cockpit. When I entered I saw Tony playing Mah Jongg on the computer.

"I guess we are relaxed. Did Tom get to take a break?"

"Yep! I just got back in her about an hour ago. Everything is ready."

"How are you feeling?"

"I'll be alright."

That is all I could get out of him. It appeared that something was really bothering him but I could not tell if it was physical or mental. Since we didn't know what to expect we were getting into full suits for the burn. I watched the computer screen for a while and then got up and went and ate some food before heading for the equipment space. In there I found Hank and Michelle already getting dressed in their suits. I went over to the communication station and made an announcement that everyone needed to suit up in full gear within the hour. I hung up the mike and went and retrieved my suit and started the process. Everyone took turns in the bathroom and then the lower body suit went on first. After that it took two to help with the upper suit. Soon all seven of us were suited up. I took the helmet and headed for the cockpit telling Hank and Carl to wait and assist Tony. When I arrived Tony left to get suited. We were now within the hour before rocket blast time. I was in comms with Lincoln and all preps were made for the system to do its thing. It was all going to be automatic with us monitoring the system to be able to over ride it if needed. With about twenty minutes to go Tony came in and got himself seated. I made the announcement that everyone needed to go to their seats and get secured. Then I strapped myself in and we all waited. In time the countdown monitor was inching its way to the one minute mark. Then I made the last announcement to be prepared for heavy turbulence in less than one minute. We could only figure the force of the engines trying to slow us down would create very heavy shaking. I mentally was trying to get ready for it. I told Tony,

'here we go.'

Then the clock hit 5 seconds and we both braced ourselves. The firing of the rockets in the reverse main engines started on time and then the vibrations started as we watched the speed indicator very slowly start spiraling downward. As the vibrations got more intense we could feel the craft yawing from side to side slightly but the bucking motion was getting far greater than we expected. I knew that things in the craft that were not secured properly would be everywhere. As the Mach meter showed 25 it seemed to stabilize the vibration some. We did not seem to be shaking as much as before. The speed indicator was now flying downward. You could not keep up with the numbers. I looked at the clock and saw we had less than a minute left in the burn. It was all working as they expected it to. We were very grateful for that. One can have only so much confidence in technology without being able to test your theories until you actually are performing them. We were checking all the controls and indicators and resetting the ones that were tripping when all of a sudden the engines quit. I looked up and saw the time indicator had reached 0 and the speed indicator was only four mph faster than it was supposed to be. I started to have a great respect for our engineers. Even more now than before, since I was at their mercy. It was also crossing my mind that those entities we encountered also did indeed have something to do with the fuel left in our engines. I didn't know how but I was praying words of thanks at that moment because it told me that the trip home was now going to be alright. We looked at the horizon of Mars out the side and front windows. It was like we were orbiting the Earth but the color of the planet was all wrong. We heard and felt some retro rockets going off in short bursts knowing they were setting us up for the orbit angle. I got up and looked out the side window at Mars. It seemed so desolate out there but we embraced the facts of why we were here. I announced over the intercom that we were here and all went very well. Everyone could remove their suits and go about their business. I sent Tony to get out of his suit first. I sat there watching the horizon of Mars as we drifted over it. I felt the retro rockets fire again and this time for about eight seconds. I looked at the speed indicator and saw it drop numbers. I knew then that we were dropping to line up to be in orbit. It was awesome to have everything computer controlled and it work. To sit back and enjoy the ride but knowing in a few days we would be deep into experiments and EVA's and sending down the rover on its mission. I took a peek at the log program for tomorrow and there was a section in there that only said 'See Lincoln for Instructions'. I sat there looking at it and then it dawned on me that it had to be referring to the satellite that was such a secret this whole mission. After about a half hour Tony came back and I left to shed the suit. In the equipment room was Sarah waiting for me to assist.

"You're going to help me get this off?"

"Oh yeh! Let's get to it."

She started to help get me out of the top half of the suit. It took a lot of pulling and working the arms in the right angles to slide out of this monstrous suit. Soon we were down to the bottom half and she made a soft comment about getting to the good part. I gave her a soft slap on the side of her face and she responded in kind but to the back of my head. After I was free from the suit she walked up next to me and grabbed my groin with her hand and looked me in the eyes and softly said 'later in the lab'. I smiled and told her she was on. She told me she had some work that needed done so she would see me later. She smiled and left the equipment room. I finished with the smaller items and got into my blue jumpsuit and headed back for the cockpit. When I entered Tony and Lincoln were discussing the burn and going over the fuel numbers to verify we had indeed only used the one set of reverse engines. They were trying to figure out how we slowed down to the correct speed on less fuel than was indicated before. I reminded them that we came out of Mach speed early so we were going to have to get closer to Mars before we could go into orbit. They told me that I needed to check my numbers and take a better look because somehow we were right where we should be if we had done the normal burn. That is what they were talking about when I had entered the cockpit. Again another mystery that we could not explain. They set up the EVA for tomorrow to discard the empty rocket sections and to look over the skin to see what damage if any we had taken during the time when we had been hit by a few meteorites. The rest of the day was organized into setting up for the two EVA tomorrow. So relaxation was definitely in store for later. Tony left to get some sleep and then I realized that I was going to be there for the next eight hours. I decided that Sarah was going to have to come to the cockpit and we would see what could be done there. I also remembered the camera I had put in place there. I didn't remember it when the lights were running around in the cockpit but I remembered it now. I went over and sent the recorded file to the computer and labeled it cockpit lights. I then checked it to make sure it was transferred and then erased the system and started the recording process again. I copied the cockpit lights file to a CD to give to Sarah. I created a note to put on the outside hatch that said out to lunch and put it aside for later. I finished up the computer files I needed to get us into tomorrow and sat back and relaxed for a while. It was more than half way into my shift and I figured that Sarah would be by eventually. I was sure hoping she would. I waited and waited and now I had about two hours left in my shift. I got up and grabbed the note and put it on the outside of the hatch and swung it closed but not locked. I headed out and as I passed the eating area I saw a few of the crew sitting around talking. They acknowledged me as I headed for the science lab. I had a folder in my hand to make it look like I was delivering it there. I entered the lab and found it was empty. I looked around but there wasn't anything there to indicate she was coming back soon. I left the lab and headed for the sleeping quarters. I went past mine and down the corridor to hers. I peeked around the curtain and saw she was sleeping. I stood there for a moment and decided to leave her be. I left the area and went back to the cockpit leaving the hatch wide open now. I took the sign and threw it away. I sat in the seat and just rested and daydreamed about what might have been. It wasn't too long after that when Tony came into the space and after we discussed the events that needed done before tomorrow came I left the cockpit. I wasn't hungry so I grabbed a drink and headed for my quarters. I entered the space and saw a note attached to my desk. I picked it up and read it. All it said was,

'lab 2 AM'.

I looked at my watch to see it was already after 1AM. I stood there and thought about it for a minute. Tom was supposed to be on watch now so how was she going to do this. I sure didn't want him coming in on us. I wandered around for a few minutes and then headed for the shower. I did a load of laundry in the great special machine that didn't use water but they came out smelling good anyway. Soon it was a few minutes after 2 and I headed for the lab. There was no one around at all. Everyone who was on the EVA team was getting extra hours of sleep so there should only be 2 crew members up right now. I entered the lab and there she was standing there in a lab coat. I asked her where Carl might be hanging around and she told me she switched shifts with him since he needed to be alert for the EVA in the morning. I locked the door behind me and made my way over to her. Just as I approached her she opened the lab coat to reveal a very see thru negligee.

"Where did this come from?"

"I brought it in my bag just in case I needed it."

"And why would you thing you might need it?"

"Because six months before we left on this mission I fell in love with you mentally and have been trying to figure out how to tell you."

I unzipped my jump suit and stepped out of it and we embraced. For the next hours we caressed and made love and then tried to just snuggle next to each other holding on tight but the gravity thing was getting the best of us. We finally got dressed and after spending some time kissing and still caressing we settled down to a serious conversation concerning what she had said earlier. We both agreed there was an attraction that we could not overlook but we had this little problem of us both being married. After looking at all the facts we determined that we were both convinced neither of our spouses would be there when we returned so we justified everything we were doing. I needed some sleep but I just didn't want to leave her. Eventually we both left the lab and we both headed for our own quarters and went to bed. I wasn't sure about her but I never went to sleep. I just rested thinking about our love making session the whole time. I heard my alarm go off and I just wanted to ignore it but I knew we had a busy day ahead so I got up and after putting my jump suit back on I strolled out and got some food to eat. Sarah was already out there eating. I sat across from her facing her with Karen next to me. We played eye games and eventually I could not take any more and excused myself and headed for the cockpit. All I could think about was getting this mission over with so I could spend real time with her on the Earth where gravity wasn't a major deterrent. I caught myself drifting a few times when Tony was talking about issues but I managed to cover up the fact that I just wasn't listening to him. Life was very good all of a sudden and I didn't want anything to change it.

CHAPTER 20

WE WERE RUNNING THROUGH THE FLIGHT PLAN AS THE CREW was preparing to commence the EVA to set the antenna arrays out for better communications with Earth. Then they needed to set and align the solar panels towards the sun. And the third part of the EVA was to open the rover compartment. All this would take about five hours by the plan. All three were going out on this EVA. So I was waiting for the signal that they were ready. It was taking a long time for that notification to get to us. I called Carl and asked him what the delay was. He informed me Karen was having problems. He didn't say what they were just she was having problems. I got up and headed for the equipment room. When I arrive I saw two of them fully suited and Karen was there only half suited.

"What the hell is the problem here? This EVA was supposed to start thirty minutes ago. Now lets get your act together and get dressed, now!"

She looked up and I could see she was crying.

"What the fuck is wrong now?"

"I just can't do this. I just can't go out there."

I walked over to her and grabbed her arm.

"You have fifteen minutes to get your act together. You have trained to do this job and you *will* do this job. We did not travel over four month for you to sit on your ass and cry. Get your ass out there and now."

I pointed to the other to get her dressed. She stood up and they started to suit her up. I stood there and watched.

"How is it going to look back on Earth when they find out you quit and became a loser. You are just having jitters because it is now for real. There is nothing different today than five months ago in training. You have already been out there on EVAs already. You keep your head on the job and don't get distracted. You are the one that is making history here. Make us and the world we know proud of you."

I stepped back and let them finish getting Karen in the suit. When she was all suited up I left and returned to the cockpit. I told Tony what I had to do and that it hurt me to do it but they could not manage with just the two of them. He agreed with me and we waited for their signal that they were ready. It took about ten minutes before Carl notified us they were at the pressure hatch ready to go. I gave a little pep talk speech praising them for their work in advance over the intercom and then gave them the go ahead to start. Lincoln was told that the EVA was getting underway and we watched as the cameras were showing us their progress. It took about a half hour to get them all outside and ready. We were monitoring the vitals of Karen extra close. All was going well and they started to put out the antenna array and after about forty-five minutes they aimed it at Earth and we watched as our signal strength went up twenty fold. We did a remote lock on and the antennas motor started to move slightly. When ever we were in sight of Earth we would be locked on automatically now. Tony left for a while still showing signs of there being something wrong. Then they moved over to the rover compartment and started to undo the many bolts that secured it. This took over an hour but finally they opened the two panels and after folding them back they secured them in the open position. Now was the fun one. They had to pullout each of the six solar arrays and unfold them so they would stretch out the thirty feet and then align them towards the sun. This also would be remote controlled once they were expanded. This took about thirty minutes for each panel. After almost four hours they were all finished and came back to the hatch and entered it ending our first EVA at Mars. When they were all inside and secure the EVA had taken over seven hours total time. That was amazing. It was one of the longest EVAs ever done. We were wrapping up the data and setting all the controls for the solar array which was giving us a lot of power right now. All the batteries were being recharged and everything was working great. We were finishing communications with Lincoln when Karen came into the cockpit. She came up to me and planted a kiss on my cheek and gave me a big hug. She started to cry and was thanking me for not giving up on her and she was telling us how awesome it was out there. I told her that the stage fright was not new and she just needed to forget about it because we had already put it in the past. She left in a happy but really tired state. The three of them were heading for bed since they had to do it all again tomorrow. We went over the flight plan for tomorrow and there it was staring us in the face. That section where all it said was to obtain instructions from Lincoln and it showed five hours of EVA time allotted for this. After we talked about this satellite thing for a while Tony left to go get some sleep and I settled down and rested in the Captains seat there. Lincoln was sending a lot of data and updating the computer system so some one needed to stay and monitor the computer to ensure the files were being accepted and actually modified. I watched as the system program for tomorrows big EVA was loaded into the computer. There seemed to be a lot of things that the crew needed to do to get it ready for launch. But then it was completed and the system and the file was pass coded so I was not able to open it and read it. I was pissed about that. I was the captain of this mission and they were withholding data from me concerning my mission. I was planning on calling them to tell them I was going to refuse to deploy the satellite unless told what and why it was with us on this mission. It didn't take too long before Lincoln called and we got into an argument over the satellite. We went to a secondary secure channel and continued the argument.

'LINCOLN – TALON HERE.'

'GO AHEAD VINCE.'

'I WILL NOT BE GIVING THE ORDERS FOR AN EVA TOMORROW. WITHOUT KNOWLEDGE OF THE PURPOSE FOR AN EVA THERE WILL BE NO EVA.'

'CAPTAIN YOU HAVE YOUR ORDERS. THERE WILL BE AN EVA TO LAUNCH THE SATELLITE AND IT WILL BE TOMORROW.'

'TALON OUT.'

I cut the communication off. They tried many times to call us on all the secure channels but I would not answer them. Then they called on the main unsecured channel.

'TALON – LINCOLN.'

'TALON HERE.'

'REQUEST CHANGE TO CHANEL 7.'

'NEGATIVE OUT.'

There was not another call for quite a while. I knew they were furious with me but then I was way out here and definitely in control. I figured they would lay some bullshit on me about disciplinary action when I returned but I didn't care. I was planning on retiring from the space agency anyway so I was not going to be railroaded into changing my mind. It was over an hour later and I started to hear their calls again on the secure channels. I again did not answer any of them. Finally they called on the regular channel.

'TALON – THIS IS LINCOLN.'

'AND THIS IS TALON.'

'WE WILL BE SENDING YOU A MESSAGE SOON. YOU NEED TO RESPOND AS SOON AS POSSIBLE.'

'ROGER.'

That was it, that was all they had. I guess the message on the computer would be the big threat. I waited for it to come in and after about a half hour it popped in the mail box. I looked at the mail box and saw it referred to me looking at a file in the system under a folder named 'targets'. I went in the system and looked around for this folder. It took me a while because it was hidden in the equipment log documents. What were they up to hiding this so deep in the system. I opened the file and the first page came glaring out at me in a bold red color and flashing.

'This document is Top Secret and unauthorized disclosure will be dealt with criminal charges.'

I started to scroll down the pages and I saw where it was twenty-three pages long. I read the first three pages and it was all about the background of intelligence gathering stuff. Then I hit page four. There were pictures and graphs about the satellite. The next several pages explained the pictures and the graphs. Then it went on to list the capabilities and the purpose for the satellite. I sat back in the seat and read that section again. When I moved on to the last part of the file I was reading about the satellites mission and how it was going to be used. Finally I read the last page which was the part I believed they didn't want us to know about. It listed what was attached to the satellite and how many and their destructive power. I was just finishing the last page when Tony came into the cockpit. I told him what I had done and that they had sent a folder for me to see to convince me otherwise. I also told him that I had just finished reading it and it was for me only but I wanted him to read it and be by backup if something went totally wrong concerning this satellite. He agreed and between the two of us we made a promise never to discuss what was in this folder. It took him a while to read it and I saw him read sections of it a second time like I did. After he finished I closed the file and folder exiting out of the program it was in. As soon as I did that I watched the computer take that folder and delete it. I went back in to see if the folder and file were still there and they were not. Lincoln was playing a very smart game here. We looked at each other and talked about it for a few minutes and decided we needed to go ahead and launch the satellite. Based on what we read we did not like the purpose but we agreed on the reasoning behind it.

'LINCOLN – TALON.'

I called on the secure main frequency.

'LINCOLN HERE.'

'FILE READ AND ACCEPTED. EVA SCHEDULED FOR TOMORROW.'

'ROGER.'

We sat there and tried hard to understand how and why this monster satellite was created. It obviously has been in the making for quite some time to have been on this mission. We knew we were going to Mars for three years now so they had to start planning that long ago also. I left and tried to get some sleep but was haunted by the thoughts of it being on board for four months and we didn't really know what we were carrying. When it was time for me to go back in the cockpit I was exhausted. I did not sleep a wink. I went over to Sarah who I saw by the food god and told her my situation. She took me to the clinic and gave me two pills and I took them. Then she handed me a small pack with about five pills in it.

She told me to take these in about five hours or whenever I feel like I couldn't keep my eyes open anymore. She was worried about my condition. She also told me to drink a lot of fluids but I told her that wasn't possible stuck in the cockpit. I left and went to the cockpit and for the next three hours got ready for the next EVA. As soon as we were ready to send them outside, Tony left to get some rest. I was in there alone and I knew with no one to talk to I was going to be in trouble keeping awake real soon. I started to sing as I was monitoring their walk. I was watching as they opened the casing to the satellite. Soon the camera I sent out with them was activated and sending back clear video of the satellite. I was a very large satellite and it had three rectangular boxes in a triangle formation around the base of the satellite antenna array. I knew from the file just what those boxes were. They started to work from the script each of them had and started to assemble the items that were attached to the inside covers to the satellite. There were five attachments that needed to be done. After about two hours all the attachments were done and the crew now moved the boom arm and attached it to the frame of the support mechanism holding the satellite in place. I then asked them to look at the sides of the craft for damage during the flight. They spent about a half hour looking over the skin and then returned to the hatch and back into the pressure chamber. After another hour they were all back in and out of their suits. Two of our fixed cameras were on the satellite. Lincoln was informed the EVA was completed. It wasn't long after that we watched the arm remotely being controlled by Lincoln and lifting the satellite up out of the compartment and then releasing it with a swing action sending it slowly away from TALON. When it drifted far enough away we could see the small retro rockets fire and off it went. We did not know where it was heading but based on the equipment it had on board we did not think it was staying in Mars orbit. But then we would never know since we probably would never see it again. Sarah made sure I was getting water during this time and then after it was over I crashed for a good ten hours. The couple of hours spent before I finally got some sleep were spent looking over the papers again and again concerning the satellite. I was still very uncomfortable knowing I released a monster. I knew it had to be a secret government project and I had the feeling that the only reason we made this trip was because the President and his cronies wanted this thing in orbit. The next few days were uneventful. There was nothing but science experiments scheduled from orbit. Day six started with the rover being detached and sent to the Mars surface. Most of the day was devoted to getting the rover to talk to us. We were having a terrible time making communication with the rover. It took over eleven hours before we received a response from the rover. But once we did we started to give it orders and it started to respond. Carl, Tom and Sarah would be very busy for the next month having it do experiments and then retrieving the data and analyzing it. I knew there were long hours in store for them. Tony and I decided on twelve hour shifts since most of our job was just monitoring the action happening all around us. We were not going to ask Lincoln for their permission this time. There were two move EVA planned but not for another week. We went into automatic mode. Tony and I were just monitoring experiments, the rover, and moving data all around the computer system to get them in the right files for transfer back to Lincoln. The time was flying by because everyone was super busy and no one had any idle time to waste. I went to the food machine and found very few selections for a meal and realized no one had time to restock the unit. I found out where the stock was at and got the instructions from Carl and did it myself. It took me quite a while but then we all had food to eat again. I did a walk through the storage area and looked at all the packs. Most of them were already used and now were being filled with finished experiments. The ones that were extra were going to be stored again before we headed back to Earth. There were two days designated just for cleanup and securing everything. The next two EVA sessions went according to plan and everything was now finished. There was another week of experiments to do and the data from the rover was coming in fast. There were a lot of experiments the rover was doing that we never saw the data on. Some of it went straight back to Lincoln. We had to move the rover to another location that would take it two days to get to. That process started and we were waiting for it to get there for the last three days of its mission. Tony told me that we was keeping track of the satellite on radar and for the first three weeks it was orbiting Mars but for the last few days he was not able to pick it up again on radar. I was amazed how smooth everything was going and should have kept that to myself since with only four days left in Mars orbit we lost contact with the rover. We were trying all three of the frequencies but it quit responding to our signals. After two days we set the rover controls on an automatic signal system and hoped to get it back before we left. Tom also told me that we were getting alarm readings from the main propulsion system in the backup control room. All the indicators in the cockpit were reading normal. We did not understand why the alarms were going off since that system was not active nor would it be until we were getting ready to leave orbit. We figured it was a glitch and Lincoln agreed and we ignored it. The last two days in Mars orbit were frustrating days. We were still not in communication with the rover and things were disorganized. It was like everyone on board was having mental issues. No one was thinking correctly. We were trying to figure out if it was due to fatigue or was there some kind of reaction to the area. But then we were in a closed environment except for those three who did the space walks. So I asked Sarah and Michelle to set a monitor on each individual and check everyone twice daily. The last thing we wanted to do was bring back to Earth something foreign to the world. Tests and retests were done over and over again. Everything was coming up negative. Every once in a while the computer was telling me that changes were made to files that affected our communications system and our propulsion systems but then I could not get any more information or path to follow concerning the alert message. Reports were showing problems and then saying nothing was wrong. It was very confusing and I was getting frustrated with the system. I passed everything on to Lincoln and they said they were running tests as well because they were definitely showing system problems. But like us they had not been able to isolate the problem as of yet. Their messages were simple ones but they showed concern in the way they were written. I had to trust that everyone on board was doing their job and I saw nothing lately to make me thing otherwise but I still had doubts. My thoughts went to Tony and the problems I had with him earlier in the mission.

Lately he seemed to be on course and was working well with me and the crew. I wanted to believe that his issues were resolved but then I was too busy myself to be monitoring his actions all the time. I wanted to talk to Lincoln about this but I was afraid that Tony might hear it and then I definitely would have a problem. So I decided to just keep it to my self again for the time being.

CHAPTER 21

I ROSE TO THE ALARM GOING OFF AND WAS SURPRISED THAT I HAD slept that long. I was slowly coming around to full consciousness when Sarah popped her head around the curtain.

"It's our last day at Mars, do you want to make it memorable?"

She was smiling at me. I looked at my watch and then up at her.

"I wish you had come in earlier, I only have a few minutes before I need to be in the cockpit for when Lincoln calls. We have to run the check list. Sorry."

She looked around behind her and then slid in the space and closed the curtain.

"You know Tony will send someone in a few minutes and it would not be good for us to be in here together."

She came over and planted a huge kiss on me and then grabbed my crotch and left. I poked my head out the curtain and softly yelled at her.

"How about a rain check?"

"Let me know when it starts raining,"

was her response as she headed for the science lab. I finished getting ready and headed for the cockpit. When I arrived Tony was already in conversation with Lincoln. They were discussing the rover. He told me they were considering us staying another two days to keep trying to raise communications with it. I flatly said no to that one. Not for a mechanical thing that we already had a tremendous amount of data from. I reminded them that every experiment had already been conducted and all tasks except the remote one were completed. I did not see the advantage of floating around for two more days hoping for a change that I felt would not come. So we argued for a while longer and then I reminded them our burn time was less than an hour away and we needed to cut the talk and get ready for it. They finally gave us the ok to prepare for departure burn. I made the announcement and everyone went and took their positions for the bone jarring blast again. We ran through the check list again and made sure all the switches were in the proper positions. When the time came it was again set to be automatic. Since communications was on such a delay Lincoln made it simple by having the burns run off of the computer activation programs. The solar panels and the communication arrays were on an exploding bolt system and would detach from us when we started our burn. We sat there and waited for the final minutes to count down to our booster rocket propelling us up to the Mach 60 level again. We watched the last few seconds go down to zero and then nothing. Nothing happened. We looked at each other and then started to check the computer status. It was showing a count up as if the burn occurred. I got on the radio and called Lincoln.

'LINCOLN – TALON.'

'LINCOLN.'

'WE HAVE A NO GO ON THE BURN.'

'REPEAT PLEASE.'

'I SAY AGAIN WE HAVE A NO GO ON THE BURN.'

'ROGER.'

I knew they were seeing the same false indicators as we were from the computer. I had Tom go immediately and check the system backup to see if there were any indications there of a failure. He reported that everything looked normal. We went over the switch locations and all checked out again. Then after waiting about a half hour the computer recycled and they tried again to fire it. Nothing again, just the false count up showing once more.

'LINCOLN – TALON WE HAVE A NO GO ON THE BURN AGAIN.'

'TALON IN FIVE DO A MANUAL FIRE.'

'ROGER.'

We reset the computer manually and set it for five minutes and started the count down. When it hit zero we threw the switches to fire the booster engines and we got nothing. We were still just sitting there orbiting Mars.

'LINCOLN – TALON THE MANUAL FIRE FAILED. WE HAVE A NO GO ON THE BURN.'

"ROGER TALON WE COPY."

We went to the secure channel and tried to go over the check list one more time to make sure something wasn't missed. After an hour every switch and every toggle was checked both in the cockpit and the backup system. I sent Tony back to the secondary control system during this check to confirm all the settings were the same back there and he reported it all check out. I remembered from before that Carl told me the main propulsion panel back there was flashing yellow indicating a failure in the system. I also remember the system giving me an error in the propulsion system for a moment earlier in the day. When Tony got back there he said the buttons were all flashing yellow. I told Tony to shut down the secondary system and we would try again. He told me he would secure himself back there and to go for it now. We had to wait until we were in the right aspect trajectory to get back to Earth but when we were ready I reached up and threw the two main rocket fire switches and the rockets fired and we started to move. As we moved faster and faster I called Tony and told him to watch the panel for any problems. He told me the whole system was turned off at the moment but he was smelling smoke. I watched the speed indicator and it was starting to climb faster and faster. Tony called and said he had a fire and was using the fire suppression system to extinguish it. I watched all the indicators and none of them were indicating a fire. I started to worry about the computer monitor program since it seemed it had failed. We were passing Mach 35 and Tony said the fire was extinguished but he was in duress due to not being able to secure himself and the smoke was heavy back there. I called Carl to see if he could manage to get to Tony and report on his situation. He said he would try. The vibrations started to ease and the G force was also getting easier to deal with. We were now at Mach 45 and had about forty seconds left in the burn. Soon it was over and we were flying through space back toward Earth. At least I sure hoped we were. I was not trusting anything at this moment. Tony called and said he and Carl were alright and they were going to check the auxiliary system before he came back. I looked at the speed indicator and saw it was only indicating Mach 58 and the actual speed was about 1310 mph less than it was on the trip out. This was not a real major difference but it would mean we were not getting home on time. It initially looked like a four or five day delay but we had to run the analysis to be sure. Tony came into the cockpit and he said the back up system control room was gone. The fire had destroyed a lot of the wiring. We called Lincoln and passed on the two crucial pieces of information we had. Lincoln was extremely concerned about the back up system but said we were still within their parameters on the speed. I also told them about not getting any indications of the fire or the problem with the back up system in the cockpit. I suggested they check the programming from their end. They agreed they would run a diagnostics on the whole system. We settled down and started the check list for the return flight plan. There wasn't a lot to do on the return flight. There still were experiments to perform but we had a lot of down time to deal with now. Tom came in and told us the fresh water system did not seem to be working at the present time. I told him to find Carl and the two of them to go and check it out. I looked at Tony and told him that four and a half months to get back was a little too much without water. I asked him if it was just one evap system or both. He said that all the evap lights were on indicating failure. He just looked at me and started to work on the computer without saying anything else. I knew he was running diagnostics himself now. We were both doing what we could to find out why the systems were failing and with out warnings. I started to think there had to be one thing that was linked to everything that was the culprit. I got everyone involved in some way to help. We were still working on our individual items when Lincoln called and told us that they had done a scan of the system starting with a month ago and have retraced all the changes that were made to any of the computer programs. They had a few things they were looking at that might have contributed to the failure. They indicated they would get back to me whenever they had solid clues. I thought about what they had said and determined they were sending me a message they wanted to talk to me alone. Instantly my thoughts went straight to Tony. He was always the common denominator in all the previous incidents so I started to wonder about what he did this time. I thought again that I was over reacting. Tony would not put everyone in jeopardy. I knew him too long for this to be the situation. At least I sure hoped I was right. So I waited for a while and then made my move.

"Tony, we are not getting anywhere here. I guess we will have to wait for Lincoln to see what they actually come up with. In the meantime we need to get back on our schedule. You have been up for over twelve hours now so you need to get some sleep. So it is almost noon by my watch meaning that we could get back to eight or twelve hour cycles again starting now."

"I think twelve hour cycles will be OK."

"Alright then, you go get some sleep and I will monitor everything for a while. Knowing Lincoln we probably won't hear from them until tomorrow."

He finished up doing whatever he was doing and then left the cockpit. I waited a good half hour before I called Sarah to the cockpit. When she arrived I told her that she was the only one right at this moment that I knew I could trust. I needed her to do some work for me and to tell no one. I needed to know where Tony was right now and asked her to hang around after she told me outside to make sure no one came into the cockpit when she returned. She looked at me funny and I told her I would explain later but I needed to know that Tony actually headed for bed. I made it clear that she was not to give any indication she was spying on him. She left and came back about ten minutes later telling me Tony was in the equipment room looking around the computer system that failed. I told her to get Carl for me right away. When he arrived I gave him direct orders to have him go to the equipment room and under my orders to not let anything be modified in there. He was to stay there until I got back to him. No one was allowed to enter that space except he and I. I wanted to make sure Tony did not change anything. Then Sarah had returned and took a seat in the cockpit as I asked her to do waiting for another set of instructions. I knew that Tony could monitor anything I said or did from that room. I soon was told that Tony had an argument with Carl and he was heading towards me. I waited a few minutes and then Tony walked in the cockpit.

"What the hell is going on here? Why are you giving orders to Carl to keep me away from the equipment?"

"There were no such orders given. I gave orders to Carl to go in and monitor the system in the equipment room and to make sure nothing was changed or to report if anything was disturbed or happened in there. I didn't know you were in there but under the orders I gave him everyone is included. So why were you in there messing with the system when it is shut down?"

"I was checking it to see if I could figure something out. Why are you questioning my authority?"

"I am not at all questioning your authority, just questioning why you were in there when you knew it was shut down. Are you aware of something that caused it to catch fire? You sure are acting like you are trying to cover something up and got caught. I know you better than that or at least I thought I did."

He stood there and stared at me with a very red face. He was furious but was it because I caught him or because he thought he was above questioning. He turned and started to leave without saying anything else.

"I asked you a question Anthony. I expect, as Captain of this craft, to receive an answer."

He did not stop at the hatch but continued on out of sight. I turned and called Lincoln on the secure channel.

'LINCOLN – TALON.'

'LINCOLN HERE.'

"THIS IS VINCE, I AM ALONE AND READY TO DISCUSS THE ISSUE AT HAND.'

'STANDBY.'

I told Sarah to stand outside and make sure no one came in the cockpit. She left and went outside. I sat there for a while and then I heard the Director of Lincoln Flight Operations on the radio.

'TALON – LINCOLN CONTROL, PHIL HERE.'

'VINCE HERE PHIL.'

'WE HAVE RUN OUR PROGRAMMING AND HAVE FOUND MODIFICATIONS HAVE BEEN DONE THAT HAVE ALTERED AND

IN SOME CASES DESTROYED PROGRAMING AND HAS CAUSED EQUIPMENT FAILURE. THOSE MODIFICATIONS HAVE COME FROM TALON.'

'I UNDERSTAND WHAT YOU ARE TELLING ME. ARE YOU SURE AS TO WHEN AND WHO HAS MADE THE MODIFICATIONS?'

'YES, ALL THE MODIFICATIONS CAME FROM THE COCKPIT COMPUTER AND ANTHONY HAS BEEN SIGNED ON EACH INSTANCE.'

"ROGER, CAN ANYTHING BE DONE TO COUNTER THE MODIFICATIONS?'

'NOT THE ONES THAT HAVE ALREAD CAUSED DAMAGE. THAT DAMAGE IS NOT REVERSIBLE. ALL PROGRAMS FROM THIS POINT ON HAVE BEEN SCANNED AND FIXED. ALL PROGRAMS ARE NOW LOCKED AND I WILL SEND YOU THE PASSWORD IN YOUR PERSONAL FILE. READ AND DELETE IT IMMEDIATELY. NO ONE ELSE CAN MAKE ANY CHANGES TO ANY PROGRAMS. ALL EXPERIMENTS, ALL COMPUTERS ON BOARD ARE LOCKED AND WILL REMAIN SO FOR THE REST OF THE TRIP.'

'ROGER, UNDERSTAND. WILL READ AND DESTROY. WILL TAKE APPROPRIATE ACTION CONCERNING ANTHONY IMMEDIATELY.'

'ROGER, VINCE THIS IS SERIOUS. HE HAD THE OXYGEN SYSTEM PROGRAMED TO FAIL BUT WE CAUGHT THAT. HE CAN DO DAMAGE THERE MANUALLY SO BE CAREFUL. ADVISE WHEN COMPLETED.'

'ROGER OUT.'

I sat back in the seat and all I could come up with was,

'holy shit'.

I opened my personal file and found the folder that was just sent and read the password and then deleted the folder. I watched as the computer went through an update knowing that when it was finished everything would be locked. I went to the hard copy of the manual that covered what to do if someone needed restrained. I finally found it and read it over a couple of times. I called for Tom to come to the cockpit. When he arrived I told him to read the manual and showed him the section to read. He looked at me and then read it.

"What is happening here? Who are we going to restrain?"

"The trouble we are having with the system and the fire we had were done deliberately. I don't know why but one individual on board wants us all to die. We must not let that happen."

He looked at me and then he looked at the co-pilot seat.

"I saw Tony in the systems room where the backup computer is located two days ago sitting there at the computer. It looked like he was working on a program. I didn't say anything and he didn't see me. Is he the one we are talking about?"

"Yes! You are now my second in command. Let's go and get this over with."

We left the cockpit and went to the storage room and in the rear was another room that was small but where we kept spare space suits and extra survival gear. We started to clear out the room. It took us a while but finally we emptied it. I went to the small chest we had as an armory. It was for emergency purposes only. I took my keys and opened the chest. I removed the harness and strapping items to secure a person if need. I took the several locks from the chest. I looked at Tom and said lets go and find him. We went to the main area where the food system was and saw Michelle and Karen sitting there. We went past them and over to the berthing area and to Tony's quarters. I reached and moved the curtain back and saw he was not there. I looked at Tom and we headed for the science lab. We entered the lab and saw Sarah in there working. I asked her if she had seen Tony, and she answered that she saw him at the food machine about thirty minutes ago. We went back out to the main area and decided to check the cockpit. Just them Carl came round the corner and told me that Lincoln was calling us. We hurried to the cockpit and when we entered we heard Lincoln calling and we also saw three yellow lights flashing and the alarm going off. I looked up at the lights and saw they were all for the pressure hatch used for EVA's. There were two hatches and both alarms were going off and flashing. That meant the hatches were open and only the outer hatch to space was left beyond that. We went as fast as we could move to that part of the space craft. When we arrived we did not see Tony but we immediately closed the inner hatch and started to seal it. Just as we did I felt great pressure on the hatch. I told Tom to watch it since it was indicating a breech on the other side. I hurried back to the cockpit. When I arrived there Lincoln was still calling us. I hooked up and responded.

'LINCOLN – TALON, VINCE HERE.'

'TALON, HAVE BEEN CALLING FOR A LONG TIME. YOU HAVE A BREECH TO THE OUTER EVA HATCH. YOU ARE IN GRAVE DANGER.'

'ROGER, WE FOUND IT. INNER HATCH SECURED. MIDDLE AND OUTER HATCH OPEN, NEED RECOMMENDATION ON HOW TO CLOSE MIDDLE AND OUTER HATCH AT THIS POINT. ANTHONY MISSING AND PRESUMED KNEW WE WERE AWARE OF HIS SABATOGE. BELIEVE HE EXITED THROUGH OUTER HATCH. WILL CHECK TALON AND ADVISE FURTHER.'

'UNDERSTAND! NEED TO DONN SUITS AND PROCEED AS IN EVA FROM INSIDE. USE LIFE ROPE PROCEDURES AND DOUBLE SAFETY GUARDS. REMEMBER YOU ARE AT MACH 58. SUCTION FROM THE VARIANCE OF THE THREE SPACES MIGHT BE EXTREMELY DANGEROUS.'

'ROGER, WILL ADVISE WHEN READY FOR EVA.'

I left the cockpit and headed back to the equipment room. I was met by everyone except Tom. I explained the situation to everyone and told them what needed to be done and it was imperative it was done quickly. They all scrambled to get their space suits on. I went in the EVA area and found Tom with his hand on the hatch.

"There is a great deal of pressure on the other side. I am not sure this hatch will hold."

"Go and get into your space suit. Everyone needs to be in full EVA gear now."

"How about you?"

"I will be there in a minute."

I stood there just thinking about what was happening and cursing

Anthony for creating this mess. I then left and headed for the equipment room to get suited up. After about forty minutes everyone was in full suits and on packs. We made our way to the EVA hatch area. We were thankful that the hatch held and gave us the opportunity to survive. We tied three ropes individually to each person and then we chained us all together in a line. I told them that since I was the Captain I was responsible to make this happen so I would be the first one and the only one to go out. Carl stopped me and told me there was no way they would let me go out there. He said he was going to do the job and for me to be at the back anchoring the line. They all agreed that I needed to be in the back since I was the only one left to get us home safely. I finally agreed and moved to the back. We tied the three ropes off to the craft and we slowly started to open the inner hatch. The pressure was really strong and we knew the hatch would be sucked in as soon as the latches were close to being open. We were just praying the hatch remained in tack on the bulkhead. Everyone was pulling on the hatch as Carl undid the latches. We managed to let it swing open hard but not rip off the hinges. The space inside the outer area was an L shaped compartment. The middle hatch was in front of us open and then the outer hatch was around the corner to the right. We slowly eased Carl and Hank right behind him into the middle hatch area. When they arrived Carl stated the outer hatch was missing. It had been completely ripped off. We pulled him back and for the next thirty minutes tried very hard to pull the middle hatch closed. The sucking action wanted to pull all of us out the hatch and yet we were trying to pull the hatch closed in the opposite direction of the pressure. It just wasn't going to happen. Tom then mentioned that if we flooded the space with oxygen we might lessen the pressure just enough to pull the hatch. Karen was next to the hatch opening so I told her to hit the pressure dump valve on the wall next to the door. She reached up and gave it a smack. It did not move at all. She tried several times but nothing. No one else could reach the valve. Suddenly I saw Sarah holding on tight to the ropes swing up her legs and then come back down. She did this several times until her feet were at the height of the valve. When she did it the next time she threw her foot forward and hit the valve. It was enough pressure to activate the system and oxygen started to dump into the outer pressure chamber and then we all pulled with everything we had. The hatch started to slowly move in our direction. When it reached the halfway point the pressure was low enough for us to pull in closed. Then as fast as he could Carl and Hank secured the latches. As soon as they finished I turned off the oxygen flow to the outer area. We then backed out and secured the inner hatch. We had to stay in our suits until we could get the craft filled again with oxygen and suitable for us to get out of the suits. Finally we saw the green light come on and the gauges all were reading acceptable levels and we started the process of taking off the suits. The whole process took over three hours and I didn't know about the others but I was exhausted. After I got out of the suit I just tried to lie on the floor for a while. Sarah came over and asked if I was alright. I told her no and then started to laugh. I mentioned that I felt like every part of my body had been beaten with a baseball bat. She told me that she had something that would help me with that feeling and told me to come to the clinic when I could manage to get up. I floated on the floor for a while until Tom and I were the only ones left there. I told Tom I would meet him in the cockpit as soon as I got my energy pill from the doctor. He told me to bring him one too and he left. I headed for the clinic and eventually made it there. I entered to find Sarah writing in a book on the desk.

"I'm here for my energy pill."

She looked up at me and shook her head. She got up and went to the cabinet and opened it. I told her to give me one for Tom also. She looked at me and went back to the cabinet. After a minute she locked it back up and turned towards me.

"Here, take this now."

She handed me two pills. I looked at her and looked around for something to get water in.

"The water is over there."

She pointed to the container on the wall. I got a drink and took the two pills. She then came up to me and gave me a big hug.

"You do realize that you saved the lives of all of us today?"

"I did what I, as the Captain, had to do."

We talked about what really happened and then she gave me one pill to take to Tom. I left and headed for the cockpit. When I entered Tom was talking to Lincoln. I sat there and listened to their conversation. He told them what we had to do and that the outer hatch was gone. Lincoln told us that they knew something was wrong since their sensor light was still on for that hatch and that we were drifting off course to the right. Apparently the open hatch was creating a very slight drag as we traveled through space. We spent hours talking to them going over everything that happened and what need to be done to survive the rest of the trip home. It was during this time when we realized that our oxygen level was now less than sixty percent. All the other levels were critical as well. We were going to have a lot of work to do trying to figure out how to survive for over four months on what we had left. The mission just became a survival mission rather than a celebration for reaching Mars. I sat there with Tom and we went over every system and wrote down every level that they were presently at. Then I went into the system and pulled up the file that showed all the system levels for yesterday. I sat there and compared the two files. I went over every system several times to make sure I was reading them correctly. Then I sat back and I let out a big sigh. Tom noticed that and spoke up.

"That sigh tells me we are in deep shit."

I looked over at him and handed him my papers.

"According to my figures we don't have enough water, air, or fuel in the retro rockets to make it back home. It looks like we will be about two months short on water and almost a month short of oxygen."

He looked over the papers for quite a while.

"I also figured that we will have to course correct about eight times and that we have enough retro fuel for six firings."

I leaned forward and put my face in my hands. Tom leaned over and put his hand on my shoulder.

"We have faith in you and Lincoln to resolve this. Now go get some rest. Get out of here for a while."

I looked at him for a few moments and then I got up and headed out of the cockpit. I went straight to my quarters and started to write in the diary. I had a lot to write this time. I put everything down from the problems to Tony and all my thoughts about him. I spent several hours putting it all down in writing. We did not search the craft for him but I knew that if the outer hatch was opened there was no way he was not sucked out into space. I was going to have to review all the cameras to see if they confirmed that, but not now. I finished my writings and went straight to bed even though I knew I would never get any sleep.

CHAPTER 22

WE WERE WORKING HARD ON THE COMPUTER DOING ANALYSIS calculations and running scenarios on everything we could think of. Lincoln was doing the same and every time we seemed to come up with the same answers. Those answers were not good. After about ten hours of this I started to come down from the pills and was really getting tired. Tom from time to time was drifting off and was fighting sleep with everything he had. We told Lincoln we could not go on any more and we needed sleep. They agreed and said they would continue to work on the problems. Both Tom and I left the cockpit and we went straight to sleep. I felt a hand on my shoulder as I opened my eyes. I looked up and saw Sarah standing over me.

"Sorry to have to wake you Vince, but I think you really need to come to the cockpit now."

"Please tell me that I did get a few hours sleep at least?"

"You have been sleeping for seven hours. Tom is still sleeping but I will wake him too in a few minutes if you want me to do that."

"What is going on that requires you to wake me, I want to know?"

"The haze is back and is right next to us right now."

"You have to be shitting me. You woke me to tell me the haze is back. God damn it Sarah. I am exhausted. I don't need to look at a haze just because you are obsessed with this thing."

"I need your support right now. I have a problem and I need you, please, come to the cockpit."

I looked at her and she was looking like she was scared. I got up and together we went to the cockpit. When we entered the cockpit there were two lights in the cockpit. I stopped just inside the hatch and looked at her.

"Do you see them?"

"Yes I see the lights."

"No, them!"

She looked at the lights and just stood there.

"You see forms, don't you?"

"Yes, there are two male forms standing there."

She grabbed my arm and turned me towards her.

"Vince, they are talking to me. I can hear them."

I looked into her eyes and saw she was scared.

"What are they saying that has you so scared?"

"One of them is asking to join us. I don't know what that means. I am afraid to answer them."

"Ask them what they mean by joining us."

She looked forward towards the lights and just stood there. She then spoke without taking her eyes off them.

"It says like they did before. It says it over and over, the same thing."

I looked at the lights.

"I can not see you. Why? Can you let me see you?"

I waited to see what would happen. There was nothing changing at all. We stood there for a few minutes and nothing changed at all. Then all of a sudden Sarah started to cry and I heard her say,

'Yes'.

Then we watched as the haze started to drift over us. Soon we were engulfed by the haze as when we were on the trip towards Mars. I then remembered that after this had happened we had things done to the craft that we could not explain like the oxygen level and the fuel issues. I watched as the lights were seemingly passing through the cockpit at will. Then another light came in the cockpit and started very slowly moving towards Sarah. I heard her gasp and then reach out her hand. I watched her hand enter the light. I could see her hand and the light was transparent enough that her hand was always visible inside the light. She started to smile and her voice was quivering as she was trying to say a name. I heard her say,

'Aunt Lilian'.

I looked at her and then at the light that was inches in front of her. I watched her face as she was smiling and nodding her head. It appeared they were having a conversation but she wasn't saying anything. I watch for about five minutes and then the light drifted away and I heard Sarah say,

'goodbye'

very softly. I stood there still looking at her.

"Well, what just happened here?"

She turned and looked at me.

"I just saw a vision of my Aunt Lilian. She told me how much she loved me and how everyone is so proud of me being on this mission. We just talked about the family."

I couldn't believe my ears. She just had a conversation with a vision in the form of a light. There was no response for this. I know if I questioned her more that she would turn from the happy place she seemed to be in right now back to where she was before. The other two lights were still in the cockpit.

"Can you ask them why they are here?"

Sarah turned to the lights and stared at the lights. After a few moments she said again,

"They want us to know why Anthony left us. They want to let us know we will be alright. They said they need you to release your energy that is holding them back."

I looked at her and shook my head.

"I don't understand what that means. I want to see them, I really believe they are there. What energy are they talking about?"

She looked at me and told me to relax and let my spirit go free. Not to think so hard and so much because it blocks them access to you. I went and sat down in my seat. I leaned back and closed my eyes and tried to relax. I was there for a couple of minutes and then I heard Sarah telling me they were ready now. I opened my eyes and turned my head. There they were floating in the middle of the cockpit.

"Do they understand who we are and why we are here?"

"You can talk to them Vince. I don't have to ask them for you."

I sat there and looked at one who seemed to be looking at me. All of a sudden I could feel a chill come over me and then I was hearing words in my head.

'You are here to seek knowledge of life. We are here to let life know how great you are.'

I looked at Sarah and asked her if she heard what was just said. She said no that she has figured that they speak through thought and therefore one on one is all they can do. I looked back at the vision.

"Do you understand why we are out here?"

Sarah spoke up and told me all I have to do is think the questions and they will understand. While she was talking I was getting my answer again.

'You are here to seek knowledge of life.'

So I started to try and control my thoughts and only think about what I wanted them to hear.

'I feel great love here, did you know us before now?'

'You are the people that are connected to our life, and our life is you.'

I was not understanding at all what was being told to me. It all sounded like riddles and I was getting confused and frustrated. I was having great anxiety again and the visions started to fade away. I closed my eyes and relaxed again and tried very hard to open my mind and free it of all thoughts. When I felt calm I opened my eyes again and they were there again. Sarah told me that they want to know why the evil was forced out of our presence. I looked at her and told her I just didn't understand what they were asking me. Then I saw a third vision come into the cockpit. I moved and focused on it.

'You have great power and love. I will help you with your needs. The evil has gone and the good is you. Let us keep the good.'

Then I watched the vision pass through the hatch and into the craft. It disappeared on the other side of the curtain. Sarah was in conversation with one of the visions the whole time this was happening. I started thinking about the problems we had. I thought about each one and in some detail. Then I looked at the vision in front of me again.

'I know you helped us before with our problems. Can you please help us again?'

I thought those thoughts several times over. Then I eventually got a thought response.

'You are safe and the love is strong about you.'

All of a sudden the visions turned and drifted out the front of the craft. I looked at Sarah and she looked at me before looking back out the front windows.

"I wonder why they are here and just what they are. I don't understand their coming and goings. How only some of us can see them and then, now, hear them or what appears to be them. Nothing I heard made a lot of sense to me. I guess I just don't understand all this."

"It took me a while but I understand them completely. I know who they are. I am just confused why I could see my aunt because she is still alive."

"You think these are ghosts?"

"No, not ghost, spirits of the dearly departed ones that we loved. I think we have crossed the path of the mystical cliché, you know, the stairway to heaven concept."

I sat there and thought about what she had just said. I didn't agree with her but I understood her concept of thought. I decided right then and there that I would talk to all the crew members about this. I felt everyone had their own opinion and belief and that was the way I believed it should remain. As we continued to talk Carl came into the cockpit.

"You are not going to believe this one. It is like nothing had ever happened. I can't believe what I just watched in the storage compartment where the backup computer is. I was in there just looking around at the gauges trying to figure out how bad our water and oxygen levels really were. In came this light and then another and another. They moved around the system control panel and the computer control system. After about ten minutes of watching them move around I suddenly realized that the oxygen and the water level meters were showing a lot more than they did fifteen minutes earlier. Then all of a sudden the computer system lit up and so did the systems control panel. I still don't understand how and what happened but it is all working."

I looked at him and didn't say a word. Sarah started to giggle and she smiled and clapped her hands.

"They fixed everything again just like before but on a much greater scale this time."

She kept clapping and I finally got her to settle down.

"I know what our situation was two hours ago and I believe I understand the concept of what has just happened. Now I want to review everything and see what our current situation is. I will get back to you guys later."

I motioned then to go check their areas since we went through the hatch opening I wanted to ensure nothing was damaged or destroyed. Sarah and Carl left the cockpit and I dialed up Lincoln.

'LINCOLN – TALON.'

'LINCOLN HERE, GO AHEAD VINCE.'

'I DON'T KNOW WHERE TO START WITH THIS ONE BUT I NEED TO SEND YOU A VERY LONG MESSAGE TRYING TO EXPLAIN THE LAST FOUR HOURS OF OUR LIFE.'

'ROGER, WE ARE MONITORING THE SYSTEMS UP THERE AND WE SEE CHANGES THAT WE SURE NEED EXPLAINED.'

'GIVE ME SOME TIME TO GET IT TOGETHER AND I WILL CALL YOU WHEN I AM READY TO SEND.'

'ROGER, I GUESS YOU ARE GOING TO TELL ME THE HAZE DID THIS AGAIN, RIGHT.'

'NO, NOT THE HAZE. LET'S JUST SAY THE LIGHTS WITHIN THE HAZE.'

There was no response at all to that. I sat back in the seat and just wanted to think for a while about everything. After a while I started to write an outline of everything in chronological order. Then I went back and wrote what happened under each heading. It took me over two hours to complete it. In the time it took me to write this the lights had finished roaming around the craft and had exited and were outside the front window again. I saved it all in the computer and then made a copy and sent it to Lincoln. I called them and told them it was coming. I saw I had been in the cockpit for almost ten hours now. I knew that Tom would soon be there to take over. I looked out the front windows and saw the haze was still there. But now instead of seeing lights drift past the windows I was actually seeing figures. I got on the intercom and made a general announcement that I wanted to have a talk with everyone in an hour. I set it for the main area near the food machine. When I was finished talking on the intercom I realized I was hungry. I hadn't eaten for over twelve hours and it was getting to me now. I called Lincoln and advised them that for two hours we would be on the mobile freq. I then wrote a letter to Susan and explained that I was aware of our relationship and that even though I was in space I still knew what was happening on Earth so if she wasn't there when I returned that was alright. I understood and only asked she leave all my possessions in the house when she left. I told her I was a changed man now because of this flight and I didn't know whether she would like the new Vince or not but the new Vince was the one returning. It was about two pages long and I put it in a folder named 'letters to home'. I was going to let everyone write a letter and include it in a file to Phil back in Lincoln to print and mail for us. It was time to go talk to the troops so I left the cockpit. When I arrived in the main space they were all there. Tom walked up to me and handed me a couple of sheets of paper. It was hand written and appeared to be in Anthony's handwriting. I looked up at him and he told me he just found these on his desk when he got up. I looked around at the crew for a minute. Some were eating and others milling around talking. I went over and got two selections of food and found a seat. After eating one I started to talk. I told everyone about the encounters Tom, Carl, Sarah and I had with the lights. I asked each one to write something in the computer log about their personal experiences with the lights or visions they encountered. If they had none then write about that. I went on to tell them that what ever they were they had just saved our lives. I left nothing out explaining the oxygen levels and the water issues. I explained what had happened on the trip out and then now again in detail what had happened recently. I told them they needed to believe in what they felt comfortable in believing. There was no preaching going to be done here and there were no forcing of feelings on one another to be conducted. If you believe we encountered aliens, then so be it. Each one of the crew understood what I was telling them and agreed to keep it a personal experience. I passed on that the trip now was going to be slow because we didn't have much to do for the several months it would take to get there. Most of our work was already completed. As I was talking everyone was noticing that there were several lights in the area just moving around but not coming very close to us. I saw them and decided to ask a basic question. I wanted to know, by show of a raised hand, who saw more than just a light in the room just now. I saw three raised hands, and then I raised mine. I also asked if anyone did not see any lights at all. No one raised their hands. I again stated that they were our life savers and they were welcome to stay as long as they wished. I then told everyone that I planned on sending a folder back to Lincoln with letters from us to our family or friends. If anyone wanted to write a letter they could do so on the computer and place it in the folder named 'letters to home' under the tab Personal. I made it very clear that nothing about the lights was allowed to be in the letters. After all that was said I told everyone that was it and to enjoy the rest of the day. I went back to eating my food and then just wanted to get some sleep. Tom told me he was heading for the cockpit and he would take over now. I thanked him for his support and told him I had sent a message to Lincoln requesting his status and rank be changed to Commander and title be listed as Co-pilot. He thanked me and left. I wandered around for a few minutes and then saw Sarah at the door of the lab. She was waving for me to come there. I wandered over there and entered the lab. She was standing next to the desk holding some papers in her hand. I walked up to her and she handed them to me. I started to look through them and just wasn't sure what I was looking at.

"I have been talking to my entity and they told me to give you this. This was on my computer when they left. I think it looks like plans to build something."

I went through the papers again and looked closely at the ones that had a lot of figures and measurements.

"I don't know what this is. I can see that it is not instructions to build something. More like charts and graphs to show something or somewhere. I will add it to the other ones to have it reviewed by Lincoln."

I went to her computer and found the pages and then copied them to two folders, sending one to Lincoln with a brief write up on it. I also asked Lincoln if they were keeping any personal information from us on any of the crew members. I hinted that we had some information and were looking for verification but did not tell them what. It took them about twenty minutes to get it and call us back. Tom called and said Lincoln was on the radio wanting to talk to me. I made my way to the cockpit and gave them a call.

'LINCOLN – TALON.'

'VINCE, PHIL HERE, ARE YOU ALONE?'

'TOM IS WITH ME.'

'THAT'S ALRIGHT, HELLO TOM. -VINCE I RECEIVED SOME INFORMATION A WHILE AGO BUT DIDN'T WANT TO UPSET A CREW MEMBER DURING THE MISSION. ONE OF YOUR CREW HAS LOST A FAMILY MEMBER.'

'ROGER UNDERSTAND, WHICH CREW MEMBER?'

'FIRST ANSWER ME THIS, WHAT INFORMATION COULD YOU HAVE RECEIVED KNOWING THERE WAS SOMETHING WE HAD NOT TOLD YOU?'

'DR. MEYER SEEMS TO HAVE HAD A CONVERSATION WITH, WELL, LET'S CALL IT A VISION. SHE TOLD ME IT WAS HER AUNT BUT WAS CONFUSED SINCE HER AUNT IS STILL ALIVE. LET ME STATE SHE BELIEVED THESE VISIONS ARE RECENTLY DEPARTED INDIVIDUALS FROM EARTH PASSING TO THE OTHER SIDE, WHERE EVER THAT MIGHT BE.'

There was a considerable pause before he answered.

'VINCE, THE INFORMATION I HAVE IS FOR DR. MEYER. CAN YOU GIVE ME THE NAME OF HER AUNT?'

'I BELIEVE IT WAS LILIAN.'

'THEN I WOULD SAY THERE MIGHT BE REASON TO RESEARCH HER THEORY A LITTLE BIT MORE. HER AUNT LILIAN IS THE FAMILY MEMBER THAT PASSED AWAY.'

I looked at Tom and we both sort of said,

'no way'

at the same time.

'ROGER PHIL, I COPY THAT. YOU NEED TO READ MY LOGS THAT I HAVE SENT YOU AND THIS MIGHT BE BEST KEPT

UNDER WRAPS FOR A WHILE. THIS IS NOT EASILY EXPLAINED AND THE PRESS WOULD NOT TREAT THIS WELL.'

'ROGER, WE FEEL THE SAME. SORRY FOR THE NEWS BUT THAT'S ALL FOR NOW.'

'ROGER'

Tom and I talked about a few things and then I left to head back to the lab. When I entered the lab Michelle was in there and they were talking. I walked up to them and asked if I could speak to Sarah alone for a minute. I told Michelle she could come back in after I was done talking to her. She said she would be back a little later and left. After she walked out the door I turned to Sarah and reached out and took her hands.

"Sarah, I have some news that Lincoln has passed on to me. I think you might have already thought about this but still it is not good news."

"It's about my Aunt Lilian isn't it?"

"Yes, the reason you were able to see her is that she passed away. They didn't tell me when but based on your understanding of what these visions are I would say it was before she appeared to you."

She looked at me and put her head down but she did not cry.

"I have talked to her again and I am alright about this. I knew the second time that this had to be the case. I asked her a few questions and she never answered me. It was as if she didn't know she was dead. I then knew."

She moved forward and we embraced each other and she held on tight. I kissed her on the side of her head and she responded by turning and kissing me hard on the lips. After a few minutes we separated and I told her I would send in Michelle so she had a female to talk to for a while. She smiled and thanked me. I turned and left the lab and saw Michelle hanging out in the area. I went over to her and told her she needed to go back in the lab because Sarah needed her friendship right now. She looked at me with a puzzled look but didn't ask anything. She just went around me and entered the lab. I headed for my quarters. I went in and grabbed a few things and headed for the shower. After I was all cleaned up I went to bed. It had been a very long day and even longer several days. I was exhausted and needed to get away from everything for a while. I had ten hours left on my down time and I wanted to sleep the whole ten hours. I was trying to clear my head when Sarah popped in around the curtain.

"Are you sleeping yet?"

"Not yet, close but not yet."

"I need you!"

"Is it possible to talk later or can I ... ... well OK. Let me get up and we will talk."

"No, you don't understand what I said. I don't want to talk. I want you to make love to me."

I looked at her and tried to sit up but ended up getting out of the cocoon completely. I reached out my arms and she came close.

"Did anyone see you come in here?"

"I don't care anymore. I need you right now more than I have ever needed anyone before."

She started to undress and I did the same. For the next half hour we engulfed each other as one. Afterward we just laid there and were talking. Well, more like whispering to each other. After an hour we got up and dressed. I wanted her to stay and just be in my arms for the night but we knew that could not happen. I peered out the curtain and saw Michelle walking around. I watched her for a few minutes just roam around and then she went into another space. I told Sarah it was clear and she left and headed for her quarters. I crawled back into the cocoon and tried to sleep the last six hours of my time that was left for me. It didn't take very long because all I had in my brain was Sarah so I was very relaxed.

CHAPTER 23

FOR THE NEXT TEN DAYS WE WERE STREAMING TOWARDS EARTH and the haze was still over us. Actually we were inside the haze since it was all around the craft. While we were being engulfed by the haze we needed to make no course changes due to the hatch being missing on the EVA port. It was like there was a vapor or air shield covering the hole. We were approaching the two month mark of the mission home. Sarah and I were seeing each other regularly and we noticed that Hank and Michelle were sneaking off from time to time also. We still were waiting for Lincoln to give any response or tell us what they thought about all the data we had sent down to them. The following day we started to notice changes happening again. Sarah came to the cockpit and told us the visions stopped coming by yesterday and she felt the haze was shifting and moving away. We watched the front windows from time to time and late in the day we saw we were now at the edge of the haze. She told me that she had her last contact with them a few days ago and saw less and less of them. Sarah had been right and it was moving away. The lights were still in the haze drifting past but we no longer were being visited in the cockpit either. I called Lincoln and told them our current status and that we should start to expect the craft to be affected by the missing hatch again soon. It took about three more hours but Lincoln said they were starting to detect a slight course shift again. So we checked everything one last time and sent the report to what our levels were for all our supplies. Over the next three weeks we watched the haze disappear off in the distance. We calculated the angle and the trajectory of the haze and then compared it to our trip to Mars and they almost matched perfectly. We did track analysis to see if we could determine where it was aiming at out there in space. Nothing came back at a target point from our search. We knew it changed course while we saw it so could only figure that it had that ability to change any time it wanted to but since we really didn't know where it was headed. We actually had no idea what we were looking for. If Lincoln had figured something out, they did not tell me. So we determined that the haze was in a predetermined space and was not likely something that just happened to appear. I wrote a log entry and highly recommended there be another mission just to verify what we saw out here. Since we had all our systems back after the latest encounter we made an attempt to contact the rover left on Mars. Lincoln told us that they had found that Tony had sent it directions to get lost and they think it did just that. In the letter that Tony had left for Tom he mentioned that he was instructed to not let the rover and the satellite complete its mission. We didn't know whether he succeeded in sabotaging the satellite but we knew he did succeed in the rover. Tony said he received a lot of messages in his sleep that we all were trying to destroy him and he just could not let that happen. So the mission had mentally destroyed Tony's mental capacity to reason and unfortunately we did not catch it in time to save him. All those times I though that there was something wrong and I just waited to see if he would correct it himself was now a mistake on my part. I knew that maybe if I had acted on my beliefs that he still might be alive and we would not have been put in danger. But then hind sight was always your second choice when something goes wrong. You can always come up with the right fix after the fact. It was being brave enough to act at the present that fails you. We went another several weeks and everything was near normal. There were no problems except the drifting and there was a great peace among the crew. We were starting to think about what our life was going to be like when we arrived home. A whole year away from everyone we used to spend our daily lives with. I sent a message off to Lincoln to try and get them to respond to all the things we had questions about including the letters we sent out. Several were asking if any return letters were written back to us. Finally Lincoln responded with a written message to my folder. In it they referred to the haze and said only they were still investigating it and would not respond until they had time to talk to us personally when we returned. As far as the way our life systems kept regenerating fuel and oxygen, well they determined it to be false readings from the indicators. Then came the mail issue. Lincoln responded that only four pieces of mail were received in reply and they would forward them tomorrow. They indicated that Carl, Tom, and Karen were the only members of the crew that received mail. I went to the cockpit and called Lincoln on the radio and asked them to get Phil for me. When Phil called I asked him if he was in contact with Susan, my wife. He told me that he had not seen her since the week before we launched. He also told me that our house was vacant so she was not there. I thanked him for his candor and told him we needed to have a good stiff drink when I returned. He said he already had that covered. I knew then that she was gone for good. I was at the top of my career and I was now at the bottom of my home life. He asked me if we were holding up ok and I responded that all the crew members were mentally very stable but we all were changed. None of us would be the same when we returned after our experiences. He understood that very well and said we had a lot to talk about later. I tried to keep myself very busy over the next few days trying not to fall into a depression. I was lucky that Sarah was making sure that did not happen even though she had no knowledge of my conversation with Phil. The trip was starting to slow down mentally. We were about seven weeks away from rendezvousing with the space station. That was going to be the check point before we came home. We needed to stop there and check the craft for damage and to get rid of the booster rockets that would be empty at that point. So we would have one more EVA and then the short trip home two days later. I called a meeting and when everyone was gathered I went over the last scheduled plans we had before arriving home. We discussed that fact that we will be getting there about ten days later than the scheduled arrival date due to the slightly slower speed home. We went over everything and then we talked about the press and that almost everything that we experienced on this mission was to be kept secret. That meant that the press and the world did not know about any of our problems or the haze and its effect on our lives. So nothing at all is to be said about the mission.

There will be a debrief and then we will go over the scenario that will go out to the press. Everyone understood and acknowledged what we needed to do. After the meeting was over Sarah came up to me and asked what happens with us. I told her that as far as I knew I was going home to an empty house. I told her that where she went home to was up to her. I did mention that we needed to make sure of things before we made a move that could be harmful to either of us. She agreed that she would go home and see what the situation was there and then call me. I agreed to check out my house and wait or call her if there was someone there. I knew we would talk about this several time more so I didn't repeat any of the plans. I told Sarah that we needed to put together a package of pictures and events that each of us could keep from the trip in secret. She said she would work on that and make up folders for everyone. I was going to have to find a way to get them back off the space craft without them being taken from us when we returned. After a few days of thinking about it I created a file in the computer and then hard copy folders for each of the crew. I planned on sending the file to Phil who I believed I could trust to hold for me. I also was going to put the hard copies in envelopes and put them in a pack and seal it for Phil only to receive. I could intercept that when it was delivered. We did a lot of planning and thinking about what we wanted in these packages. Soon we had three weeks left and we could see the Earth large in the windows. We made the thruster firings to correct the off course drift and actually went past the designated line knowing we would drift back on course in the coming days. We saw that there was very little fuel left in the retro rockets. I have some of the crew start early to secure all the packs and seal the ones up that had the experiments in. Tom and I were spending more and more time preparing for our arrival at the space station. The days were really dragging on very slowly but we knew it was getting closer. We looked at the calendar we had on the wall of the cockpit and saw we only had two weeks left and also saw that in two days we were originally supposed to be home. The atmosphere amongst the crew was getting subdued. There was excitement and at the same time no one was talking. Everyone was keeping to themselves and just doing busy work to keep their minds off the days dragging by. I called Lincoln and made a request for Phil to contact me.

After a few hours he called on the secure channel and I told him that I was sending personal letters to be delivered and asked him to take care of it for me. We set up a file name for me to deliver the folder to and then I send the packages to him directly. I put a cover letter on it to make sure he understood what I wanted him to do. About two hours later he called again and acknowledged he had received the files and folders and stated that all was good and would be delivered as requested. I sat back and Tom and I knew that we had a friend that could be trusted. Lincoln started to get us ready for the burn to bring us out of Mach 58. As it was we were at the point when we should have been doing it today. But at the slightly reduced speed we still had eleven more days to go. We should have been home now but the slower speed meant the longer trip but we were dealing with it. So the next week went by very slowly with everyone doing nothing but thinking about home. Well, I shouldn't say everyone because I was not looking forward to walking into an empty house but then I was looking forward to having Sarah in my life and not having to sneak around to even give her a kiss. We were in the final stages of making sure everything was secure for the burn. We knew the last time we had missed a few things but this time everything was double checked. I went through the check list with Lincoln one last practice time. Finally the day came and everyone was given the hours to sleep before the burn. There wasn't anything to do anyway. Our biggest concern was the hole in the side of the ship. We were going to fix it when we arrived at the space station but going through the burn and the drastic slow down was a concern on stability. We decided to blow oxygen into the outer space at the hatch like we did that enabled us to close the middle hatch. It should give us some help in keeping us from twisting out of control. It worked when we were boosting up to the Mach speed so we expected it to word in slowing down as well. We now had less than an hour before the burn and everyone was ordered into their space suits just in case and were now getting to their seats to buckle in. Tom came in and took his seat and we were ready. I went over everything he needed to concentrate on again and we then waited. The time came and we watched the countdown hit zero and felt the jerk of the massive reverse engines kick into gear. We instantly started to feel the build up of pressure from the G Force hitting us and then the vibrations started.

We knew we had about twelve minutes and then it would be over. The first seven were the worst and that seven minutes felt like eternity. I threw the switches and blasted oxygen into the voided space where the hatch should have been. I kept an eye on the oxygen gauge to make sure we didn't use it all up. After five minutes we were down to thirty percent left and I was getting ready to shut it down when it hit twenty percent. Soon the vibrations started to ease up and we hit the twenty percent mark so I threw the switch to turn the oxygen flow off. I could tell from the gauges and the computer readings we were off course. Then the burn started to come to an end and the Earth was glowing bright in the front windows. I saw Tom sitting there with a big smile on his face. He turned and looked at me and I smiled back stating,

'We made it home. My god we made it.'

Lincoln called and told us we were off course by a lot more than expected and they were scrambling to configure the computer to adjust for the correction. I looked at the Mach indicator and it was at 10 and the speed indicator was still falling fast. Then the engines stopped and we slowed down to within twenty MPH of the target goal. All I could think of was how great the engineers and scientist were that developed all this to actually make it happen as they planned. I had a great respect for everyone in the space industry to make such a feat happen. I threw on the intercom switch and yelled,

'Honey we're home'.

I could hear the laughter and clapping coming from just outside the cockpit where four of the others were seated. The other two, Carl and Michelle were in the space were the back up systems were located. Lincoln called and gave us the corrections and we fired the retro rockets and tried to set the angle to put us in orbit around the Earth and still rendezvous with the space station. The burn only last a few seconds. It was far short of the time we needed to get on the right trajectory. After about an hour it was determined we were in too low of an orbit to adjust for the rendezvous and we had to abort that part of the mission. We were barely in orbit according to the gauges. Lincoln sent up the new configuration for the computer and they said since the weather was good today they were going to bring us straight home. First we had to attempt to replace the hatch. Tom went back to the EVA portal and the crew joined him there. They all pitched in and they started the EVA to remove the middle hatch and place it in the outer hatch location. The way the door was ripped off the hinges made it possible to remove the old hinges and just bolt the new assembly in place. We got very lucky on that one. The frame was only slightly bent out of shape. It took about five hours but they managed to put the hatch on. It was not the exact fit we hoped for but very close. Close enough that we did not think it would cause us any problem during reentry. They sealed the cracks from the uneven seal with the compound we had to fix any heat shields that might have had to be replaced. So the decision was made to come home now. Everyone was really happy about that decision. We fired the jettison rockets and got rid of the booster rocket tanks. Three hours later we watched as the computer finished the upload and we were ready. We started the burn to come out of orbit and start the decent home. It took about forty minutes for us to fall out of orbit knowing full well the small gaps were still a concern but we had great confidence it would hold. Our decent was great and we touched down at the cape just after 1 P.M. We rolled down the runway and came to a stop near the end. We removed the helmets to the suits. I sat back and listened to the cheering coming from behind us. Tom turned to me and started talking.

"There were so many issues on this trip that had disaster written all over them. You saved our asses each and every time. Thank you from me and the crew for being so strong and never wavering from your job."

He reached out his hand and I shook it. I just smiled at him and really could not think of a response. Then we could hear the CAPCON coming across the radio,

'TALON THIS IS MISSION CONTROL. WELCOME HOME! YOU HAVE JUST RETURNED FROM A HISTORIC MISSION THAT THE WORLD WILL NEVER FORGET. GREAT JOB VINCE, TO YOU AND YOUR CREW. AGAIN WELCOME BACK TO MOTHER EARTH.'

'THANK YOU MISSION CONTROL. WE LOOK FORWARD TO STEPPING OUT ONTO MOTHER EARTH AGAIN.'

Then over the secure radio we heard mission control tell us that do to the urgency of the landing all the festivities that were planned will not be happening but that there were a few people there to greet us including the Vice President. We acknowledged that and said we would be out shortly. We made our way out of the cockpit and everyone went to the equipment space and got out of the space suits and we put on our blues. After that we heard the outer hatches being opened and voices calling in. I answered and we headed for the exit. There were several men in white suits to meet us there and with smiles that welcomed us home. We walked out and down the ramp and were escorted into the RV for the trip to the reception area. Our legs were just a tad unstable as we walked over to the reception area. We were greeted by all the dignitaries and after the normal array of speeches we finally got the hell out of there and to the living quarters. Each one of us went through a lengthy physical and then we were met by Phil Nelson. We did not mention any of the mission issues but were hopeful that all the experiments would be useful for future missions. We played it up since the press was all around us for most of the afternoon. He did whisper into my ear to come to his office later and smiled at me. I knew that meant he had our folders there for us. We spend five days at the cape being debriefed and writing statements. We were in many meetings about what we saw and went through and all were ended by their statements of keeping everything top secret and making us sign statements to that effect. They wanted to gather all the information and come up with something reasonable before they let that information out to the world. But after we were done with all the meetings we all knew that they were planning on covering up everything and it would never be released. They made us sign so many papers to not divulge anything until they made it public that it became very clear it was never going to happen. We managed to get our packages from Phil and he thanked us for making one up for him to keep as well. He did urge us to keep the folders very secure and private. Finally we boarded a private jet and headed back to Lincoln. When we arrived in Lincoln there was a huge reception and then a parade and more interviews. This was our homecoming event and they dragged it on for a long time. All the crew members were greeted by their families and friends. I saw Sarah standing there with two elderly individuals and of course I was all alone. No Susan showed up for my arrival. I thought my son might have made the trip but he did not either. I learned later he was on a business trip in Europe. I walked into the front entrance of the main building and sat down in the reception area while everyone was having their joyous reunion. Leanne saw me and brought me a cup of coffee.

"Wow! Real coffee! Now I know I am home."

She made some small talk and then made a comment about having two letters for me in her office. She left and returned with the letters and handed them to me. She made a comment about being sorry for having to give them to me like this but I had to get them sometime anyway. I looked and there were no other names on the envelopes but mine. I knew they were from Susan. I opened both of them before pulling out the contents. I saw one was a letter and the other seemed to have just loose papers in it. I pulled out the papers and found our marriage license and then a copy of a pending court issuing a decree for a request for divorce. I put them back in the envelope and put both in my pocket. I didn't want to read the letter right now. I heard the front door open and saw Phil enter. He came up to me and said that there was going to be a private hearing on our mission in a few days. They wanted us to have time to settle down after the trip before they started to get into what happened out there in space. He told me that he knew we just went through all this but we had to do it again. I told him I would be ready whenever they called the house. He said they were extremely interested in finding out what really happened to Anthony. I told Phil about the letter Anthony wrote before he left the craft. I told him a copy of it was in my baggage for him. I asked that it never be revealed to anyone what he went through mentally before he left us. He needed to be remembered as an astronaut on a mission that was nothing but great for him. He agreed and we talked about other crew members and how it was going to affect their home lives. He told me there was a pack in his office addressed to him but he figured it was mine. I told him yes it was the crews' things from the trip and there were things in there for him as well. We made plans to go through it later. He got up and left. I started to go back outside and saw Sarah coming towards the front entrance. I waited at the door for her and when she arrived she told me her parents were here but there no longer would be a Robert in her life. She was straight faced when she told me that but then immediately broke out with a smile. I told her that I just received divorce papers and there would no longer be a Susan in my life. We talked for a while and she told me her parents would be here for a couple of days so she would be over when they left. I told her I would be waiting. She left to go back to them and I wandered out to where the rest of the crew was and after talking to each of them I watched as they departed the area for their homes. I finally was standing out in the parking lot all alone. I heard someone come up from behind me and turned to see it was Phil.

"I guess you need a ride home?"

"It does look like that is the case."

"I'm sorry about Susan, I didn't see that coming. What are you going to do now?"

"I pulled out the envelopes and he looked at them in my hand.

"She filed for a divorce. So my life now will start over. But first I need to end this one that gave me such a great ride."

"What! You are not thinking of quitting. We need you now. With the implications you brought back with you, there will be years of work you will have to do to sort that all out."

"Well, maybe so, but I don't want to do it as an astronaut. Maybe just as a contract civilian."

"How about as a Deputy Director of Operations? I have it on good information there is a position available that needs to be filled."

"Are you telling me Sturgis is gone?"

"He had an unfortunate incident and his last days were last week. I will tell you all about it later."

I looked at him and he was smiling at me. I nodded my head and told him that sounded like a good desk job. I also mentioned it was the right thing to do to make sure I kept quiet about all the things we went through on the mission. He never gave me a response to that one. I picked up my two small bags and told him I was ready. We walked to his car and he gave me a ride to my house. We made small talk on the way and when we arrived there were banners in the front yard and my neighbors were all standing in the street.

"How did they know I was on my way home?"

"I think Leanne might have made a phone call or two."

He smiled and pulled into the driveway. I got out and greeted all my neighbors and then they told me that there was a BBQ in my back yard tomorrow so for me to relax tonight and everyone was bringing everything to my house in the morning. I thanked them and said my goodbyes as they left and I went in the house with Phil who handed me my keys. Everything felt musty for being closed up so long. But nothing was changed. I went to the refrigerator expecting a disaster there but inside was only a twelve pack of beer and a box of fried chicken.

"Linda and I cleaned it out months ago and the beer and chicken is fresh from yesterday."

"I guess you knew what I needed and just didn't feel I needed any more stress."

"Let's just say Susan and Linda talked about a month after you left on the mission and we came over and made sure things were right for your return."

"Thanks!"

"So, now I will leave you and you try to enjoy the next few days. Get some well deserved rest and I will see you and the crew on Monday morning."

"I will be there, and thanks again for everything. I intend to sleep for a long time right now."

"First help me get that pack out of my trunk. I didn't want to leave it in my office for someone else to see and insist it be opened."

"Right!"

We laughed and after taking the pack and placing it in my living room he left. I looked around the house and saw that nothing but her clothes and personal items were missing. I ventured out to the car port and started up the car to make sure the battery was good. It started right up. I guess that Phil took care of that as well. I went back inside, drank a few beers and emptied my bags. I looked over the many photographs I snuck out of there. I looked at all the lights and the figures in the pictures. I knew my life was changed and I expected everyone else on that mission was thinking the same. They all had the same set of pictures. Sarah made sure we all got a copy of them. I put one next to my bed and crawled in and went to sleep. I woke up to noise outside my window. I looked at my watch and saw it was after ten in the morning. I had slept for about fifteen hours. I got up and showered and just stood there under the hot water for a long time. My legs were still trying to get used to gravity and my head hurt. I knew the headache was from real air instead of the mix we breathed for a year in the craft. I walked out into the back yard and there were dozens of people setting up tables and umbrellas. I said my hello's and thanks and strolled in and grabbed a beer for breakfast. The afternoon went fast and soon I was alone again. I called Sarah's house but no one answered. I watched some TV but found myself bored so I went through the pack and sorted out everything in piles for each crew member. Soon the backyard party started and for the afternoon I was surrounded by the neighbors and friends. Susan's daughter Deb and her husband Ben came by and stayed a while. We had a good conversation and all was good with them. We planned on staying friends for the future. The next day was spent in and out of bed all day. Monday morning came and I arrived at the Space Center complex at eight. Everyone was already there. I walked into Phil's office and Leanne told me they all were in the conference room. When I entered there was a party atmosphere going on. There were balloons on the ceiling and a big breakfast spread and a huge cake and the whole administration building employees and the training crew were there. I saw my fellow crew members sitting at a table and then they saw me standing in the door way. There was a celebration for us and I took it in stride with the others. In the afternoon the meetings started. We all were in meetings and debriefing sessions for days. It was almost two weeks with everyone under the sun attending them. We even had a special secret meeting with a bunch from Washington. Everything discussed there was classified Top Secret and they wanted it to stay that way. I felt that we had just created our own Area 51 right here in Texas. When it was over the crew and I got together at my place and discussed what we went through. We knew then that nothing was ever going to be told about our mission and our findings and beliefs. That the mission to the world was a boring slow trip out and back. That Mars was a place we didn't need to go back to since they did not want a repeat of what we experienced. They did not want to have to cover up another mission. It was going to be a sham and a huge cover up. I could not believe that such a great experience that we encountered was never going to be made public. That the findings of what everyone would consider a possible vision of the after life was going to be squashed for ever. Most of us thought that the world needed to know and then they could make their own decision whether to believe it or not. But then we also saw the other side in that there would be a large group that would tear down the agency and all of us for our beliefs in what we saw or maybe in their minds made up. The Psychologist that ended our conversations when we were at the cape made a statement that made us all think about why we would not go public with it. He said whether people believe or not there will always be the ones that will be relentless in their criticizing of us to make us all look like we went crazy out there. That alone might destroy future missions to Mars. Everyone took the things I had sorted out for them when they left. Sarah moved in with me and we settled down as a couple. We framed a lot of the pictures and kept them in our bedroom. She became a crusader for the fight to have another mission. In the next few months we knew that Michelle has filed for a divorce from her husband and that the others were now expecting new additions to their families. I received the promotion to Deputy Director of Operations and retired from the military. Sarah continued with a position at the university teaching Biology and stayed on the inactive list as an astronaut. We were making a happy life together and I was starting to enjoy life again. Carl was promoted and stayed with the space program. Tom and his wife built a huge family and he eventually retired from the military and moved to the mountains of Colorado. Henry and Michelle got married after her divorce and along with her first child they had three more. He still is in the military but no longer involved in the space program. Karen, well, I know she retired from the military but she never married and we never heard from her after the mission ended. As for Anthony's family, the Government took good care of them and we heard Gabriella remarried and was living in Virginia. One of their children entered the Air Force Academy. The letter he left us was never made public so his memory was left in good standing as an accident. So the crew tried to arrange a reunion a few years later but it never came about. There never was another mission to Mars. The memories of what we had and what we experienced started to fade away. Life was the same as it always had been for the rest of the world but for the seven of us that were on that mission, life could and would never be the same again.

The End

ABOUT THE AUTHOR

He was born and lived in and around Pittsburgh, Pennsylvania. After High School he entered the service and served four years with the U.S. Coast Guard. He went to college and obtained a ASET degree in Electronics Engineering. Worked for NCR Corporation and for many years was part of the development team that designed the new age of cash registers you see in stores today. He left the business world to go back into the military to pursue a dream that they could offer. For the next twenty-three years he worked in Communications and Computer Operations with a departure for almost eight years when he joined the Government's Federal Agent Corp. He has traveled extensively and gained a vast experience of knowledge from his encounters. After retiring he went back to the Computer Industry and worked as a consultant for major industries until he decided it was time to relax. He spent more than twelve years working for the Walt Disney

Company. A truly unique experience into the world of entertainment and the Hospitality Industry. He is now completely retired to pursue a love he has always had in writing. His current book, The Talon Incident, was a dream that came to him over several days. It was so compelling he had to put it to print. His future works will go in other directions and some will be taken from real life experiences based on his travels.

Printed in the United States
by Baker & Taylor Publisher Services